The House

at the Heart

of the Lakes

CW00822877

The Hotel at the Heart of the Lakes

Ellie Wood

Harper
North

HarperNorth
Windmill Green
24 Mount Street
Manchester M2 3NX

A division of
HarperCollins*Publishers*
1 London Bridge Street
London SE1 9GF

www.harpercollins.co.uk

HarperCollins*Publishers*
Macken House,
39/40 Mayor Street Upper,
Dublin 1, D01 C9W8, Ireland

First published by HarperNorth 2025
1

Copyright © Ellie Wood 2025

Ellie Wood asserts the moral right to
be identified as the author of this work.

A catalogue record for this book is available from the British Library.

PB ISBN: 978-0-00-862633-4

This novel is entirely a work of fiction. The names, characters and incidents
portrayed in it are the work of the author's imagination. Any resemblance to
actual persons, living or dead, events or localities is entirely coincidental.

Printed and bound in the UK using 100% Renewable Electricity by
CPI Group (UK) Ltd

All rights reserved. No part of this publication may be reproduced, stored in a retrieval
system, or transmitted, in any form or by any means, electronic, mechanical, photocopying,
recording or otherwise, without the prior permission of the publishers.

Without limiting the author's and publisher's exclusive rights, any unauthorised use
of this publication to train generative artificial intelligence (AI) technologies is
expressly prohibited. HarperCollins also exercise their rights under Article 4(3) of
the Digital Single Market Directive 2019/790 and expressly reserve this
publication from the text and data mining exception.

This book contains FSC™ certified paper and other controlled
sources to ensure responsible forest management.

For more information visit: www.harpercollins.co.uk/green

On the summit of a Cumbrian mountain
you're that little bit closer to the stars

Prologue

'Shall we buy it?' Anna said, tilting her face towards him in the spring sunshine and raising her eyebrows, as though they were simply standing by a stall at a farmers' market.

Dominik frowned. Thought he'd misheard for a moment. That the birdsong was playing tricks on his ears. '*Buy it?*' he asked, but she'd turned back again, features bathed in the bright daylight.

He looked at her, there beside him on the shore. His Anna. His *wife*. He took her hand. Glanced back at the view before them. *Is that even possible?* he thought to himself as her question looped through his mind again, like a song thrush in the sky. *Was she actually serious?*

The island opposite them seemed to shimmer in the March morning. The white building at its centre half hidden by the trees, the lake surrounding the little circle of land glittering like a dream.

'You mean before we've even finished the honeymoon . . .?' he asked with a laugh, expecting her to squeeze his fingers fondly, say it was a joke, a fantasy to be shared like a dessert.

But Dominik knew Anna better than that. She believed dreams could be spun into something solid, the same way grains of sugar could be transformed into glistening strands of gold. Look at the two of them, after all. She'd been a memory in his head for so long. Now she was here, next to him.

He smiled as he stared at the hotel across the water. A stone's throw from their home in Buttermere, yet the place they'd decided to stay for their week away after getting married. 'Well, this is the most beautiful place in the world,' Anna had reasoned when they'd booked it. 'Why would we go anywhere else?'

He'd spent so many years more than a thousand miles away from the Lakes, and now they were together he didn't ever want to leave. Not when even Katrine and Mateusz had encouraged him to come. His precious children. All grown up and seemingly twice as wise as he'd ever been. He couldn't wait to show them this spot. Tell them how he and Anna had imagined living there, across the water. Pictured themselves swimming off the private beach, strolling in the gardens as they grew older. Perhaps even welcoming guests of their own to the seven picturesque suites, watching their jaws drop in awe as they landed on the little wooden jetty and stepped onto the island for the first time.

His son and daughter would smile and say it looked magical. That it was nice to see it. What a location. Perhaps he could take them for a meal, share a little of the dream with them too.

Though if he was honest, the hotel looked more impressive from this vantage point opposite, in Keswick's Crow Park. The building was a ramshackle mansion in reality, in need of much love and care. Faded, but still with a charm.

Anna had said earlier that it had been handsome in its heyday, and Dominik hoped she didn't think the same about him.

Had she honestly suggested purchasing it? It was more than they could manage even if they could find the money. But surely Anna didn't mean it. They were on their honeymoon. It was supposed to be a break from reality. He knotted his fingers through hers, as the warbling birds filled the sun-soaked silence, and Derwentwater's reflection twinkled in her eyes.

Chapter 1

'Good morning, the Lake Island Hotel. How may I help you?'

Katrine's intonation was the same as her dad's, thought Anna, watching as her stepdaughter tucked the phone under her chin to take the booking. She paused in the entrance hall, head tipped to one side, taking it all in for a moment, as she sometimes did. As Dominik had taught her to do. He always saw the glimmers in an ordinary day, forever panning for tiny diamonds of joy. She smiled. Everything that surrounded her now had once been just an idea in their heads. They'd pored over plans, suggestions flurrying like fireworks in an ink-blank sky. And gradually, they'd made it a reality.

She took in the reception desk, a live edge slab of solid oak, its tactile curves welcoming guests as soon as they stepped through the door. Just as she'd envisaged it. She caught the flickering glow of the open fire in the lounge to her left, flaming with the last of the logs Dominik had chopped by hand when they'd cut back the overgrown grounds; it was never left to go out. The staircase straight ahead of her led to the seven bedrooms they'd spent months discussing how to decorate, spreading out fabric swatches and daubing paint-shade squares on the walls. They'd made up their own names for the colours: 'bat's breath' and 'mole's nose' – in-jokes that still conjured a smile.

'Yes, of course, when were you looking at coming to stay?' she heard Katrine say to the person on the phone, her voice echoing Dominik's warmth. Anna sat down on the scatter-cushioned sofa while she waited to speak to her, looked out across the lawn towards the landing stage where the lake lapped at the island as though the real world clutched at the pebble-stoned shore but never really touched the island.

'Great, and can I take a name?' Katrine continued, dipping her head as she typed on the desktop, dark hair shining in the light. The central ceiling lantern looked like a halo above her from where Anna was sitting by the window.

'Anna, good morning!' called Katrine when she'd finished the call, her bright words bouncing across the burnished-wood floor.

Anna stood up and walked towards the desk, arms outstretched to embrace Katrine.

'Beautiful day,' said her hotel manager, glancing beyond the panes of glass, positivity percolating through the air like perfume.

The March morning had dawned cold, the kitchen garden iced with sugar-sprinkle frost, but now that had melted away into a spring-warmed day.

'That was a request to hire the whole hotel for three nights in June,' Katrine murmured, tone low. Discretion could have been the make of her suit.

Anna raised her eyebrows.

'We're already getting quite booked up for summer.' Katrine bent to scroll through the reservations system, angling the screen so Anna could see how busy they were. 'See?' Katrine grinned over her shoulder.

Anna nodded. Felt a swell of pride and the unexpected prick of tears. Shook herself. 'Is it for a special occasion?' she asked. 'How many guests?'

Katrine's forehead furrowed. 'Didn't say. It was an assistant I spoke to. Paid the deposit, though.' She pointed at the amount on the computer.

Anna felt a shot of relief as she looked at the figure in front of her. 'Well, that's good news.' Recouping the cost of the refurbishment was a challenge she knew she had to under-take gradually, like conquering a particularly high mountain, but it didn't make it any less daunting.

'They didn't hesitate when I explained the breakdown of the price, the fact we have to take into account blocking out the restaurant and all the other rooms.'

Anna pursed her lips as she listened, piecing together the unspoken information.

'Said their client wanted exclusive use and all staff would need to sign a non-disclosure agreement.'

Anna's eyes met Katrine's briefly before they flitted back to the monitor. She scanned the rest of the customer infor-mation file Katrine had filled in while she was on the phone. Frowned at the name the reservation had been made under.

Beatrix Potter.

Anna glanced up at Katrine. The facts were tessellating. She stepped away from the desk, as though she was standing back to see a mosaic more clearly. *A call from a personal assistant. A lavish booking made on behalf of someone else. Under a fake name.*

Who do you think it is? said Katrine's beam.

Anna pursed her lips and shrugged: *Hard to say.*

The phone rang, diffusing the frisson of excitement that had fizzed in the foyer only a few seconds before.

'Good morning, the Lake Island Hotel?' chimed Katrine, sitting back down at the desk.

Anna folded her arms, wondering whether William Wordsworth was on the other end of the line this time.

'What, someone *famous*?' said Harry, sitting next to her on the sofa.

Katrine nodded. 'I think so,' she whispered back, even though they were home now. She'd changed out of her work clothes but always kept her tact.

'Imagine if they're properly A-list,' Harry continued. 'A Hollywood star.' His eyes were wide.

'Well, they might be.'

'Imagine: LA to Derwent Bay.'

'I'd rather be here,' said Katrine.

Harry's eyes crinkled at her over his cup. 'Bet it costs *a lot* to rent the *entire place*,' he murmured.

Katrine took a sip of her drink, stopping any more on the matter from spilling out. 'I've no idea who it is,' she said, shaking her head.

'You wouldn't tell me if you did know.' He nudged her leg with his toe.

This was her favourite time of day: snuggled up together for a debrief, back in Keswick, in their cocoon for two. They'd planned to watch a film that evening, but had simultaneously draped their tired selves over the upholstery in such a way it signalled the movie was mutually postponed.

'I reckon they're a singer,' mused Harry. 'A pop star shooting a music video in the mountains.' He swept a hand

4

through the air, reimagining the sitting room as an artistic set instead of a motley collection of their combined belongings. 'All atmospheric and full of drama.'

Katrine grinned as she pictured the scene.

'Possibly a romantic reunion by a misty lake.'

She laughed. In the early days, when they'd shared their stories on snatched dates in between their shifts, he'd told her that he'd dropped out of drama school many years back, decided it wasn't the life for him. Yet moments like this made that hard to believe. He seemed to relish having an audience, even of one, and she delighted in the fact his performances were reserved only for her.

'It could be anyone,' said Katrine, tucking her feet up underneath herself.

The moon gazed through the window, as if wondering who the celebrity guest was, too.

'It might be a girl band,' said Harry, with a carefully judged note of teasing hope.

She swatted him on the arm, and he leaned over to kiss her smile.

'Anyway, how was your day?' Katrine said, rubbing her eyes to stave off sleep, savouring these minutes when their routines were suspended.

'Yeah, fine,' replied Harry, fatigue sighing from him as another Friday spent ferrying guests from one side of the water to the other faded. 'There were lots of checkouts this morning, so busy-busy, then a few couples and a fiftieth birthday this afternoon. All very friendly.'

'Good.' Katrine settled back against the cushions; not all the guests remembered their manners along with their luggage. But as the boatman taking people to and from the island, Harry was responsible for both the start and finish of their stay. And in the same way, he bookended her every day.

'The birthday party was a really nice family,' said Harry. 'First time in the Lakes. Full of excitement.'

She smiled. Remembered the glittering wonder in her dad's eyes when he'd shown her the hotel when he and Anna had just bought it: a long-held wish in a shabby shell. *Five years ago now.*

Harry yawned a silent sleep-cry.

'Bedtime,' said Katrine, standing up.

Harry did the same, took her cup.

Neither of them reached to draw the living-room curtains; in a few short hours they'd only need opening again.

And as they settled into bed, over on the other side of the globe, a fourteen-hour flight across the Atlantic, the much-talked-about mystery visitor to the Lake Island Hotel was only halfway through her day.

Chapter 2

The car should have arrived ten minutes ago. Rachel felt the corridor lurch: no lunch and too much coffee. Her head banged. When had she last drunk any water? There never seemed to be enough time for anything. Gaia's needs came before her own, as though her boss was a glitter-gowned baby. *Goes with the territory*, others in the industry had warned her. *The flipside of the shiny gold coin.* She braced herself for Gaia's reaction as she knocked on her hotel door; three quick raps as she pushed down the stress pulsing through her body. 'It's me,' she said, though she hadn't felt herself for months, not since she'd taken this job.

'Come in,' someone called from the other side, Savannah the stylist, maybe.

Rachel took a deep breath. Clutched the clipboard to her chest as she shouldered her way in.

But her employer was still in hair and makeup.

What?

The limo would be here any second. Why wasn't she ready?

Rachel glanced around; took in the swarming team of assistants, the tense, hairspray-scented air. Sweat sparkled at her temples; the lightbulb-lined mirror glared back at her.

'What's happened?' she asked.

'You tell me,' demanded her boss from the makeup chair, blue eyes boring out of the glass.

Rachel swallowed. Being confronted with two Gaia's was terrifying, even if one was just a reflection.

Rachel blinked at the makeup artist. He bit his lip, head bowed, carried on delicately dusting bronzer across his client's cheekbones. She caught her own pale face reflected back at her, squinting in the blinding brightness. Whatever the problem was, she was certain of one thing: it would all boil down to being *her fault* in the end. If being Gaia's PA had taught her anything, it was that. It was a role as impossible as trying to catch a skyfull of rain with two cupped palms. Like attempting to quell the wild sea in a storm. *I'll stick it out till summer*, she told herself at times like this. *Three more months.* She'd see the trip to England through – she'd always wanted to go to the Lake District, after all, people said it was amazing – and there surely had to be a silver lining to this saga somewhere. *Then I'll leave.* She'd thought she'd be able to last a full year, at least, but nine months was more than enough. Then she'd be reborn, say goodbye to all of this, she promised herself, meeting her own gaze in the glass.

'Someone's in my dress,' said Gaia beside her, voice so level it could be mistaken for calm. But Rachel had learned to read the full range of anger on the Gaia Richter scale.

Her boss's false lashes made the stare she fixed her with even more penetrating.

'That can't possibly be the case . . .' mumbled Rachel, mouth dry. She'd double checked with the designer. She always did. She fumbled with her phone, sweating fingers slipping on the screen. Scrolled through emails. Hundreds of them. She leaned against the side of the dressing table as dizziness fuzzed the edges of her vision.

'Look.' Gaia thrust her own phone towards her.

Sure enough, there was a photograph of a woman posing in exactly the same jewel-strapped midnight-silk sheath Rachel had arranged for Gaia to wear to the premiere. The woman's features were in profile, her chin tilted gracefully. Rachel couldn't be one hundred per cent sure, but if she had to guess, then the person wearing the dress did look very like . . .

She glanced at her boss, expecting to see a red-carpet shade of sheer rage on her face, but to her surprise, tears glistened in her eyes like miniature versions of the gemstones that embellished the copied dress.

'I can't wear it, too. What am I going to do?'

Think, Rachel told herself.

'This is so embarrassing. My career is over.'

'No, it's not.' Rachel almost reached out to put a hand on Gaia's satin-robed shoulder, but stood up straight instead. She had to fix this. Her reputation depended on it. But how? She didn't understand. The fashion house had said it was a one-off. Assured her they weren't dressing anyone else for the event.

Gaia dabbed French-manicured nails at her mascara, the rest of her look pared-back to complement the showstopping gown. 'I'm going to look so stupid, in front of *everyone*.'

For all the glitz and glamour, Rachel didn't envy Gaia one little bit. She pictured the paparazzi with their flashing cameras and baying shouts; sharks searching for a shipwreck, looking for that million-dollar shot.

Think.

It was useless calling her contact at the label. The clock was ticking. The car was due.

Time for Plan B.

Her phone buzzed in her hand. The driver was outside. She strode over to the wardrobe and yanked open the doors. Miles always made fun of her for always having a safety net in place, but then he didn't work in showbusiness. *And neither will I, once this summer is done.*

The backup options hung in the closet like unpicked players waiting to be called onto the pitch.

'It's the end of *everything*,' wailed Gaia as Rachel held up a plunging ruby jumpsuit with an elegantly cut cape.

'I *hate* it.' Gaia held up a hand.

You chose it! Rachel wanted to scream but it wouldn't solve the problem. She zipped the protective cover back up, as though to shield the outfit from her boss's wrath.

'Right, well that leaves this one.' She pulled out a frothy fantasy of a princess dress, fit for a ball. Full skirt, sweetheart neckline, delicate tulle ruffles that cascaded in a fairytale train.

'But I want to wear *this*!' said Gaia, thrusting her phone out again, the image still displayed on the screen.

Unless I Photoshop your face onto it, I'm afraid it's not going to happen, Rachel wanted to retort. She passed the coat hanger she was holding to the stylist, who approached Gaia with the caution of a lion tamer.

'I don't want to wear it!'

A toddler tantrumming in haute couture.

'You'll look stunning,' cooed Savannah. 'Completely out of this world.'

Rachel tried to slow her breathing as she called the driver, asked him to wait just a few more moments.

Savannah inched towards Gaia with the gown. 'Let's just try it on . . .'

The room fell quiet as the stylist eased her into the outfit with expert care.

'There!' said Savannah, standing back to take in the actress's finished look.

'A vision,' declared Mark, a makeup brush still clutched in his hand for good luck, not yet daring to believe the situation had been resolved.

Gaia didn't speak, and for a second Rachel feared she was going to rip off the dress, but instead she burst into tears.

Mark's shoulders sagged as he stood there, unsure whether to rush forward to touch up her melting face or take shelter.

Rachel put her hands on Gaia's shoulders, steered her back to her seat. 'Let's do your breathwork exercises, come on, now. In for five, there we go. Nice and slow.'

Mark stared at her expectantly, like she was casting a spell.

Savannah showed her snow-white teeth, would have frowned had she still had that function in her wrinkle-free forehead.

Gaia closed her eyes.

'That's it, then out again,' continued Rachel, blowing out a breath of her own, trying to slow her heartbeat, too.

Mark covered his face as tears fled down Gaia's freshly foundationed cheeks, rendering the last two hours of his life an utter waste of time.

Savannah's eyes fluttered over the hand-stitched folds of the borrowed frock, the fragile fabric balled in her boss's fists.

But Rachel was more concerned with the first outfit. How on Earth was someone else – and not just *anyone* else: *her* – wearing an identical dress? She just *couldn't* be . . . but the images of the stars already arriving at the event didn't lie. Rachel had seen it with her own eyes.

She jerked her head at Gaia's phone – a dangerous pest in a black-screened slumber – now lying still on the dressing table. She looked from Mark to Savannah and back again, palms upturned. 'What happened?' she mouthed.

They shook their heads. *We don't know.*

It was up to her to find out. It always was.

'Breathe in for five . . .' she soothed again, mind spinning. Her lungs filled with Gaia's signature fragrance – a bespoke selection of essential oils that could have been called Expensive Taste. But there was something else. Rachel thought of the picture that had been snapped on the red carpet and already shared around the world. Live-streamed, splashed on celebrity news sites. A showstopper of a dress worn by none other than *Victoria Cole*. Actress. Model. And ex-girlfriend of Gaia's new fiancé, Federico.

The distinct aroma of sabotage pervaded the room.

'Gaia! Over here!' roared the photographers jostling alongside the red carpet. 'Gaia! This way!' 'Gaia! Give us a glimpse of that ring!'

Rachel watched as she put her left hand on her hip, twisted from side to side to a firecracker of flashes. The metal barrier barely contained the crowd competing for her attention.

Rachel readjusted the train of her boss's dress each time she swivelled this way and that, bending down to smooth the silk ripples back into an elegant river, then stepping out of the sightline, away from the spotlight.

'Gaia! What are you wearing?' came a shout.

A journalist with a microphone millimetres from her employer's mouth.

Gaia's lips parted.

Rachel called the name of the label. Used to anticipating every want or need. A habit she couldn't *wait* to break.

And then there he was. The door of the limo opened to a white-gold blaze of lights and an explosion of clicks. Rachel shielded her eyes as the media competed to capture the couple of the moment. *Like trying to photograph a comet before it left the sky.*

Federico's arm was draped around Gaia like the most desirable shawl. She put her hand on his chest, tipped her head back for a kiss. A luminescent flare from the bustling cluster of press. The combination of the two of them so much more dazzling than either one alone.

Rachel hitched her handbag higher up her shoulder, her back ached from the weight of it, the contents a collection of items to fix every what-if. A surge of tiredness swelled within her, but the night was yet young. There were the speeches, the screening, the reception and the after party still to go. Her feet throbbed, she'd had five hours' sleep and been up for fourteen. She couldn't remember the last time she'd seen Miles for more than a few rushed minutes. Her stomach gave a twist. But she'd triumphed in spite of the earlier dress disaster. Gaia had got her wish, eclipsed every other guest in attendance. Rachel just needed the rest of the evening to go smoothly, then she could finally get home to her boyfriend and her bed.

They were being ushered inside now.

Gaia gave one last wave to the gathered crowd. The goddess of glamour.

Federico flashed a grin. The most famous film producer ever to come out of Rome.

Rachel scurried after them as they entered the foyer of the theatre, allowing herself a split second to take in her surroundings. This was what she'd wished for. Slaved away in all those internships to achieve. She tried to appreciate it, just for a heartbeat.

The hum of a hundred high-stakes conversations.

The wonder of the life-sized game of snakes-and-ladders playing out in front of her.

There were faces she recognised from movies she and Miles had watched together over the years, alongside people she admired from every sector of the business: celebrated screen-writers and industry-shaping directors.

So much talent in one room. The figures at the forefront of the movie-making world.

But her attention kept sliding to those on the sidelines just like her.

The assistants were shepherding, each following a star.

The unheard, unheeded ushers were urging everyone to take their seats.

'Where are *we*?' asked Gaia as they entered the auditorium, looking round at Rachel rather than at the rows of reserved seats.

'In the middle,' Rachel reassured her. 'The best in the house, of course.' She gave a nod.

Gaia turned to grin at Federico.

Rachel smiled at everyone and no one as the three of them took their places, painting on an ever-professional expression like a layer of makeup.

Other members of the audience were filing in now, filling the lines of plush red chairs, finding their celebrity friends in the sea of sequinned frocks and tailored suits, casting aside the seating plan if the current arrangement didn't please them.

But Federico leaned forward, extended his hand in *her* direction. 'Rachel. How are you?' he asked, his dark-haired good looks straight out of a Ferrari advert.

She was so surprised that he'd addressed her, she didn't respond straight away. Was so unused to anyone even half as well-known as him remembering her name.

Gaia was glaring at her from her seat in between them. *Don't you dare let me down*, said her burning stare.

Her smoky eyeshadow complimented her personality perfectly, thought Rachel, as her fireball of a boss blinked back at her.

'Federico, hi,' she said falteringly, almost checking behind her to make sure she was indeed the Rachel he meant. She stretched out her fingers and shook his hand firmly. 'I'm really good,' she replied, used to lying in the name of politeness. 'Thank you for asking . . .'

Gaia frowned, like that was an affront – she always took offence if there was the opportunity.

Federico turned his attention to a man in the row in front of them, who was reaching over to embrace the film producer, congratulate him on this latest release.

'The man of the moment!' Rachel heard him say as she busied herself with gathering up the goodie bags that had been by their seats, stuffing them alongside her already-groaning tote. More stuff to carry around for the rest of the night, less space for her aching feet.

Federico radiated the warmth of Italian sunshine. If there was anyone who could melt her boss, it had to be him, thought Rachel.

Then Federico sat back in his seat.

There was someone standing in the aisle now, on the other side of him. Making their way to the empty chair to his left. Pretending not to have noticed him.

Impossible, thought Rachel.

'Feddy!' came a squeal from the woman as she suddenly looked in their direction.

He stood up to greet her, ever the gentleman.

The woman wrapped her tanned arms around his neck and her diamond-paved jewellery winked in delight.

Victoria Cole.

Gaia was a good enough actress to be able to stifle her gasp.

Rachel's throat was Death-Valley dry. Why had she brought water for her boss, but none for herself?

Federico stepped back, introduced them both.

But there was no need.

Rachel researched everything – the reason she'd got this ridiculous job in the first place – and Gaia was all too aware of who Victoria Cole was, she just couldn't believe she was the woman who was wearing *her* dress.

But it did look *stunning* on her, thought Rachel. The fabric clung to Victoria's supermodel figure as though the silk was one with her flawless skin.

Gaia seethed in serene silence.

Rachel swallowed.

Victoria gave them all a perfect pearl-toothed smile, then twisted to air kiss a guest on her left – and showcase the plunging back of her gown.

Oh my god. Rachel put her hand to her mouth.

It wasn't a duplicate of the dress Gaia had been going to wear at all. It was *far* more dramatic and daring. The front might have been very nearly the same, but the back bore no resemblance: it had been designed to upstage Gaia and steal the spotlight – and possibly her fiancé.

Chapter 3

Dominik wasn't there to see the apricot dawn kiss the mountains good morning. But Anna was awake, watching the hills come to life in the early spring light. She went to the window, a frame for the ever changing view beyond. A mercurial masterpiece more mesmerising than anything man-made. Today, Derwentwater was painted in a peaches-and-honey palette. At the moment, anyway. It would shift with the minute, time reminding her that nothing stayed constant. The world always moved on.

Downstairs, Anna set the kettle to boil. Dominik's day had always begun with a cup of black tea with lemon and sugar, and now that was how she started hers, too. She reached for the mug with his initial hand-painted on the side, herbs entwined around the capital letter. Forever inseparable from his garden.

It had been the only element of the hotel that they could wholeheartedly agree on, too. While bedrooms and communal areas were good-natured battlegrounds, and kitting out the restaurant was clearly Anna's domain, the kitchen garden was a shared passion, and the part of their joint venture where their visions aligned.

She took a sip from her steaming cup, looked out over the box hedges towards the raised beds beyond, bare squares of brown soil at this time of year. It was hard to believe vibrant vegetables had been thriving there a few months before. The cycle never ceased to amaze her, even though the pattern of the seasons was something she was well versed in.

These continually tended patches of earth supplied almost all of the plant-based produce for the hotel's restaurant, Moy. Anna had come up with the name, which meant 'mouth' in Cumbrian dialect, vetoing Dominik's idea of the Polish term 'Usta'. A different word, for exactly the same thing. So much of the world was like that: underneath the surface, people's feelings, hopes and dreams didn't differ all that much. Since then, she often wished she'd gone with his suggestion, but it was too late for that now. She should have been less stubborn and admitted it was better at the time, that it linked well to the sister restaurant in Buttermere, Hesta, it sounded similar on the tongue; cemented the past as something to be proud of, not a period of time to be pushed aside.

She had the final say, he'd said, she was the one with the restaurant-running experience, the half of the partnership who'd put up the money for their project.

But Anna had long since hung up her whites, she'd passed her Head Chef's apron to Jackson three years ago now, swapped the buzz of service for the hush of the garden, the precision of the kitchen for the unpredictability of the outdoors. Screened off from the rest of the hotel by the pleached fruit trees that divided the space, it was where she felt happiest. Yes, that plot of land she and Dominik had planted together had become the beating heart of the whole place. And working away there with soil-stained hands, surrounded by all they had built, was when she felt closest to him. Almost content.

Anna pulled her wool cardigan more tightly around herself. Her breath clouded the cool glass, misting the scene before her. Everything could alter in a second. She thought of the hotel. All their efforts so far. It could all be swept away in an instant. Such a delicate balance, a careful equation. Enough customers and the right attitude. Attention to detail plus a dose of pragmatism. She sighed. Always so much to do – a list the length of the lake.

Derwentwater was shrouded in cloud on the other side of the pane: a temperature inversion. Hot air confronted with cold. The beautiful result of normality being turned upside-down.

She wrapped Dominik's cashmere scarf around her neck as she left their annexe in the grounds of the hotel and headed for the kitchen garden. Productivity was the key. *No point sitting there, feeling like it's all piling on top of me*, she thought to herself, keen to make the most of her early start. The sight of a robin resting on top of the greenhouse made her smile. She was never alone on the island, not really. 'Keeping me company?' she said, as its chocolate-drop eyes glinted back at her.

Inside the glasshouse, her neat rows and ordered shelves made her feel as though everything was under control. All was as it should be. Whatever was happening inside the hotel, in here, she could find comfort in the way the seasons came around like a clock. Predictable. Each quarter bringing its own set of rituals to keep her busy.

Spring was Anna's favourite time of year. Sowing seeds her favourite task. Such an optimistic act. The fruit always proof that miraculous things could grow from only a tiny kernel of hope. She needed to start off the sweetcorn and spinach. Plant the parsnips and leeks. She pictured the bright colours of the vegetables that would soon begin to flourish in the soil, as she worked away. Peppers and pumpkins. Kale and cauliflower. Gardening made you look forward to the future, marvel at everyday wonders: the amethyst skin of a ripe aubergine, the ruby-like spheres of sweet cherry tomatoes, rich baubles of beetroot.

And then Dominik was there beside her. She wasn't sure when she felt his presence, didn't need to look up from her job of planting chilli seeds in soft compost to know he was there next to her. 'First time trying to grow these,' she said with a smile. She pictured the fruit being ready to pick come the summer, as though positive thinking was as crucial as heat and light. Perhaps it was. 'Hope they'll be okay in the Lake District,' she added with a chuckle. The cold, wet climate wasn't what you associated with exotic chillies, but with a bit of love and a watchful eye, hopefully they'd thrive. Or at least survive. She heard Dominik's soft laughter as she flattened the compost with her fingers.

Two hours dissipated like mist.

The next time she looked up, she saw Katrine, making her way towards the hotel's back door, arriving for her shift. Soon guests would start coming downstairs for their breakfast. Anna stood upright, set down her tools. 'Right, that'll do for the moment,' she murmured, though Dominik had already disappeared. Anna started to walk back to the annexe, boot-soles crunching on the gravel path, birds greeting her with a good-morning song.

'Everyone happy?' Anna asked Katrine as she passed through the lobby a little while later with a basket of logs.

Her stepdaughter nodded. 'No complaints so far –' she flicked back the cuff of her jacket – 'though it is only ten past nine,' she added with a grin. 'The day is young.'

'Unlike me,' quipped Anna as she carried the wicker container of wood through to the lounge, though at sixty years old she was fitter and healthier than she'd ever been. In the three years the hotel had been open, she'd spent her days outdoors, keeping both her mind and body busy by striving to get to grips with the rhythms of the garden – a far cry from her previous life where she hardly ever left the stainless-steel interior of Hesta's kitchen.

Maybe she should have looked up sooner, she wondered as she stooped to restock the log pile by the hearth. Searched for Dominik before. But maybe if that had been the case, they wouldn't have had the courage to take the plunge and plough their combined efforts into establishing this place. When they'd finally been reunited, time had seemed extra precious, and what better way to spend it than making their dream come alive.

She remembered something from the night before as she stood up and walked back through the entrance hall. Dominik wasn't around to tell, so she shared her recollection with the next best thing: Katrine.

'You know, I dreamed we had to paint the whole hotel *pink* last night.'

A frown formed underneath Katrine's fringe. 'I do hope that's not some sort of premonition,' she said.

Anna shook her head, thinking of the booking they'd had yesterday. 'Me too. Can you imagine?'

'Yes, but I don't really want to,' replied Katrine, eyes wide. Being the manager meant being on top of everything at all times, and always anticipating the next issue, big or small.

21

That would be a thousand times worse if this famous guest that was due to come in summer was a complete diva. The excitement that had stirred in her the previous day seemed to curdle in her stomach in an instant.

'The entire hotel,' Anna continued, not helping the matter. 'Every inch. Vivid magenta.' She chortled. 'Wouldn't that be total *madness*!'

Yet across the ocean in LA, such an instruction would have seemed quite normal to Rachel had it come directly from Gaia's red-glossed lips. In fact, she was used to turning far more preposterous requests into reality, had got used to her employer's increasingly outlandish demands in the past six months. Even on a day-to-day basis, Rachel knew that Gaia always needed her hotel suite scenting with three freshly lit rose-petal-fragranced candles, equally spaced, and that a vase of exactly twenty-six cut stems of white floribunda – one for every year her boss had graced the earth – should be displayed in each room, in a precisely described dome arrangement. Gaia was a self-proclaimed 'English rose,' and she'd be damned if anyone was going to forget it. But these everyday idiosyncrasies were nothing compared to what she was capable of when the mood truly struck her.

Rachel had heard Gaia wondering out loud whether to have a completely gold-themed wedding when she married Federico the following year, featuring a handcrafted carriage and a specially commissioned thousand-thread carpet, and part of her felt guilty that all of that would be the next PA's problem. They'd have all of this to look forward to. As soon as the recce to Cumbria was over, then Rachel would be out of there. The new assistant would still have twelve full months to sort everything before the big day next summer. And

Rachel would be free, released from worrying about whether a particular make of champagne was the right shade of gold to be served to Gaia's guests.

The sound of her boss's voice brought her back to the present. 'I'm hungry,' Gaia said, like a two-year-old who'd just learned to talk. They were outside the venue now, standing on the sidewalk, and the early hours air was cool on Rachel's skin – a welcome change from the false warmth of the afterparty.

Rachel felt her jaw tense with the effort of trying not to scream in response to her boss's statement. She'd carried a bagful of Gaia's favourite snacks around for the whole evening, for them all to be refused, and she hadn't touched a single canapé at the reception or any of the food at the afterparty. Rachel looked at her watch: quarter past two in the morning. Her exhausted brain tried to come up with a plan. She'd thought all that remained for her to do was corral the happy couple into the waiting blacked-out limo and then she could call it a night. She unlocked the phone that was permanently clamped in her hand. 'I'll order you something now. Japanese?' she asked, feeling a rising panic at the probability of finding a vegan sushi establishment still serving after midnight that wasn't a million miles away from Hollywood Boulevard.

'Hmmm, I don't fancy that,' said Gaia, her pear-drop earrings trembling as though they were the ones in trouble.

Rachel bit her lip.

'It's okay,' said Federico to them both. 'I know a place that'll still be open.'

He was a superhero not a movie producer, thought Rachel.

'They do the best pizza,' he said to Gaia, as though being able to source one at any time of night was all part of being Italian.

Gaia smiled at him. He seemed to have the ability to please her whatever he said – a power Rachel would never possess.

'Would you like to come?' he said to Rachel, his manners as impeccable as his tuxedo.

'No, thank you, I'll leave you to it,' she replied, as Gaia shook her head at her.

As if I'd want to *voluntarily* extend this night even more? thought Rachel to herself.

'You can go,' said her boss, and Rachel felt like doing a fist-pump. *Finally*.

'If anyone can make chillies grow in the Lake District, it's you,' said Jackson to Anna when they caught up later that afternoon. They were sitting at a table in the restaurant, empty now it was three o'clock and the hotel guests had finished lunch. She and her head chef were updating each other on developments on both sides of the kitchen's solid stone wall, which separated it from the orchards and growing beds beyond. They discussed planting schedules and crop production, as well as ideas for new cultivations and future recipes.

From the start, Anna's concept for the hotel's restaurant was to showcase Cumbrian ingredients in simple yet delicious ways, but Jackson revelled in coming up with ever more exciting twists to delight their diners. Their collaboration continued to go from strength to strength and she couldn't be prouder of him for all he'd achieved – in fact, she was hardly able to believe he was the same boy that had once railed against Hesta and the style of cooking they employed, before performing a complete turnaround and becoming the best apprentice she'd ever had. She'd never imagined stepping back from the stove before she reached sixty, or that she herself would never cook in the kitchen she and Dominik had created, but there had been something satisfying about handing the baton to the next generation, someone she'd mentored from the start, who'd begun at the bottom at Hesta and worked his way up the culinary ladder. Jackson was innovative and enjoyed experimenting with different flavour combinations and thinking up new ways to celebrate the fresh, seasonal food Anna grew in the garden.

'But enough about cooking for now,' said Jackson suddenly, looking up from his scribbled-on notepad. 'I hear we've got a *celebrity* coming!' He raised his eyebrows as though that would help elicit their name from Anna's lips.

'How do you kno...?' She trailed off. News always travelled swiftly on the island, as though secrets bloomed in the soil here, bursting forth before their very eyes.

'Harry told me,' admitted Jackson with a grimace.

Of course, thought Anna. The two of them had become firm friends; the hotel staff formed a close-knit family, the only people on the island apart from the guests.

'I won't say anything to anybody,' promised Jackson solemnly. He mimed fastening his lips together like he was closing a zip. 'Katrine's emailed us all a form to sign this morning.'

Anna nodded.

'Not that I actually know anything,' he added with a shrug.

'We've only got a pseudonym so far,' she replied.

'And you've absolutely no inkling at all?' he whispered, as though the hotel itself could hear.

She shook her head. 'I don't see the point of speculating either.'

'I just want to know who I'm cooking for.' Jackson's eyes shone in the restaurant's lights.

25

'We'll find out soon enough. But any information will be on a strictly need-to-know basis. And I'm sure I can count on you to be professional.'

Jackson hadn't let her down once since he'd started as a commis chef at Hesta all those years ago.

'What happens on the island, stays on the island,' said Jackson with a mock salute. There was something about the hotel seeming to be removed from everyday life that set it apart from the rest of the world. A sanctuary from reality. It was surely why their enigmatic guest had chosen to come here – wanting somewhere secluded from prying eyes and away from the gossip and chunter of somewhere more accessible.

'Right,' said Anna, satisfied. 'Then let's get back to these starters, shall we?' she said, spreading her palms across the scrawled-on menu in front of them.

'Just one more thing before we do that,' said Jackson.

Anna glanced up. She had little time for rumour or hearsay. Whoever was coming to visit was no different to the regular guests that usually graced their doors, in her eyes. Everyone deserved the same respect and attention to detail. 'What?' she said, letting out a sigh.

'How are *you*?' asked Jackson, to her surprise.

'I'm fine,' she replied, so fast he knew it was a reflex.

He frowned. '*Really*, how are you?' he asked again, refusing to focus on the menu till she looked at him.

Anna swallowed, for there was another big day looming that none of them would celebrate.

Chapter 4

The day broke in great cracks of pink and scarlet; broken-hearted colours befitting the occasion. The anniversary of the event none of them could have seen coming. Here again, another four seasons and 365 turns around the sun later. Three years in total since it had happened.

As the morning sky bled red beyond the mountains, Anna flung back the covers, determined not to feel sad. The hotel was a place of happiness, that was what she and Dominik had wanted right from the start. She didn't intend her emotions to get the better of her, especially not when the hotel was fully occupied and the restaurant was booked to capacity. People were here to enjoy themselves; her staff were depending on her. There was no way she was going to dampen the atmosphere being maudlin.

The first rays of dawn turned the dust motes in the air to glitter. The garden was calling; nature always knowing when she needed it most. She left her phone on the bedside table, on top of the stack of books Dominik never read, and made her way downstairs.

The stretched-out branches of the trained fruit trees were like arms reaching to envelope her, and the soaring birdsong of the early morning chorus lifted her soul. An hour or so outside, cocooned in the island's beauty, was exactly what she needed to root her to the present.

'Oh,' she exclaimed as she saw a figure in front of her, over by the far wall. Goosepimples prickled her neck: a mixture of the cold air hitting her skin and the shock of seeing someone unexpected in her garden haven.

It was Will from Fell View Farm across the water in Buttermere.

What is he doing here? She usually knew everyone who was booked to cross over to the island each day – staff, visitor or supplier.

He had his back to her, was crouched down on the frost-dusted ground.

She walked towards him, wellies scrunching along the stone chippings, but he didn't look up, was too busy constructing something on the gold drenched grass on the very edge of the garden.

'Good morning,' she said as she came to stand beside him.

He pushed himself to his feet with a huff. 'Anna, hello.' His cheeks were flushed a rose colour like the clouds. He indicated the pile of what looked like cedar-wood planks. 'Um . . . I wanted it to be a surprise . . .'

It appeared as though he'd been assembling something, but she wasn't sure what.

He scratched his stubbled chin, shuffled his boots on the gilded grass.

'I was . . . er . . .' he said, to the espaliered apple and pear trees that surrounded them, instead of her. His blush deepened to match the sky.

Anna scanned the patch of land where they were standing, looking for the answer. This was perhaps the warmest, most sheltered spot on the whole island. Here, protected by the garden wall, was the place where the sun spent the most time, and even at this hour, there was a warmth to its rays.

Will swallowed.

It was unlike him to be so stuck for something to say.

'I was building you a beehive,' he blurted out, stuffing his hands in his coat pockets.

It was Anna's turn to be speechless.

Will squinted at her in the little slice of sunrise where they stood. 'I wanted to . . . do something nice to . . . to . . .'

And then Anna understood.

'. . . to mark the occasion,' he finished.

The word 'memorial' hung unspoken between them.

Anna swept a dew-drop dampness from her cheek.

'I should have asked . . .' muttered Will, rubbing his forehead. 'I don't know what I was thinking . . . It seemed a good idea at the time . . .'

Tears burned the back of Anna's eyes. 'It's a lovely thought.'

Will's gaze was on the pile of wood – as unrecognisable from the finished idea as the hotel had been when Anna had first bought it. He'd wanted to create something, when so much had been lost. Do something nice for her, and for Dominik.

'Thank you,' she murmured as Will crouched down again, his attention once more on putting together the beehive's cedar pieces.

Anna turned towards the pebbled path; began to walk back the way she'd come. 'I'll put the kettle on,' she said to him over her shoulder.

He looked up and smiled.

How long had it been since she'd last seen him? she wondered as she made them both a mug of tea in the misty-windowed warmth of her annexe home. Ages. *Months.*

They'd got off to a rocky start back in Buttermere, when he was her restaurant supplier and she was his buyer, but eventually they'd gained a sort of tentative understanding of each other. Realised they weren't quite so different after all. That they both had a passion for the area, a love of local produce, an appreciation of the natural landscape. They may not have become *friends* as such, but there'd been a thaw, even the first shoots of mutual respect by the time she'd opened the hotel. And since he'd stepped back from the farm, handed over the reins to his daughter, Rose, he'd been helping here and there with the hotel garden, as an extra pair of hands mainly, occasionally offering advice on what to grow and how. But this was the first time he'd visited of his own accord, she realised, as she stirred in the milk. She would *never* have envisaged him being involved at one stage, she thought, as she set down the teaspoon. They'd clashed so many times in the past. But if life had taught her anything at all, it was that you couldn't predict what would happen in the very next moment, let alone the future.

Katrine's head was bowed, her brow creased in concentration, when Anna walked past Reception a couple of hours later.

'I don't want to interrupt,' Anna said softly, placing a hand on the solid-wood surface of the oak desk. 'Only checking you're still on for dinner.'

Katrine glanced up. 'Definitely. It's tradition . . .'

Anna nodded. 'And Harry, too?'

Katrine beamed at the mention of her boyfriend's name. 'He's honoured to be invited. Can't quite believe he's going to be cooked for by *Anna Carleton*.'

Anna traced the lines in the slab of burnished wood. 'Oh, it'll just be something simple.'

'To you.' Katrine grinned.

'I was thinking some kind of pierogi,' said Anna.

'Dad's favourite.' A dreamy expression came over Katrine's face as she pictured a freshly made plate of the delicate dumplings.

'Mine won't be as good as his,' said Anna. Dominik's were the best she'd ever tasted, filled with caramelised cabbage and wild mushroom.

'I bet they're better,' said Katrine kindly, eyes shining in the chandelier light.

Anna felt a burst of affection for her stepdaughter. 'So, just come round when you've finished,' she said, glancing over at the computer screen. 'I'll stop distracting you.'

Katrine rubbed her forehead. 'Oh, you're not – I just had an email the length of the Magna Carta so I was working my way through that.' She angled the monitor so Anna could see as she scrolled right to the bottom of the message.

'Goodness me.' Anna raised her eyebrows. The signature at the end had an address in Los Angeles. 'Is this from . . .'

Katrine nodded. 'An assistant called Rachel, wanting to check "a few things" before her VIP client comes to stay.'

But then the phone rang, and as Katrine reached to answer it, greeting the caller with a cheery good morning, Anna glimpsed Will out in the garden through the far window. He'd been working away there since she'd taken him his cup of tea about two hours ago.

* * *

Will came to join Anna on the garden bench, and the sun beamed back at them above the fells.

Anna gazed at the beehive bathed in the spring light. 'It's beautiful.'

'I'm glad you like it,' said Will, turning towards her. 'I thought I'd just build one to begin with,' he added. 'See how you get on.'

Anna nodded. 'Jackson'll be thrilled, too. Our very own Lake Island Honey.'

'Sounds good, at least,' Will replied. He looked up at the sun-streaked sky. 'We'll bring in the bees when it's a little bit warmer.'

How was it already a quarter of the way through the year? wondered Anna. Time slipped by so quickly, yet some days crept by at a crawl. Back when she and Dominik had been setting up the hotel, March had meant seeing joyous bursts of life everywhere they looked: the first clusters of wild daffodils; vibrant swathes of bluebells. Confetti blossom and branches covered with sticky buds. In between all the hard labour there had been spring swims and woodland walks and they'd marked each milestone – a completed room, a ticked-off chore – against the backdrop of the Cumbrian countryside. But now the nights getting lighter, just meant the days were longer.

'Well,' said Will now, standing up. 'I'd better be off.'

Anna bent to collect up their crumb-covered plates and empty coffee cups.

'Thanks for the cake.'

'And what do I owe—'

'That's a gift, obviously.' Will glanced at the beehive before meeting her gaze again.

'But I'd thought about getting some—' began Anna.

Will held his palms up. 'Good. And I'm pleased to help. If there's anything else you need a hand with, just say . . .'

'Thanks,' murmured Anna as they started walking back along the path towards the hotel.

'It's no trouble. I'm glad to be busy . . .' Will trailed off as though he hadn't intended to admit as much.

The crockery Anna was carrying clinked as they lapsed into silence, nearing the point where their routes would diverge.

'Right, then, see you soon,' said Will, beginning to weave his way towards the front of the building, back in the direction of the jetty. He raised an arm in a farewell wave.

'See you soon,' Anna called like an echo, watching as he disappeared around the corner.

She shielded her eyes with her fingers as she watched him leave. The midday sun was glinting off the glass of the lounge's large side window, almost blinding her, as though the hotel itself was trying to make her believe in patches of brightness again.

Chapter 5

Rachel closed her laptop and rubbed her eyes. The rest would have to wait for now. She'd booked first-class flights and a luxury car transfer for the Lakes trip at least. She struck a line through those bullet points on her list, but no longer got the same hit of satisfaction she had when she'd first started in the role.

Coming to bed any time soon? x

Miles was texting her from the bedroom. That was what their relationship had shrunk to. She scraped a hand through her hair. She needed to call it a night. She scribbled yet more jobs on her notepad, in an attempt to stop her thoughts endlessly swirling in her head as she tried to sleep. *Passports. Pounds sterling. Source scented candles.* She stretched her arms above her head as a yawn escaped her lips. *Find Lake District florist. Ask about hotel security. Check vegan menu.*

Her phone buzzed again.

Gaia.

I think Feddy's going to break up with me.

Rachel wanted to tap back: `Well, maybe try being nicer`. But her boss was already typing again.

`I need a cab home from his.`

'*Please*,' Rachel added aloud. She opened her taxi-booking app with a sigh, scrolled to select an executive car—

`It's okay Feddy's got me one.`

Rachel slumped back against her chair. Then yet another message popped up.

`Can you come round to mine?`

'What, *now*?' muttered Rachel, tiredness making her body ache. It was gone 11 p.m. She clenched her jaw.

Gaia sent a crying face emoji.

Rachel blinked at her phone screen. Gaia's apartment was in the Hollywood Hills on the other side of the city. But there wasn't really an option other than to go. It would only make her life more hellish if she didn't, and she desperately needed the rest of her employment to go smoothly. Then she'd get her reference and *run*.

She grabbed her notebook and shoved it into her handbag. Double-checked her diary for the following day. The *Vogue* photoshoot. Oh god, she really had to stop Gaia from working herself up into a state ahead of that. Puffy eyes weren't a good front-cover look. And her boss would only be more of a nightmare if the pictures turned out anything less than perfect—

Her phone pinged again.

Rachel took a deep breath.

But this time it was Miles.

`Night x`

Chapter 6

Anna laid the table for three, put out the best linen napkins that weren't often used, one beside each place setting. She lit a cream pillar candle in the centre, surrounded by a circle of fresh foliage from the garden. Arranged a vase of daffodils beside it. The blue and white pottery one Katrine had given them. The doorbell chimed as she was stoking the fire; filling every corner of the house with light and warmth.

She didn't let go of Katrine until her stepdaughter stopped hugging her first. Then she stepped back to usher Harry in from the cold. 'Welcome, welcome,' said Anna.

'Mrs Carleton,' he said with a smile as he stretched out his arm to shake her hand.

'Oh, you're not at work now, Harry,' said Anna, reaching to embrace him too. 'Plus you're practically part of the family.'

Anna felt her heart squeeze as she witnessed the look he and Katrine shared in that moment: unbridled love.

'What can I get you to drink?' Anna asked as she led them from the hallway to the open-plan living room.

'Ooh, cosy in here,' exclaimed Katrine.

'We brought a bottle,' replied Harry, holding up a bag. He glanced across at Katrine, as though to indicate the contents had been her choice. He handed the carrier to Anna.

'Thank you,' she said.

'We'll have some of that,' said Katrine with a smile. 'I'll open it,' she said, touching Anna's shoulder.

'Can I help with anything else?' asked Harry.

'All under control I think,' said Anna with a shake of her head. She went over to the stove, dropped her homemade dumplings in the pan of boiling water.

'Looks amazing,' said Harry, coming to stand beside her. 'Thanks for having us – me, particularly. I know usually you and Katrine—'

'It's lovely to have you here, too—' Anna jumped at the signature popping sound of—

'Champagne,' declared Katrine, holding out a glass for her to take.

'Goodness me,' said Anna. She felt a wave of emotion bubble up inside her. An unfamiliar fizzing sensation: *gratitude* for the situation she found herself in, for the unconventional little unit she'd become part of, as she looked at the people that were currently gathered round her kitchen counter with her.

Katrine chinked her drink against the others' when they all had a glittering glass in their hand. 'To family,' she said simply.

Anna repeated Katrine's words as she raised her sparkling cup of hope.

'To family,' said Harry, before taking a sip.

Katrine shone, and Anna wished Dominik could see her.

Harry looped an arm around his girlfriend's shoulders and Anna directed her attention towards the pan of pierogi. Little pillows packed with pure joy. They were floating now; almost ready. She scooped the little half-moon shapes from the water. Stirred the caramelising cabbage and onion accompaniment.

'Smells delicious,' said Katrine, looking over Anna's shoulder. 'She grows everything herself, you know,' she said to Harry proudly. 'The potatoes as well, all of it. Made from scratch.'

'I can't wait to try them,' replied Harry appreciatively.

'You two sit down and I'll bring it over in a minute,' said Anna, above the sputter and crackle of the frying pan.

Katrine carried the bottle of wine over to the table along with each of their glasses.

Harry politely poured tumblers of water.

'Here you are,' said Anna, presenting them each with a plate of perfectly crisped pierogi, now resembling small round-edged sunrises, warm and golden.

'Oh wow,' breathed Katrine. She cut into one and took a bite. 'Tastes like home,' she said, looking over at Anna.

'This is the most delicious thing I've ever eaten,' said Harry. 'It'll be all downhill from here on,' he said with a humorous sigh.

'I think these are the best ever, Anna,' Katrine added generously.

Anna felt heat flush her cheeks; a combination of standing so close to the cooker and receiving so many compliments.

'That was incredible,' said Harry as he scraped up the last morsel of spiced apple pie from his plate. 'Thank you.'

'It's my pleasure,' replied Anna with a smile. A contented warmth spread through her as she sat back in her chair. The evening had been full of animated chatter; lively speculation about the identity of the person who was coming to visit in the summer, a fun-filled bet as to whether it would be a high-profile figure they'd have heard of, or somebody so trendy they wouldn't have a clue who they were. The amber candlelight cast their faces in a happy glow, illuminating their laughter, a flicker of Dominik's spirit in the sound of their voices.

Harry stood up to clear their empty plates.

'Oh, leave that. You two get back, it's late,' said Anna, reaching out a hand to still him.

'Are you sure?'

'Absolutely.'

'It's been a wonderful evening,' said Katrine, stretching her arms above her head. 'Very special.'

'It has,' agreed Anna.

'I've enjoyed it a lot,' said Harry with a nod.

'You'll have to come again soon,' added Anna. 'We don't need a reason to get together.'

'You must come to us next time,' said Katrine. 'Spend an evening back on the mainland. See our new place.'

'Oh, no pressure at all cooking for Anna Carleton,' Harry said with a sideways glance at his girlfriend.

'I'd eat anything,' said Anna, batting the air.

'Thanks – setting the bar low for me,' said Harry, a twinkle in his eye.

'Then, Keswick here I come,' declared Anna, as another flutter of gratefulness enveloped her.

Derwentwater was liquid obsidian, the stars white sapphires above them as Harry and Katrine walked down to the jetty, their breath clouding between them as they talked.

'Well, that was lovely,' Harry said, as the lake greeted them with glistening ripples and soft gurgles.

'It was,' agreed Katrine.

Flashes of molten night glimmered between the slats of the wooden walkway as they neared the boat, the water serenading them with its hushed splashes of song. Otherworldly reflections danced on the surface, the playful moon painting everything in sight a silvery shade of magic. The journey across to the other side was only ten minutes, but when you were out here on the island, the mainland felt a million miles away.

Harry took Katrine's hand to help her onto the boat. Not because she needed it, but because this was the first sliver of time they'd had to themselves all day. Wavelets whirled around the jetty posts as he pulled her close.

She kissed him beneath the winking sky.

'Anna should cook at Moy sometime. She's amazing,' he said as he unmoored them.

Katrine blinked at him; dark tendrils of her hair tugged back by the breeze.

'Has she ever thought about it?' Harry continued, but when Katrine didn't reply he wondered whether his question had been carried away by a breath of wind.

They began to cut their way through the shimmering ink-well of lake that separated them from Keswick, making their way home.

'You know the story,' Katrine said, her beautiful black locks blurring with the midnight sky.

'Not really. I know she used to mentor Jackson, that she brought him in to run the restaurant here because he'd impressed her over at Hesta . . .'

Katrine nodded.

'We don't have to talk about it if you don't want,' said Harry with a shake of his head. Navigating a relationship was much more complex than piloting a boat – there were no red buoys to mark the rocky bits to steer around. He concentrated on the speckle of lights that gleamed across the way.

'No, it's okay,' she said. 'She didn't want to be in the kitchen anymore, after what happened . . .'

Harry's eyes widened. 'After your dad died.'

Katrine nodded. 'She preferred to be out in the garden, planting things, away from people saying how sad it all was and how sorry they were.'

Harry nodded. 'That makes total sense,' he said as the golden glimmer of the bay up ahead sped closer.

'She was head chef when the hotel opened. Just for that one night. Dad collapsed in the middle of service, in front of a packed-out restaurant on that very first evening.'

'Oh my god,' said Harry. 'I had no idea. I knew it had been sudden but—'

'There was nothing anyone could do. He could have had the hole in his heart for ages, the doctors said.' Katrine smiled. 'I thought that would have been sorted once he found Anna again.'

Harry's lips twisted as he took it all in.

'Maybe all the excitement of it didn't help,' continued Katrine. 'So many years of hard work finally coming together. Perhaps it was too much.' She bit her lip. 'The fact the hotel was fully booked and it was all real after so long.'

'Poor Anna . . .' said Harry. 'The shock must have been—'

'It ruined her for a while. She hung up her apron after that. Wanted to be alone in the garden she and Dad had built. But gradually, she started to see it differently. I don't think you get over something like that, but she said she was very lucky to have found Dad again, and to have had the five years they did spend together,' said Katrine.

'The strength that must take,' said Harry.

'That's Anna,' replied Katrine with a shrug.

Chapter 7

A sharp pinch of pain woke Rachel – the combination of constantly being hunched over some kind of screen and a few snatched hours of sleep spent awkwardly slumped in an armchair in Gaia's living room. She looked about her as she rubbed her eyelids, realised she still had mascara on, was dressed in the previous day's clothes. For all its plushness, the velvet curves of the statement piece of furniture she'd curled up in provided little comfort. Rachel hadn't even had the energy to crawl to the spare room. Gaia's apartment was so large, it had seemed like an insurmountable task, and she'd passed out where she was. Her iPad was still flipped open on the enormous oval coffee table in front of her, her notebook and pen beside it. She shuffled upright, her spine aching, feeling the weight of her responsibilities press down on her like the high ceiling was caving in. Despite the huge rooms and sheer scale of the place, Rachel always felt suffocated whenever she was here; the apartment's curated perfection making it feel like a show home or the set of a film. *But that view.* That was something else. She had to admit she was just the slightest bit envious of that, at least. She and Miles looked out onto a backstreet scattered with litter and long-discarded dreams, where the walls were decorated with the kind of graffiti that railed at the world, rather than sold for thousands to art collectors at auction.

Rachel sighed. She longed to throw the great sliding windows wide, let fresh air flow freely through the gargantuan villa's veins, but knew she would risk Gaia's rage if she disrupted the state-of-the-art aircon, the carefully curated humidity and filtration. She stood up, didn't dare touch the spotless panes of the bullet-proof doors for fear of leaving fingerprint smears on the panes. The blue-skied morning stared back at her, framed by the floor-to-ceiling surrounds, the city stretching out to the horizon in a manmade sea of metal and glass. Trees dotted the foreground, flanking the view of downtown LA, and Rachel fleetingly wondered how the Lake District hills compared to the Hollywood ones. She couldn't really imagine what Cumbria was like, found it hard to picture a world that didn't orbit Tinseltown – even the skyscrapers in the distance seemed to be reaching upwards desperately hoping for a handful of stardust.

Rachel made a mental note to research their summer destination some more; she'd looked at images of the Lake Island Hotel online – checked out the décor, dining options and facilities available. Begun to explore transport and logistics. But what about the landscape? 'Natural' was an offensive word in Gaia's circle. Rachel thought of the hours spent in hair and makeup, the elaborate outfits, the illusion and artifice. Moviemaking was modern magic, but maybe a spell in the countryside was exactly what Gaia – and she – needed—

A buzzing jolted her from her reverie, reverberating through her body. *Her phone.* Where on earth was it? Rachel scrabbled to find it as the vibrating continued. God, what was the time? Her sleep-deprived mind struggled to snap into action. Then there it was – her fingers closed around the metal case; it had slipped down the side of the seat cushion. She pulled out the phone with a breath of relief. But when she saw the time displayed on its electronic face she dropped it as though she'd left it out on the panoramic balcony in blistering heat. The *Vogue* photoshoot. They should have been on the way by now.

She fumbled for the phone again, noticed the caller's name this time. *Miles.*

She clicked to answer it. 'Hello.' Her head and heart pounded a guilt-ridden rhythm.

'Where are you?' he said, though he didn't really need to ask. 'Not *again*,' he added with a sigh, when she paused before answering.

'I . . .' began Rachel, recalling the tornado-strength spiral Gaia had been in when she'd arrived the previous night. What time had it been when she'd finally got her to bed?

'Look, I don't want to hear any excuses,' he continued before she could explain. Rachel could hear his final straw about to snap on the phone; his tone was brittle, the affection in it worn thin along with his patience. 'I just wanted to know you were okay.'

Was she okay? Rachel flinched as her neck twinged again. 'I'm . . . fine,' she replied. She didn't have time to justify the situation to Miles. She had to get through today, and once she'd handed in her notice, she could start to repair their relationship, stitch the gaping holes in the fabric of them back together again.

'I've got to go, Miles. We're already late for—'

'Well, that's just it. There's only one "we" in your world, isn't there, and it's not you and me.'

'Miles. Please. This won't be forever.'

'No, it absolutely won't.'

Was he going to break up with her? Rachel felt claustrophobic, like the carefully controlled air-handling system had sucked all the oxygen from the atmosphere. She put a hand to her chest. She'd come here last night because Gaia had been fretting about Feddy, and now her own relationship was on the line. 'I had to come or else—'

'Or else what, Princess Gaia would have had to put her own pyjamas on?'

Rachel winced at the comment. Was that what his true thoughts were about her job? That she'd sacrificed so much – of herself, of their time together – for something utterly inconsequential. Gaia wouldn't be thriving in her career as she was without people like *her* peddling away in the background supporting her.

'What's in this for you, Rach?' said Miles, more gently now. 'What are you doing this for?'

Rachel swept a hand over her eyes, felt flecks of dried mascara migrate down her cheek like dehydrated tears. Miles's words were like an injection of honesty.

'I know it's hard to believe but I feel the same way as you,' she said. 'I'm just trying to get through these last few months.'

'And then what? You'll do all this for someone else? Spend your whole life waiting hand and foot on someone who doesn't even have the decency to say please and thank you?'

Rachel opened her mouth, but no words came out. He was right. There was nothing to say her next position would be any different, any less all-consuming. She'd expected it would be hard graft in this industry, but assumed there would be an upside somewhere. Yet she was struggling to see any sort of reward whatsoever. The pay didn't cover the emotional cost; and there could never be a fair price for taking over her whole life.

'I can't do it anymore, Rach.' His voice cracked.

'*What?*' she whispered.

'This. *Us.* There isn't an "us" anymore, is there?'

The sound of her heart thudding made it hard to hear him on the other end of the line. 'You're doing this over the *phone*?' she found herself saying.

'I never see you. What am I supposed to—'

'Miles, wait . . .'

'It's too late. I'm sorry. I can't carry on like this.' He sighed. 'You might want to spend all your time surrounded by actors and people faking it till they make it, but that's not me, Rach. I'm done pretending. I want something *real.*'

'This was real to me.' *Was.* She heard her own words and stunned herself. After almost four years, was it really that simple to consign their time together to the past?

'Gaia might be your world but she's not mine,' said Miles.

'She's not my—'

'Sorry, *universe*,' he said, his sentence garnished with bitterness like a shot served with lime.

Rachel was too taken aback to reply.

'I shouldn't have said that,' he added suddenly. 'I'm just . . . disappointed. Heartbroken to be honest.'

'Well, then let's fix it,' said Rachel. 'Can we at least talk it all through in person. You're right, I should have made more time for you. And for me, too. It's just seemed impossible to even take five minutes to *breathe* at some points.'

'Okay,' muttered Miles after a few seconds. 'We can thrash it all out face to face.'

'I can't come right this second . . .' she said tentatively.

'No, I didn't think that would be the case, don't worry. When you get home later?'

'Yes,' said Rachel.

'I'll make us some dinner. I miss you, Rach.'

'Me too. I love you.'

And then Gaia appeared in front of her, a ferocious look on her face.

'I've got to go . . .' she said hurriedly into her phone. 'See you tonight. I won't be late,' she added before she ended the call.

Her boss's eyes were flaming. 'What are you doing?' she demanded. 'I don't pay you to lounge around chatting on the phone.'

Rachel clenched her jaw. She hadn't even had a minute's downtime apart from the few hours she'd been unconscious.

'Careful with that,' said Gaia, gesturing with a manicured hand at the accent chair Rachel was still sitting in. 'It was expensive.'

Rachel leapt up. What was the point of a chair if you weren't allowed to—

'You didn't *sleep* there, did you?' Gaia said.

Rachel swallowed. Was she not even supposed to rest now, was that it? This was ridiculous. Miles was right. Gaia expected her to be a robot, ready to respond to her commands and cater to every whim. 'I didn't mean to.'

'Stay in one of the spare bedrooms next time.'

Gaia had no idea how entitled she was. Next time? She didn't *own* her, thought Rachel. She should never have come last night, she realised. She had to draw a line somewhere. Maybe she and Miles would never have got to the brink of splitting up if she'd stuck to some kind of boundaries.

'The maid will deal with everything.'

Don't they have a name? thought Rachel, but Gaia was across the other side of the open-plan living space now, in the never-cooked-in kitchen with its continent-sized island.

She took a bottle of water from the fridge and strode back again, her silk kimono-style robe floating behind her, making her look almost angelic.

When she was closer, Rachel was relieved to see she was fresh-faced and rosy featured.

Her boss sat down on the enormous L-shaped sofa opposite her and delicately crossed her bronze-skinned legs. 'So, turns out I was worrying about nothing after all,' she said with a nonchalant flick of her wrist.

Rachel's shoulders tensed. She'd spent all night here for absolutely no reason. Gaia seemingly created storms just to dance in them.

'Feddy's reassured me that Victoria Cole is *nothing*.'

That sounded very much like Gaia's phrasing, rather than Federico's, mused Rachel. He seemed far too nice to talk about anyone that way. *Too nice to be going out with Gaia.* But what did she know? realised Rachel. People could perform all sorts of parts, pretend to be one character and then morph into another entirely. She'd seen Gaia do it on so many occasions. Now, her boss was sunny-faced and smiling, when only minutes before she'd worn a scowl. *A silk-kimonoed chameleon* thought Rachel. 'Right, well I'm glad it's sorted,' she replied, trying to quash the surge of resentment she couldn't help rising within her. She'd walked out of her own life, left Miles wondering where he came in her list of priorities, and raced across the city all because Gaia was incapable of being alone for a second. She needed drama like others required air. Rachel pictured the over-the-phone interrogation she'd witnessed when she'd arrived at the apartment the previous night: Gaia talking to Federico on loudspeaker – because of course nothing truly existed without an audience.

'She was trying to steal my thunder at the premiere.' Gaia pouted now, mood shifting like a mercurial sky. 'I know she wants Feddy back – who wouldn't – but she can't have him.' She jutted out her chin. 'She shouldn't have cheated with that runway model, should she.' Gaia arched her perfectly plucked eyebrow. 'He's *mine*,' she said, flashing her engagement ring.

She spoke about him like he was one of her possessions, thought Rachel, a covetable handbag or prestigious award, not a *person*. She studied the fierce expression on her boss's face, the sheer entitlement in her stance. What must it be like to have such unwavering self-belief? she wondered.

But then she saw Gaia's bottom lip tremble, only for a fraction of a moment, and another assistant might have missed it, but not Rachel. She spent too much time with her boss for the slightest change in her demeanour to go unnoticed. Perhaps her custom-made clothing didn't constitute any kind of armour against life's problems after all, and her flawless skin wasn't as impenetrable as the ballistic glass that protected her property.

Rachel lifted the cuff of the dress Gaia had given her to wear – one that had been gifted by a lesser-known fashion label and discarded in a bin-liner destined for Goodwill. 'Far too big for me,' her boss had exclaimed as she'd handed her the garment. 'But you might be able to fit into it.'

It had been one of the most beautifully made pieces of clothing Rachel had ever tried on, the handstitched darts hugging her curves to give her a flattering silhouette. But now as she waited for the photoshoot to finish, the high-neckline and long-sleeves seemed to be stifling her.

Her vision was starting to blur, she'd spent so long staring at the scene in front of her, willing Gaia to speed up. There had been countless changes of outfit, several instances of Gaia wanting to completely alter a planned 'look' and a pattern of her taking twice as much time to do anything as was necessary by anyone's standards – all while numerous nobodies like her beetled about behind the scenes bringing everything together.

Surely they had to be almost there by now? How many images of one mirage-disguised monster did the magazine really need?

They'd been booked in for a half a day – but Gaia didn't do anything by halves. It should have all been wrapped up at least a couple of hours ago by now. Surely it couldn't be too much longer until they were finished, thought Rachel, twisting her wrist to look at her watch once again, though it had only been a few seconds since she'd last done the same. Miles would be getting back from work soon. Damp sweat was making the delicate crepe collar of her dress stick to her neck. She had to make it back on time. Nothing could stop her. Not even gale-force Gaia.

She stood up, smoothed her palms against the soft fabric of her skirt. Now was her chance. If she didn't leave within the next few minutes, she'd be almost certainly losing Miles. There was only so far she could push him before they reached the point of no return. She felt a sickening nervousness like she was standing on the edge of a precipice.

Gaia was positioned facing away from her, engrossed in something on her phone while a *Vogue* employee powdered her perfectly proportioned nose.

Rachel cleared her throat, it felt as dry as the dust-covered tracks of Runyon Canyon.

'Excuse me?' she ventured gingerly, nearing Gaia with the enthusiasm of someone knowingly walking into the eye of a sandstorm.

'What is it?' said her boss, without looking up.

Rachel coughed, trying to coax her own voice to come out. 'Um . . .'

Gaia's gaze swivelled towards her with Medusa-like warmth. 'I . . .' stuttered Rachel. 'It's six o'clock . . .'

'And?' said Gaia, as her tumble of glossy ringlets shivered.

'I have plans . . .' Rachel fiddled with the scalloped hem of her frock.

'What?'

'I need to leave.'

'And I need an assistant,' said Gaia, rising up from her seat like a scorpion preparing to sting.

The make-up artist took a step back.

'If you walk out of that door you're fired.'

Rachel's resolve wobbled as she watched her reference rip in two before her eyes. But this was crunch time for her and Miles. It wasn't another occasion where she could fob him off, FaceTime him instead of taking the time to speak in person. This was make-or-break for them as a couple. 'I'm sorry but . . .' she began. *Why am I apologising?* She'd already worked more than her contracted hours. 'I have to go,' she said.

'Well, I have to find someone who *really* wants this job.' Gaia sat back in her chair, satisfied she'd played her trump card. Rachel would never dare hand in her notice on the spot like this. She cared too much. Thought everything through to the nth degree. There was no way she had the—

But to her surprise, Rachel turned and started to walk towards the door without another word.

Come on, come on, come on, she mumbled as her cab crawled through the crush of rush-hour traffic. She texted Miles to tell him she was on the way; and this time, for once, she actually *was*.

A message flashed up on her phone from Gaia:

`Don't bother coming in tomorrow.`

An unexpected thrill ran through Rachel as she realised she didn't have to deal with any more of her boss's attention-seeking antics. But as the taxi crept along the downtown tarmac, it was replaced with a sense of discomfort. She'd lost her job, her direction. What was she going to do now? All these months of stress had been for *nothing*. Where did she go from here? She rubbed her right temple. Rested her head against the window as the hum and rumble of the engine heightened her lethargy.

'Sorry, ma'am, looks like we're stuck here,' said Bobby, the Uber driver, rousing her from her drowsiness. 'Can't get through,' he said, indicating the stationary snake of cars that stretched along the street. 'Whole road is blocked.'

Rachel craned her neck to look through the windscreen. Took in the metallic jam of vehicles, and the blue flashing lights that seemed to signal you shouldn't be upset you were stuck in traffic when there were people up ahead who had found themselves in a real emergency.

She sat back in her seat. Pulled out her phone. But there was no point texting Miles again. She'd sent a hundred excuses to him since she'd started this job; this was just another one to add to the list, even though the scenario was entirely out of her hands. She sat there, motionless, yet knowingly hurtling towards the end of their story.

When she finally got home after half past seven, there was no sign of Miles, not even a note. He'd have gone to his mum's in Malibu, most likely, thought Rachel, slumping down on a stool. The beginnings of dinner had been discarded on the countertop: an open recipe book and a collection of ingredients from the grocery store. Her shoulders sagged as she surveyed the last crumbs of their relationship, scattered before her on the side – just as Miles walked in through the door.

'I thought you'd gone . . .' she said as she leaped up to hug him.

He held out a paper bag. 'I forgot the . . .'

But she didn't hear what it was he'd gone back out to buy; her face was buried in his sweater. 'I'm so sorry – I left at six.'

A sad smile twisted his lips as he stepped back from her. 'I didn't expect for one second you'd be back before now. . .' he said.

Rachel felt an ache in her stomach; the closeness they'd once shared seemed to have evaporated like steam from a burned-dry pan.

'Well, I quit,' she muttered, searching his gaze for any sign of hope. 'I said I had to leave, and I followed through with it for once.'

'Are you serious?' he said.

'Yes,' murmured Rachel, reaching for his hand.

Miles rested his back against the work surface as though otherwise, he'd have fallen down in disbelief. 'You really said no to gorgon Gaia?'

Rachel nodded. 'Once and for all.'

'I don't want you to go because of me, though,' he said with a shake of his head. 'If you're happy . . .'

'I'm not.' Rachel felt her lip wobble, was momentarily reminded of her boss, and the way a small chink of vulnerability had shown itself earlier in the day, but she pushed the memory away. Gaia wasn't her focus, not now.

But the insistent buzzing from the belly of Rachel's handbag on the breakfast bar said otherwise.

Chapter 8

'Gosh, that's good,' said Anna as she sampled the dish that Jackson had placed in front of her.

'Broad bean hummus with porcini mushrooms and a miso glaze,' he explained, pointing at the various elements on the plate as though he was speaking to someone far less well acquainted with the ingredients, the consummate professional.

Anna felt a swell of pride as she listened. 'Well done,' she said, setting down her spoon. 'It's delightful. Packed with flavour. Well put together. And broad beans will be at their peak in June. It's perfect. A fabulous starter.'

'Suitable for a vegan celebrity?' Jackson asked, hands on his aproned hips. He hadn't dared sit down; jittery energy had fizzed through him as he'd awaited his boss's verdict.

'I certainly think so,' replied Anna. 'But we'll soon see.'

Jackson grimaced. 'God, I hope they like it. There's the tomato consommé, and the artichoke and truffle velouté as well, as alternatives . . .'

'It's all sounding splendid,' Anna reassured him. 'And what have we got for mains?' she asked, sharing the responsibility, attempting to assuage his nerves a little.

'A pearl barley and buttered pea risotto, and a celeriac steak with mint-hazelnut dressing so far. I'm still working on the spiced aubergine option.'

'Marvellous. I'm excited to taste them all,' said Anna. 'And the puds?'

'I bet I'll go to all this trouble and this celebrity'll end up being on some no-dessert diet, won't they?' Jackson replied with a sigh. 'Which is a shame because I've got the *best* rhubarb soufflé you'll *ever* have tasted.' He grinned at her.

'Can't be better than Anna's, surely,' said Katrine, walking into the restaurant.

'Think it might be a close call,' Jackson tilted his head to one side. 'I've added a ginger rhubarb sauce which just makes it, in my opinion.'

There was a sparkle of satisfaction in his eyes that Anna was warmed by. 'I can't wait to try it,' she replied with a smile. She turned to Katrine. 'Everything okay?'

'I just wanted your advice – when you're finished here,' she replied. 'No rush.' Her gaze flicked from Anna to Jackson and back again. She was clutching a sheaf of papers in her hand, and a sheen of perspiration glittered her forehead.

Anna raised her eyebrows.

'Just a list of questions *this* long –' Katrine flipped through the printed-out pages she was holding – 'From *you know who.*'

'Oh, goodness me,' said Anna.

Jackson craned his neck, trying to see what was written in the novella-length email.

Katrine clasped it close to her chest.

'Wait, you *know*, don't you?' he said, looking from her to Anna. 'How is that fair?' he asked Anna, crossing his arms. 'Can't you tell me, too? I'm working away back here, completely in the dark. I might have to change the whole menu!' He raked a hand through his hair. 'What if I need to make it all macrobiotic, or find out exactly what Paleo eating *is*—'

'All right, let's calm down,' said Anna, holding up her palms. 'Take a breath please, Jackson. Katrine knows no more than you do. Neither do I. None of us does.'

'I'm just speaking to a PA named Rachel at the moment, that's all,' Katrine clarified, showing him the last sheet of paper now, pointing at the email sender's sign-off, so he would believe her.

Jackson narrowed his eyes. 'Well then, when will we find out? It impacts *everything*. If I have to start developing an entirely different range of courses—'

'I'll find out, okay?' cut in Katrine. 'You're right, we've signed the NDAs. We're sticking to our side of the deal. At some stage we have to know who we're going to be welcoming here.' She turned to Anna. 'We're bending over backwards trying to prepare as best we can, but how can we put together a tailor-made, premium package when we don't even know who it's for?'

Anna's heart was squeezing as she listened to her staff speak with such passion and care. They prided themselves on providing the best possible experience for customers coming to the hotel. She nodded in unity. 'You've answered reams and reams of their questions,' she said, glancing at the stack of papers in Katrine's grasp. 'They're going to have to answer this *one* from us.'

'Hear! Hear!' said Jackson, banging a hand on the table so that even the pushed-aside place-settings beside Anna chimed their agreement.

* * *

Rachel reached for her phone, face-down on the bedside cabinet, as though it was an explosive. She hadn't slept for more than a few fitful minutes at a time, had spent the night worrying about what the morning would bring, where she went from here. What were the prospects of finding another position with only a six-month stint of employment as a VIP PA on her CV? And if she was going to start again, switch up her career entirely, then where on earth was she going to begin, and what had all those years of internships and trying to get a foot in the door been for—

She stopped herself. Did the mindful breathing she encouraged Gaia to do. *One step at a time*, she told herself. She turned over the phone, peered at the screen with one eye. Notifications were pinging through even in the second or so it took to see the time. *Almost seven o'clock*. Only twenty-four hours before, she'd have been smashing through a full schedule of Gaia-centric duties. But not today. She sank back against the pillows. Miles was still snoring softly beside her, his alarm yet to sound, so she made her solemn vow to the ceiling instead. *Whatever happens now, things will be different*. She would not let herself be in a situation like that again. Not for Miles's sake, but for her own.

She switched on the bedside lamp and swung her legs out of bed. She stretched in the soft light, saw the dress she'd worn yesterday and wondered whether, now she'd left, Gaia would want it back. It was the kind of thing she'd do, Rachel realised, creeping towards the bathroom – just as the doorbell downstairs rang.

Miles shot upright as she froze on the spot.

'I bet that's her . . .' he groaned, voice gravelly, eyes still sleep-small in the semi-darkness.

'Don't be silly,' said Rachel, as a frisson of panic zipped down her spine. 'She's probably never even been to this part of town.'

Then the doorbell rang for a second time, doubly summoning her down.

'No reply, before you ask,' said Katrine, as Jackson walked past the reception desk later on that afternoon.

'I didn't say anything!' he said with a smile. 'But tell me as soon as you know.' He waved a scribbled-on menu in her direction. 'I'm just looking for Anna. Have you seen her?'

'In the garden, I think,' replied Katrine.

'Thanks,' he replied, before carrying on his way.

Katrine frowned back at her computer. She'd answered every single question on the list Rachel the PA had sent her, responded to every email she'd sent – several of them a day – since the booking at the Lake Island Hotel had first been made, but now Katrine had asked for some information in return, there was *nothing*.

'Everything all right?' said Harry, his Cumbrian vowels laced with concern. He was standing on the other side of the counter, one hand resting on its sturdy oak surface as though with all the celebrity-centred madness swirling round the hotel, it was an anchor to something organic.

Katrine smiled at him. 'Yeah, fine. Thank you.'

'Can I get you anything?' He reached across to link his fingers through hers fleetingly. Professionalism came first, but he could tell when she was tense and the knowledge stole away his concentration. Love meant mixing your happiness with someone else's and being unable to separate it however hard you tried. 'Cup of coffee? I'm taking some guests across to Keswick in a couple of minutes but I've got time to make you one.'

Katrine shook her head. 'What if they're early?'

'They get to chat to my amazing girlfriend.' Harry shrugged. 'That's a bonus, surely.'

Katrine laughed. 'Okay, then. Thank you.'

Her voice was a little lighter, and it warmed his ferry-frozen bones. 'One coffee, hand-crafted by an incredibly handsome man, coming right up.'

Katrine grinned. 'Tell him I'm grateful.'

Rachel glanced at the image on the intercom as she always did before she answered the door. She wasn't sure who she was expecting to see standing there – but the bald-headed, round-bellied man blinking back at her in the picture wasn't Gaia, and she released a breath she didn't realise she'd been holding.

'Hello?' she said into the receiver, sure he would be looking for someone else in the apartment block – she'd never seen him before in her life.

'I gotta delivery for a Rachel Taylor?' he said.

'That's me,' she replied, as Larry Stone showed his courier-branded ID badge to the intercom. Had she ordered anything? So much had happened in the last forty-eight hours she couldn't even remember. But she'd barely had time for breakfast, these last few months, let alone online shopping. She stared at the little square screen, trying to get a glimpse of the parcel in case that should offer any clues.

Larry bent down to pick up the package – and then her vision was filled with the biggest bunch of flowers Rachel had ever laid eyes on.

A beautiful bouquet of roses.

Oh, Miles. She felt her chest squeeze as she pressed the buzzer and bounced down the stairs to open the door. 'Oh my goodness!' she squealed as Larry handed her the fragrant spray of pink and white blooms. A small cream card was visible among the satin petals, with her name on the front. They really were for her!

'You have a great day now,' said Larry with a tilt of his head and a half-smile that said he didn't often see such genuine shows of emotion. Maybe Hollywood actresses received gifts like this on a regular basis, thought Rachel, but she had never seen an arrangement so stunning. Simple but elegant. Just what she would have chosen if Miles had asked her to pick something herself—

'Are you okay?' he called from the kitchen.

'I sure am!' she shouted back, bounding up the stairs as fast as she could manage with the huge bouquet.

'I thought Gaia might have come to kidnap you for a second—' he joked.

'Oh, Miles, they're *amazing*!' Rachel gushed. She flashed him a grin as she laid the ribbon-wrapped flowers down on the worktop. 'What a lovely surprise!' She immediately started flinging open cupboards to search for a vase large enough to display them in. 'I'd better get them in water so they don't spoil,' she said, crouching down by the sink. The jug they used for making summer punch would have to do . . .

Miles sat down on one of the stools.

Rachel was hunting for a pair of scissors now, pulling out drawers. 'Things will be different going forward, I promise. This is going to be a new start for us.'

Miles gazed at the roses.

'These must have cost a *fortune*,' Rachel murmured.

Miles nodded in agreement.

She glanced over at him. 'You *really* didn't have to . . .'

Miles looked at her.

'But they are *utterly* gorgeous,' she said, beaming at him, before turning her attention back to the flowers. She started to snip the stems one by one.

Miles watched as Rachel happily displayed the roses in the jug.

'Oh, almost forgot,' she said, smiling at him as she plucked the notelet from its little envelope.

'They're not from me, Rach,' said Miles, just as she read the words inside the card. He turned to look at the flowers once again, but all he could see were the prickly thorns underneath the pretty blossoms.

Rachel put a hand to her mouth. 'Oh my god, they're from *Gaia.*'

Chapter 9

Anna surveyed the kitchen garden, making a note of the most-urgent jobs in her jotter. Now she was three years in, she was gradually getting used to the growing cycles, becoming more familiar with the different stages of upkeep that corresponded with the seasons. She sucked in a lungful of fresh spring air and smiled in anticipation of the buds and berries that would soon be in abundance. She caught sight of the beehive by the far wall and felt a kernel of excitement for the honey-scented summer ahead. It had been a thoughtful gesture from Will, and she was grateful. The garden constantly required new life breathing into it for it to thrive, and what could be a better addition than their own colony of Lake Island Hotel bees?

Dominik's agricultural background had proved invaluable when it had come to setting up the farm-to-fork side of the business, and they had laid out the garden together, planned what would go where, pictured it full to bursting with herbs and vegetables. And now it had matured like a person, developed its own personality. The soil had decided which seeds it liked to grow best, which plants were its favourite. And the more Anna nurtured the garden, the more it seemed to nurture her back.

There was always such an endless list of tasks to do, though. She looked at the almost-bare beds, but it wouldn't be long till roots started to sprout and stems began to shoot skywards. Soon, the garden would be flourishing again.

'Afternoon,' said a voice from the gravel path, interrupting her thoughts.

'Will, hi.' Had she been expecting him? Hours seemed to slide into days so easily when she was out here; the garden always giving her a reason to look towards the future.

'I don't want to get in your way . . .' He looked at his wellies. 'But I was wondering if . . . if you needed any help?'

Anna regarded him standing there in his waterproof and boots; everything he wore was a deep forest green, as though he was made from the great outdoors.

'I was bringing the milk and butter across anyway, so I just thought I'd check while I was here.' He smiled.

'That's very kind but I haven't really thought about it yet,' she said, holding up her gardening notebook. 'Let me have a look and see what's most urgent.' She leafed through the jotter.

'Busy time of year.' He smiled at her.

'Always is,' said Anna. 'Can I let you know when I've figured out a plan of action?'

'Right. Yes, of course.' Will stuffed his hands in his jacket pocket. 'I'll leave you to it.

The birds filled the silence with their song.

'Oh, I brought you some old sheep hurdles as well,' he added. 'Thought they'd make good frames, you know, for the nets . . . to protect the plants.' He pointed to a deconstructed sheep pen, its metal fence-like pieces leaning against the far garden wall.

Anna looked round.

'That's half the battle with gardening, isn't it, keeping pests out,' Will said, then frowned as though he feared Anna might consider him one such pest. He strode towards the little pile of steel railings, seemed to rethink his offering. 'If they're just junk and you don't think they're any use, I can easily take them back with me—'

'No, no. They're exactly what I need, actually,' said Anna, going over to inspect them. 'I was wondering how to cover the fruit bushes properly, so the birds don't pinch *everything*.'

Will stilled. 'Oh, good. Glad they'll come in handy.'

Anna lifted one of the hurdles free of the stack. 'These are *perfect*. The birds ate all our berries last year. Jackson was wanting to make jam and all kinds of sauces and desserts – but they went with the *lot*.'

'Well, you'll be better prepared this summer,' said Will with a nod.

'Hopefully some of the fruit might make it onto a customer's plate.' Anna laughed.

The birds chirruped, oblivious to the plan to put a stop to their pillaging.

'Thank you, Will,' she said, carrying one of the hurdles over to the currant bushes that were just beginning to flower, having slept off the winter.

'You're welcome,' he replied, a strawberry bloom creeping up his neck. 'We sold the flock at Fell View so there's no point us keeping them.' He gestured at the hurdle she was holding.

'Big thing,' she said sympathetically, studying the set of his stubbled jaw, knowing what a momentous move that would be for him.

'Rose wants to expand the ice-cream side of the business.'

'Oh, that's wonderful,' said Anna, feeling a bubble of happiness. 'I'm really pleased it's going well.'

'I'm so proud of her,' he said, eyes welling a little. 'It's strange stepping back though, letting her just get on with it, all grown up. She keeps telling me to enjoy my retirement but I'm not sure I know how. That's why I like doing the deliveries, still being part of it, and seeing everyone.' He cleared his throat suddenly. 'Anyway, sorry, you're probably wanting to get on and I'm blathering—'

'It's okay,' said Anna, understanding the need to keep busy, feel you were moving, too, when the world around you seemed to be changing so much. It must be odd for him, watching the farm he'd spent his whole life looking after alter so much in his daughter's care. Wild Rose ice cream had certainly taken off, but Anna couldn't help suspecting Will felt left behind.

'You can help me put these up if you want?' she said, jerking her head at the hurdles.

He didn't hesitate, immediately started to follow her lead.

'Might be a good idea to hold off putting the mesh up till the bees have done their pollinating, though, to make sure you get as much fruit as possible,' he said as they started constructing a frame around the fruit bushes.

'Good point,' replied Anna. The interlinked jigsaw of the wild world would always be a source of amazement to her.

'I can bring some straw for you, too, if you like – when you're ready for it,' said Will.

Anna looked over at him.

'So the ripening fruit rests on that instead of the bare earth,' he continued. 'Stops it turning mouldy.'

'That would be great,' said Anna appreciatively, imagining laden bushes weighed down with glossy berries.

Maybe this was the year the garden would truly get off the ground.

The light was fading when she waved him off on the shore. As he turned to face her down at the jetty, she noticed the mountains were the same shade of pink as his work-flushed cheeks. 'Thanks for all you've done this afternoon,' she said. She tugged her coat zip further up towards her chin in the twilight; the day's warmth seemed to be leaving the island with him.

'Honestly, I've enjoyed it,' he said. He smoothed his silvered hair as the last of the sun winked from the fells.

After the serenity of gardening side by side together for the last few hours, an awkwardness seemed to have descended with the dusk.

'Obviously, just give me an invoice for the time you've been here—' started Anna.

'No need.' Will held up a hand.

'I insist,' said Anna.

'So do I,' he countered. He started to walk towards the ferry at the far end of the landing stage. 'It was really nice to feel like I've achieved something. Made a small difference.'

'A *big* difference,' corrected Anna. He'd pruned and weeded as though they were working in his own garden; tending the land was his lifeblood.

'Nothing better than being outside, surrounded by nature,' Will said over his shoulder.

Anna recognised that need to feel productive. She was the same. And as she watched him board the boat and greet Harry, who was waiting for him on the deck, she got the sense that Will was going home in a different frame of mind to the one he'd had when he'd arrived. His voice was brighter, his limbs lighter. Contentment shone in his eyes as he wished her goodbye with his hand held high. Maybe putting his time and expertise to good use in the hotel garden was helping him as much as her, she realised. Perhaps restoring order to the wind-ravaged raised beds, pruning unruly plants and starting to implement the plans she'd made for the coming months gave him a purpose when he'd otherwise feel a little lost.

And as she stood there on the pebbled shore with the lake reflecting the final embers of the March day, she thought she saw something of what made the Lake Island Hotel so special to the people who visited; grasped the reason why it often held a place in people's hearts long after they'd left. Here, in the middle of the tranquil water, surrounded by mountains that were millions of years old, all the pretence and pressure of the modern world was stripped away, and a new peace and perspective seemed possible.

Chapter 10

'Is that it then, one bunch of roses and all is forgiven?' asked Miles, elbows resting on the breakfast bar, his head in his hands.

Rachel came to sit beside him. 'No, of course not.' She was about to reach out, squeeze his arm, but wondered whether he wanted space instead. Somewhere along the way, she seemed to have lost the ability to understand the little signals that had so seamlessly stitched together their relationship once upon a time. Had she become so focused on reading Gaia's every facial expression, making sure she picked up on each microscopic behavioural cue, that she'd forgotten how to be there for Miles, too? She rested her chin in her palm. The marble top of the island was cold to the touch; a morgue slab where their connection lay lifeless. 'Shall we talk?' she said.

His gaze was on the jagged lines of the polished stone worktop, like he was trying to make sense of a map. 'It's just that nothing changes, Rach,' he murmured.

Rachel traced the monochrome shapes in the metamorphic rock; patterns created under heat and pressure and crystallised forever. 'It'll be different now. Let's go out for dinner later. Start over,' she said.

His eyes swivelled to the stunning bouquet on the side. 'And what are you going to say to Gaia?'

'Nothing. She fired me, remember.'

'And if she hadn't, you'd be going back again today, for more.' He put his hands over his head like he was preparing for a crash landing.

'Miles . . .' she began, but she didn't know which words would be able to repair the damage that the last few months of distance had done.

He looked up. 'You're amazing, Rach. You put a hundred per cent into everything you do . . .'

She suspected he wanted to say 'except me and you' but he was too nice for that – kind, good Miles, who she'd finally pushed away. She closed her eyes. 'I know I haven't made you feel like a priority lately but—'

'This is about you, Rach,' he cut in. 'Never mind me. You need to remember that you matter, too. There's doing your job well and then there's totally forgetting to take any time for yourself. Gaia might be famous but she's no more important than you.'

Rachel's eyes stung; a chemical reaction caused by kindness meeting complete exhaustion.

Miles got up from his stool, shoulders stooped. 'I've got to get ready for work, but we'll speak later, okay?'

Was that a good or a bad thing? Rachel followed him back out of the kitchen.

When he closed the bathroom door, she sat down on the chair in the corner of their bedroom, on top of the clothes she'd been intending to take to the dry cleaners for weeks. Her phone was lit up on the side table. She looked at the ceiling, tried to ignore its claims for her attention. She heard the shower running next door, couldn't help but imagine the memories she and Miles had made being swilled down the drain along with the water. She stood up, caught sight of her rumpled reflection in the full-length mirror. Who even was she anymore? A stranger stared back from the glass. In six months she'd become unrecognisable, shedding a part of herself with each day that passed like the pieces of clothing piled on the chair.

She needed to do something. And not for Gaia for once. She pulled on a pair of leggings and a T-shirt, and swept her hair into a ponytail. When was the last time she'd peeled her eyes off her phone screen or tablet, left her to-do list for a moment, and been outside? She picked up her mobile – saw there were several missed calls from her ex-boss – and stuffed it in her pocket. She left her headphones in her handbag; she was going to be present in her own life from this day onwards. Work was one strand, not the whole tapestry. She zipped her apartment key in her pocket, stuck a note to the kitchen counter to tell Miles where she was going – Elysian Park, around the corner – and skipped down the stairs in anticipation of feeling the Californian warmth on her skin. They could claw their way back to how things had been at the beginning, she was sure of it – they just had to both agree not to give up now. She flung open the door to a flood of LA sunshine – and came face to face with Gaia standing on the doorstep, about to ring the bell, disguised in a hoodie and baseball cap, and wearing an expression she had never seen before.

Rachel froze as though she'd suddenly found herself in Alaska. She braced herself for whatever Gaia was about to say next – that she ought to have been at work by now, that she needed to get in the waiting car straightaway – but her ex-boss fixed her with her blue-sky eyes and uttered the words 'I'm sorry' instead.

Surprise stole Rachel's speech.

'Can I come in?' asked Gaia.

Rachel leaned across to block the entranceway with her body. This was her sanctuary, the last place that Gaia hadn't managed to personally infiltrate.

'*Please*?' said Gaia.

So she *did* know how to say the word, thought Rachel. 'It's not a good time.'

'Okay,' said Gaia, not demanding to have her way for once. 'We can talk here.' She jutted out her chin. 'I want to apologise. I shouldn't have spoken to you the way I did.'

Rachel could hardly believe her ears.

'Please come back. I don't know how to cope without you.'

Rachel narrowed her eyes. Maybe now Gaia was starting to realise just how many things she juggled, the immense amount of effort it took to organise her schedule.

'I'm grateful . . . even if I sometimes forget to say it.'

You've never once remembered to show it, thought Rachel. She should have known Gaia would grovel – of course she needed her PA back as promptly as possible. But no wonder she'd won that Golden Globe Award – it was a believable performance that was taking place on her doorstep. Her former boss's bottom lip quivered as though she was struggling with genuine emotion. Rachel almost mouthed 'Bravo'.

'Please come back,' begged Gaia.

Rachel shook her head. 'I can't.'

'But—' began Gaia.

Rachel held up a hand, determined to finally speak her mind. 'I've lost all sense of balance. My home life is hanging by a thread. My boyfriend is probably about to leave me.'

Gaia gazed past her, into the apartment's ordinary hallway, the polar opposite to her luxurious Hollywood Hills abode.

Rachel filled the doorway further; she felt protective of her last little piece of privacy.

But then there were footsteps on the stairs, and Miles appeared, hair still damp from the shower, stress creasing his forehead. It was a second or so till he clocked who the sweater-wearing woman was. He looked from Gaia to Rachel and back again. Paused by his girlfriend's side and put an arm around her shoulder. 'You can't come and harass her into working for you again,' he said.

Rachel looped her hand around his waist, felt the comfort of his closeness.

'I've said I'm sorry,' muttered Gaia, her tone that of a little girl, not the great star of the silver screen. Her crumpled face was framed by a straggle of hair that had escaped her pulled up hood.

She sat down on the edge of the pavement all of a sudden, designer jeans in direct contact with the dusty kerb. If this was an act, Gaia had taken it up a notch, thought Rachel with a glance at Miles. But then she noticed something out of the corner of her eye. A person watching them on the opposite side of the street, half-hidden by a parked car. She peered across at the man, and he picked up his pace, pretending to be a passer-by simply strolling along the sidewalk, but when he jammed his hands in the pockets of his open bomber jacket, she caught a glimpse of the long-lens camera slung around his neck. Paparazzi. Poised to get an unbecoming shot of Gaia, a star in ascend-ence, but one that could be brought down by one salacious snap.

And as he reached for the shutter button on his black Nikon camera, Rachel pulled Gaia inside the apartment and pushed the door closed.

Anna was doing a thorough inventory of the Blencathra suite – the best room in the hotel, with its glorious views that stretched right across Derwentwater towards its namesake mountain – when Katrine came to find her.

'There you are,' she said. 'I've got some news,' she whispered, before closing the door behind her. 'About our celebrity guest.'

'Don't tell me,' said Anna from where she knelt on the winter-sky-shade Herdwick wool flooring. 'This needs to be ripped up and replaced with a red carpet,' she said, patting her palm on the woven fabric.

Katrine didn't laugh at her quip. 'Quite possibly,' she said.

Anna clambered to her feet. 'Go on. Who is it then?'

'Gaia.'

As mononymous as Madonna or Cher, she needed no last name. Anna knew who Katrine meant. 'What?' she breathed. 'Coming here, to Cumbria?'

Katrine nodded. 'To the Lake Island Hotel.'

Anna pressed her hands to her lips. 'Goodness me.'

'It's *amazing*, right?' said Katrine, eyes shining with pride. 'She's picked this hotel, out of all the places in the world. Not just for a holiday, but if all goes well, for her *wedding* next summer.'

Anna looked about at the Georgian panelling on the walls and the big, elegant bay window. This building was a beautiful collection of so many people's stories, hers included – its bricks like the binding of a book, holding so many narratives together, and now an A-list actress coming to stay would be another chapter.

'She actually emailed me herself, you know,' said Katrine, cutting into Anna's thoughts.

'Oh, really?' Anna raised her eyebrows.

'Yes. I've been dealing with her assistant Rachel up until now, but when she didn't reply to my message about meal preferences, I got a response from the woman herself.' Katrine crossed her arms. 'Maybe she's more down to earth than we imagine,' she mused.

'We can hope. That would be good news for all of us, especially Jackson,' said Anna. 'He's tearing his hair out trying to perfect the menu. If she's much easier to please than we feared she might be, then that's a positive.'

'Maybe we don't need to be rolling out a red carpet after all.' Katrine plonked down on the armchair that was angled to take in the Lakeland panorama beyond the window. 'Who could fail to be impressed by the Blencathra suite, anyway?' she added. 'There's everything you could possibly need.' She swept a hand round the room. 'It's unique. That's what I tell guests when they ask me about which room to choose. From the furniture to the art, the tech or the little touches, Blencathra's a one-off. Who wouldn't want to sit in front of that view, enjoy the bathroom with a double-ended bathtub, and maybe some Cumbrian coffee and Jackson's delicious shortbread and chocolate brownies?'

'We've got no spa or swimming pool,' said Anna with a grimace.

'Surely she'll forget about that when she sees the lake!' Katrine pointed at Derwentwater dazzling in the daylight. 'People come here because it's a world apart, a proper escape.' She leaped to her feet. 'God, Harry won't be able to believe it when I tell him!' she exclaimed. 'He's been guessing all sorts of names – singers, footballers – but his jaw will *drop* when it's *Gaia.*'

Anna bent to adjust the runner on the bed.

'What is it?' said Katrine softly. 'You don't want me to tell him?'

Anna smoothed the pristine duvet. 'I know that's a bit of an ask when you're a couple. I just can't help thinking the fewer people that know, the better.'

Katrine nodded with no trace of offence; she knew it was only sensible. Her beloved boyfriend was *made* to be the boatman – always full of conversation, eager to show off the hotel's attributes to the customers. One slip of the tongue and the legal agreement they'd all signed would be broken. 'I understand. If we breach the contract that's bad news. Our reputation could be ruined.'

Rachel pressed her back against the front door, hoping she'd prevented the photographer from capturing an image-destroying picture of Gaia that he could sell to every gossip magazine displayed at the newsstand.

Gaia collapsed onto the bottom step of the communal stairs. 'Was there someone watching us?' she asked from beneath her baseball cap.

Rachel nodded.

Gaia sighed. 'I can't go *anywhere* or do *anything* anymore without someone following me with a camera.'

For all Gaia's wealth and privilege, Rachel wouldn't have traded lives with her for the world.

'What am I meant to do now?' murmured Miles, leather satchel still slung over his shoulder, watch ticking ever closer to being late for work. 'If I go out there . . .'

'They'll say we're having a secret tryst,' finished Gaia, glancing up at him. 'Meeting in some *seedy backstreet* to avoid suspicion.'

Rachel tried not to bristle at her description of where she and Miles lived; it was no worse than she'd said on occasion, plus it told her Gaia had dropped any kind of act. This was authentically her: forlorn tone and all.

'They'll do *anything* to stir up a scandal,' Gaia continued. 'The truth *always* comes second to a good story.'

Rachel couldn't comprehend what that was like, always looking over your shoulder, your freedom swapped for fame.

'Call in sick,' suggested Gaia, getting to her feet and fixing Miles with a stare.

Miles frowned. 'What, so you can mess up *my* career as well as Rachel's?' He shook his head. 'No, thank you. I've got a meeting with an investor today. I can't miss it.' He glared back at her. 'I've had enough of all this.' He waved a hand at the three of them standing there. '*I* don't have any need to pretend *anything*. As long as Rachel and I know what reality is, then it doesn't matter what any *magazine* says.' He stepped forward to reach for the door handle.

'Not to you, but what about me?' Gaia cried.

She'd created such an illusion of graceful, glamorous, sophisticated perfection – and it could all be swept away in an instant – the time it took to send a snap of her being smuggled into a scruffy apartment block on the opposite side of town to her home, dressed in sloppy clothes and in close proximity to a handsome male. A scenario that was only a clever camera angle away from being converted into fact: Gaia was having an affair.

'What about Federico . . .' she wailed. '*Please.*'

Now Gaia was using politeness as currency, realised Rachel; dispensing please and thank-you like rare coins to be collected.

Miles glanced across at Rachel. *I have to go*, said his gaze. Even the face of his watch seemed to be glaring at her now. 'With any luck the paparazzi will have given up now,' Miles said, jerking his head at the door. His fingers hovered over the handle. 'I'll see you later, okay?' he said, turning to Rachel.

'*Please*,' repeated Gaia, leaping into his path. 'I'll *pay* you.'

She was so used to being able to buy whatever it was she wanted, she'd blurred the lines between people and objects that could be purchased, realised Rachel.

'Excuse me,' said Miles.

Gaia's pouting lips parted, about to repeat what she'd said, unable to comprehend that someone might be saying 'no' to her.

'I don't need your money, thank you very much,' said Miles, trying to step past her.

'You don't understand the impact this will have—' began Gaia.

'Neither do you,' replied Miles. 'I can't just drop everything for you. That's not *my* job.'

Rachel breathed out a lungful of relief. *It's not mine anymore either*.

'Just name the price!' screeched Gaia, pushing her heels against the door in protest.

'Let me past, please,' said Miles, looking to Rachel for support.

'Gaia, you're going to have to step aside, I'm sorry,' said Rachel. 'You're welcome to stay here until—'

'The newspapers are printed tomorrow?' she howled. 'Till Feddy sees some *horrible* rumour splashed across the front pages?' She waggled a hand between herself and Miles to indicate a story spun from two people caught together in one camera lens and an endless thirst for gossip.

Miles winced at the inference.

'I'll give you a thousand dollars to stay home.'

'I don't want anything from you other than to move out of the way so I can get on with my day,' said Miles.

Rachel was almost glad Gaia was giving him the full force of her stubbornness, so that he could see what she herself had been through the last few months. He had to experience it for himself to understand the strength of her will.

'Fine, five thousand.' Gaia jutted out her chin.

It was like being at an auction, thought Rachel, appalled. Where the value of other people's time was weighed and sold.

Miles's arm dropped to his side like the gavel sealing a deal. 'And what about Rachel. You'll give her the reference she deserves and leave her be if I agree?'

Gaia looked from one of them to the other with tear-glazed eyes. 'I'll double your salary if you come back.'

Rachel visibly baulked. 'No, thank you,' she said, more quickly than she once would have.

Miles linked his hand through hers.

Gaia's gaze flitted to their interlocked fingers, and she wrinkled her nose as though they'd formed a physical barrier that would stop her getting her own way. 'Miles can come to the Lake District,' she said as though she'd solved a problematic equation. 'Make it into a vacation.'

'What?' murmured Rachel.

Miles didn't let go of her hand. 'Sounds like such a great holiday waiting on you hand and foot.'

'Obviously I mean after the work part is out of the way.' Gaia batted her manicured hand. 'You could extend the trip. Stay on. I'll cover the cost.'

She was desperate now, realised Rachel. Throwing everything at them.

'You said you've *always* wanted to see the Lake District, Rachel,' Gaia said, stretching out her arms towards her.

Rachel raised her eyebrows. She really remembered her saying that?

'Now's your chance,' said Gaia softly.

Rachel swallowed.

'Don't fall for that,' muttered Miles. 'We can take a trip to Europe any time we like.'

'You'd be staying at the Lake Island Hotel, though, you're the one who told me it was the most exclusive destination in the area . . .' said Gaia.

She could certainly recall things when she wanted to, realised Rachel, so used to keeping track of every single detail of Gaia's life for her, scurrying around like a servant, that her boss didn't ever need to think for herself normally.

'Travelling first class . . .' cooed Gaia.

I know, I booked the tickets, thought Rachel.

'The trip of a lifetime,' she finished dreamily.

Rachel didn't doubt that it would be – one way or another. She blinked at her boss, suddenly uncertain as to who this woman, who she'd spent the last six months pandering to, really *was*. She looked like a lost little girl not a global talent.

'Don't be fooled,' said the frown on Miles's face. 'She's doing this on purpose, reeling you back in.'

'I need to take a break from all this, Gaia,' Rachel said, sweeping a hand through the air.

'Then that's perfect!' said her boss, intentionally misunderstanding her. 'I promise it'll be amazing! We'll have the best time – all of us,' she added, making sure to include Miles, playing the part of an apologetic character as expertly as if she was at an audition.

Rachel pushed her shoulders back and stood up straighter. 'I want to see it all in writing.'

'What?' snapped Gaia.

'Proper paperwork with the agreement all laid out.'

'Pardon me?'

That's better, thought Rachel, folding her arms.

'But I don't have an assistant anymore . . .' said Gaia with a scowl. 'How am I supposed to do that?' she asked, as though she'd been asked to do a line reading in a foreign language.

'I can set it all out for you. Lay out the terms and conditions. And then we'll consider it. The proposal. Properly.'

'Fine,' said Gaia, storming past them both and up the stairs as though she owned the place.

Chapter 11

The June afternoon was shades of November silver rather than streaked with summer-gold hues, but Anna had to accept that the weather at least was out of her control. Everything else had been practised, honed and perfected, and she was satisfied that they'd all prepared as much as they possibly could do. Each room even had a goodie bag of Cumbrian delicacies, including a miniature jar of the inaugural run of Lake Island Honey, waiting on the dressing table, and the Blencathra suite was decked out exactly as had been specified in Gaia's rider. So much for their hope that their celebrity guest would have few airs and graces. Already the stipulations were extravagant and unprecedented. Roses grown in the garden scented her bedroom, and fresh white peonies and hydrangeas that had been carefully ferried across from a flower shop in Keswick decorated the communal areas. Hundreds of candles flickered in the hearths and on the mantelpieces and dining tables in readiness for her imminent arrival.

She would cross to the island under a cloak of darkness, check into the hotel that evening, when the number of tourists milling down by the lake on the opposite shore had dwindled and the only other company was a nighttime canopy of fellow stars.

'Right, the Bleaberry room,' said Katrine, cutting into her thoughts. They were doing a final walk around before their impending guests' arrival, and a sense of anticipation fizzed among the staff, and throughout the hallways of the hotel. Excited smiles greeted them around every corner, laughter echoed about the high-ceilings, and Anna felt a wave of gratitude for the tight-knit team around her. *It would be all right.*

'So this is where Rachel, Gaia's assistant, will stay,' said Katrine, swinging open the door. 'That way she's right by the Blencathra suite.' They surveyed the flawless interior, a mix of modern soft furnishings and period features – flowing curtains framed the wooden-shuttered windows, and silk cushions decorated the bed beneath the elegant ceiling rose. An enormous white roll-top bath and walk-in shower winked back at them from the next room.

Anna nodded in appreciation.

'I can't believe they'll be here soon, after all these months of organization . . .' Katrine said, and Anna felt her stomach swirl at the idea of Gaia's gaze scrutinising hers and Dominik's dream, dissecting the hotel. Her staff had put in so much hard work too.

Katrine put a hand on Anna's arm. 'Don't worry,' she said. 'We'll do everything we can to make her stay a success. I think Dad would be amazed by all this.' She smiled at her stepmother as she led her along the cream-corniced corridor, towards Hopegill. All the rooms were named after one of the majestic fells on the mainland, rooting the Lake Island Hotel in the timeless landscape that surrounded them. 'Her bodyguard will be in here,' explained Katrine.

82

Anna nodded. 'How are you feeling?' she asked, watching the way Katrine checked every last detail, making sure each element was in place.

'Yeah, okay. I think.' She blew out a breath. 'I'll be better later, when she's all settled in.'

'Me too.' Anna led the way back out of the room. 'Well, everywhere looks stunning. You've done such a good job.'

Katrine smiled. 'Thanks. It would be a lie if I said I wasn't looking forward to them leaving already.'

Anna laughed. 'It'll be a relief, won't it? But we don't know she isn't the loveliest person on the planet.'

'True,' said Katrine. 'We'll soon see.' She paused at the top of the staircase, one hand on the shining mahogany handrail. 'I'll tell you something, I'll be relieved when Harry's back to normal.'

Anna's plan to keep the identity of their visitor as low-key as possible had been unwittingly shattered by Jackson, who had assumed Harry knew who was coming, seeing as it was him who'd first let on about someone famous planning to stay. The downside to having such a close team, she thought wryly; they were friends as well as colleagues.

'Oh no,' said Anna. 'Is he really feeling the pressure?' she replied, turning to look over her shoulder. 'Tell him he can only do his best; what she ultimately thinks will be out of our hands.'

Katrine shrugged. 'I've said that, but it doesn't seem to make any difference. I mean, I understand where he's coming from, it's a huge coup that she's coming here and we all want it to go well.'

'I know,' said Anna.

'I guess maybe it's because he's the one responsible for her first impression, he'll be greeting her at the jetty and bringing her across, and that must be making him feel stressed . . .'

'I'm sure he'll calm down once that bit's out of the way.'

Katrine nodded. 'Hopefully. He's just acting so strange. Ever since he found out who is coming to stay.' She shook her head. 'Probably has some ridiculous crush on her.'

Anna rolled her eyes. 'That'll soon wear off when she's a complete nightmare like we fear she might be.' She gestured at the abundant rose blooms festooning every surface, twisting around the banister, and cascading down the stair treads. The flames of the candle lanterns on the landing shuddered as though even they were trepidatious.

Katrine bit her lip. 'He did go to acting school for a while, you know. Maybe Gaia's success hits a nerve in some way, reminds him things might have been different if he'd stuck it out. That he could have been a big name, too.'

Anna shook her head. 'I doubt it. That was such a long time ago.'

'I don't know . . .' said Katrine, doubt dimpling her forehead. 'It's easy to wonder what might have been.'

'Everybody does at times,' mused Anna. 'But if he regretted it so much, wouldn't he have done something about it?'

'Not necessarily,' replied Katrine. 'Look at you and Dad. Took you years to get back in touch.'

Anna nodded. 'It's so easy to assume what others are thinking, though, and get it entirely wrong.'

'I know.' Katrine nodded. 'I tried talking to him and he says he's fine.'

'Well, maybe he *is*,' said Anna. But had anyone in the history of the world ever said they were fine and *meant* it?

'My phone's ringing,' said Katrine suddenly, pulling her mobile out of her pocket. 'It's Rachel, Gaia's PA. They must be on their way.'

The tinted windows of the Land Rover made the cloud-covered sky look even darker, and Derwentwater glittered like a slab of black onyx beyond the glass.

'Ugh, it's raining,' said Gaia, running a hand through her hair. 'So typical of this place.'

For someone so intent on holding their future wedding in the Lake District, she wasn't showing an awful lot of enthusiasm for being there, thought Rachel, barely able to take her eyes off the scene unfolding before her. She gazed out at the water, had never seen anything like it. Hills higher than she'd ever imagined, and greenery so lush even the privacy glass failed to dim its vividness. It was breathtakingly beautiful. Better than she could have envisaged.

'Have you been here before, Gaia?' Miles asked, twisting round in the passenger seat to speak to her.

'To Cumbria or to this specific hotel?' she snapped, replying to Rachel beside her instead, so used to her assistant fielding questions for her that the unscheduled conversation took her by surprise.

Rachel reached forward, rested a hand on Miles's shoulder. Silence filled the car once again and the question was left behind with the tarmacked track that led to the edge of the lake. In front of them, a boat floated on the liquid night, and beyond, the amber glow of the hotel's windows danced on the surface of Derwentwater in the distance.

The car came to a stop beside the pebbled shore, and Chris, Gaia's chauffeur and bodyguard, leapt out from the driver's side.

'We'll stay put for a minute or two,' explained Rachel for Miles's benefit. Chris would be scouting out the area before Gaia set foot outside the vehicle.

Her boss slumped back against the cream leather seat.

Rachel sat on the edge of hers, ready to retrieve the large dome umbrella from the car boot. If a strand of Gaia's silken hair met so much as a drop of rain, she'd be the one to blame. She wished the weather was better for their arrival on the island too, but as powerful a force as Gaia was, she was going to have to get used to the fact it was the one thing she couldn't influence.

'I hope it's sunny by the time Feddy gets here tomorrow,' said Gaia with a pout, pulling up the oversized faux-fur hood of her coat in preparation for leaving the climate-controlled interior of the car. 'I don't want him to think I've brought him somewhere *terrible.*'

Rachel glanced out at the black velvet fells beneath the sequin-scattered sky. How could anyone possibly describe this place as—

'I honestly don't know how people live here full time. It's so *miserable.*'

Miles coughed, and Rachel bit her lip to stifle a laugh.

The only thing that was in any way miserable was sitting in the car next to them, said his reflection in the nearside wing mirror.

Rachel's door suddenly opened.

'Right, coast is clear,' said Chris. 'Let's start to make a move.' His eyes continued to dart about their surroundings as he spoke.

Rachel smiled at the man standing beside him: one of her contacts from the hotel. 'You must be Harry.' She recognised his face from the photographs of the staff on the website.

'Delighted to meet you,' he said, stretching out his hand. 'It'll be my pleasure to take you across to the island.'

Miles scrambled out of the passenger seat, as Chris went around to the other side of the car in readiness to escort Gaia down to the shore.

'Welcome to Keswick, and the beautiful Lake District,' said Harry, his back straight and his chin out; employing the techniques he'd learnt so long ago to project his voice against the squally wind.

'We're excited to be here!' said Rachel, just as the door on the other side of the vehicle slammed with the force of a thunderclap.

Gaia's head was dipped, a huge pair of shades shielding her face from the rain rather than the LA sun. Tendrils of caramel hair had escaped her hood and Rachel hovered the umbrella over her as best she could as they followed their guide.

'This way,' said Harry, leading them in the direction of the landing stage. A few hardy onlookers lingered by the lakeside, but their excited conjecture was carried away by the breeze.

'Take care along here, please,' Harry called as they walked out onto the slick wooden planks that protruded out into the water. The boat ahead was nodding along with the wavelets.

'I get seasick,' declared Gaia.

'Good job this is a lake,' muttered Miles.

'I've got some ginger lozenges,' said Rachel, digging about in her bag with the hand that wasn't holding the umbrella.

Chris jumped onto the deck to check the cabins before Gaia embarked.

Rachel's gaze turned to the island, and the building at its heart. The hotel's enchanting white façade was as magnetic as the moon, she thought as they waited for Chris's signal, by the post where the ferry was tethered. She couldn't wait to explore everywhere in daylight.

When Chris returned with a reassuring nod, Harry leaped aboard and extended his hand to Gaia, as he did with all the guests.

But she swept straight past him and through to the boat's covered interior.

'Sorry about that,' said Rachel, wrestling with the umbrella before reaching for Harry's outstretched hand herself.

'No matter,' he replied, as his rain-soaked cheeks stung in the wild wind.

Chapter 12

Katrine watched the bright glow of the boat cross the lake with ever-increasing anticipation. Anna stood beside her at the window, wondering what on earth Dominik would have said about all this, and strangely, what *Will* would think too. The latter had played as much a part in preparing for their VIP's arrival as Katrine or Anna herself, decanting honey into jars like it was more precious than molten gold, helping her harvest the ripened vegetables and herbs for the Gaia-approved menu.

'Shame the weather isn't better,' Katrine murmured, breath misting the glass, her face was pressed so close to it. 'But we can't help that.'

Anna shook her head. 'It's authentically Cumbrian. To match the dishes in the restaurant and the décor of the rooms. Wouldn't be the proper experience if it was wall to wall sunshine.'

Katrine smiled. 'What is it you always say when it's like this?'

'It's "atmospheric",' Anna replied with a chuckle.

The boat was being moored down by the shore now.

Anna breathed a lungful of flower-scented air. 'Well, this is it,' she said. 'The moment we've been waiting for.'

Katrine straightened her midnight-coloured suit. 'Let's do this,' she whispered, as she squeezed her stepmother's hand.

'I'm going to go and give Jackson a head's up that they're here,' said Anna.

'Okay,' replied Katrine, feeling a shiver of nervousness slip down her spine as Anna disappeared in the direction of the kitchen. She could see five figures silhouetted by the floodlit jetty, and her insides squirmed like eels in a tarn. How was Harry feeling? she wondered fleetingly, as she watched him guide the unfamiliar party to shore. Had the crossing been smooth, in all senses of the word? She couldn't read his face at this distance. A tall, heavy-set man was striding ahead of the others, and she could make out the shapes of another man and two women following behind. Gaia was unmistakable, even in the almost-darkness. Cocooned in a blush-coloured down coat, she looked like she'd stepped straight out of an après-ski photoshoot. Beside her had to be her assistant, Rachel; she was clutching an umbrella above her boss's already hooded head, for double protection against the unbiddable outdoors. Gaia was probably so used to the specifically curated conditions of studios and film sets that she'd never experienced the full force of nature's unruliness until now. The man walking a couple of paces behind them wasn't Gaia's fiancé, noted Katrine; she'd Googled Federico in advance so she'd recognise him on sight. And according to her carefully itemised schedule, he was due to arrive tomorrow. But if there were extra members of the entourage, then she'd accounted for that; each and every room was ready. She tried to steady her breathing; she'd done her best to cover all bases. Her gaze flitted to Harry once again, hoping he'd catch her eye, share a split-second of stomach-fizzing anticipation with her. He was only a few metres away from the front door now, his handsome features gilded by the hotel's glow, his eyes alight beneath the starlit night – and his face turned towards Gaia instead.

The entrance hall of the hotel looked more like the setting for a movie than anything she'd ever encountered in real life, thought Rachel as she took in the crystal vases, twinkling candles and dazzling chandelier that hung from the centre of the ceiling and cast a kaleidoscope of sparkles across the ivory-coloured walls.

Chris instructed them to wait in the reception area, and Rachel tore her gaze away from the real log fire she could see flaming in the adjacent room, to introduce herself to the woman she knew to be Katrine.

'Welcome!' she beamed back at her.

Rachel grinned. She felt like she'd been transported to a scene from a high-budget historical drama.

'I'm exhausted,' exclaimed Gaia, collapsing onto one of the sofas before shaking off her damp coat and discarding it on the cushions without a second thought. Rachel scurried forward to retrieve it, wincing at the water droplets that seemed to leap from the jacket and shower the fabric, despite all her efforts to keep her boss dry. The rain was seemingly as desperate to flee Gaia's presence as she was.

'I need my luggage.' She took off her sunglasses and shook out her tumble of fudge-coloured curls.

'Chris will be right back over with it as soon as he's finished up here,' explained Rachel.

Miles was either rolling his eyes or marvelling again at the magnificent light fitting that shimmered above them.

'Can I get you something to drink?' asked Katrine, hands clasped behind her back as she looked from Gaia to her assistant, unsure as to who she should be addressing her enquiry.

'Surely we're not going to have to stay here that long,' said Gaia.

'Just thought you might be in need of refreshment.' Katrine smiled. 'It must have been a long journey.'

Miles gave a stifled snort, as if to say *tell me about it*.

'A glass of champagne, perhaps?' offered Katrine with a smile.

Gaia shook her head.

'Fresh mint tea?' Katrine tried instead.

'Couldn't think of anything worse,' said Gaia.

'Right, well, there's a full room-service menu in your suite . . .' said Katrine.

'Should I ever get to see it,' muttered Gaia, looking towards the staircase.

'Very shortly, I do assure you.' Katrine gave a slight bow of her head, as though Gaia was royalty and not the epitome of rudeness. 'Anything for anyone else?' she asked the others.

'A mineral water for me, please,' said Rachel.

'A double gin and tonic, thanks,' said Miles.

Harry nodded at Katrine to signal he'd pass on the drinks order to the bar staff straightaway. He crossed the entrance hall, then turned to steal a last look over his shoulder, but again, not at his girlfriend – at the glossy, blonde-locked woman sitting on the gilt-legged sofa.

'She wants *what*?' asked Jackson, hands braced against the stainless-steel worktop as Katrine spoke to him.

'"A surprise",' she repeated, standing by the swing door that led from Moy's kitchen into the dining room.

'So, nothing on the pre-agreed menu?' clarified Jackson, seething like a saucepan brought to the boil.

'Not tonight, no,' said Katrine with a shake of her head.

'So, what am I meant to give her?' Jackson glanced about the kitchen, his body aching from hour upon hour of food preparation and his brain drained from months of planning.

'There must be something . . .' said Katrine.

Jackson stood up straight, put his hands on his hips. 'But I thought the whole idea was that we had to run everything past her first, so there was nothing unforeseen.'

'I guess she's changed her mind. The prerogative of the rich.'

Jackson groaned. 'But why? What's the reason?'

Katrine shrugged. 'Maybe it's a test?' she suggested. 'See how we cope with change?'

'Jesus, she's scoping the hotel out for a wedding, not recruiting us for MI6.'

Katrine laughed, despite the situation.

'God, I thought it might be a challenging few days, but I didn't expect the prima-donna stuff to start as soon as she walked through the door.'

Katrine raised her eyebrows as if to say, *didn't you?* She looked up at the clock. Almost midnight now. The rest of the party had been more than satisfied with the selection of dishes that Jackson had served shortly after their arrival – homegrown gooseberry, oxalis and trout, or barbecued cour- gette with truffle puree and brassica flowers as the vegan option – but Gaia had retired straight to her room, seemingly to think up this precise request, as though, in her world, anything she could dream of could simply be conjured by magic – or enough money.

'How about a rhubarb and rose lolly?' said Jackson, pulling a tray of the delicate desserts from the freezer. 'They were a little extra idea I was still working on, seeing as it's going to be a summertime wedding.'

'Wonderful,' said Katrine, though the weather at the moment was hardly a heatwave.

'Good chance to see if she likes them,' said Jackson, taking out one of the presentation plates: a polished circle of oak in which the sunrise-coloured lollipops could be stuck to form a striking display.

'Oh, they look amazing!' exclaimed Katrine with a little clap as Jackson positioned three of the delicious-looking popsicles in the holder.

She waited as he swirled raspberry gel on the top of each frosted sphere, before handing them to her. 'Won't melt as quickly on a night like tonight,' he added. 'Should give you enough time to deliver them to madam.'

Katrine smiled as she took the roundel of wood; it reminded her of a miniature version of the log slab that her dad had always stood their Christmas tree in when she and her brother Mateusz were younger, and she imagined that was Jackson's intention: to evoke a similar sense of wonder in the diner.

'If Gaia's being like this now, can you imagine how a celebrity bride is going to behave?' said Jackson, bringing her back to the moment.

Katrine bit her lip. 'Not really.'

'Doesn't bear thinking about,' said Jackson.

But there wasn't any time to ruminate now; the rhubarb and rose lollipops would soon begin to dissolve. Jackson held open the kitchen door for her and she hurried off towards the Blencathra suite.

She walked up the stairs, one hand on the banister to steady herself, feet taking one step at a time. At the top, she turned the corner, and started along the corridor, trying to calm her heartbeat as she neared the Blencathra suite. She was about to raise her free hand to knock on the door, when she hesitated. Wasn't she supposed to run everything past Gaia's assistant? Did a surprise dessert count as a good reason to disturb Rachel? She hovered in the hallway, unsure what to do. Then she jumped as the door to Gaia's bedroom suddenly swung open. Katrine took a deep breath, ready to repeat Jackson's description of the dish – but it wasn't Gaia standing in front of her, it was Harry who appeared in the doorway instead. What on earth was he doing here?

'Katrine, hi!' he said. 'Just dropping off luggage.' He leaped aside, and she saw the array of suitcases standing by the bed.

Katrine swallowed down her shock like she was knocking back a shot. 'I see.' She nodded.

Gaia was over by the dressing table, inspecting the complimentary Lake Island Hotel goodies with the facial expression of someone peering into a police evidence bag.

'A special treat from our kitchen,' announced Katrine, presenting the trio of lollies, and forcing a smile onto her face while her brain filled with questions. Why had the door been closed if Harry was only dropping off Gaia's bags? It seemed strange.

He edged past her, out into the hallway.

'Ugh, are they ice lollies?' said Gaia. 'It's cold enough in Cumbria as it is.'

Katrine clutched Jackson's carefully constructed dish; tiny teardrop drips were just starting to form on the ruby-rose spheres, as if the dessert itself was offended.

'I'll take them away, no problem,' murmured Katrine, retreating from the suite. She turned to look at Harry, but he was already halfway down the corridor. When she reached the foot of the stairs, he and Anna were speaking in the rose-fragranced reception area.

'I wouldn't take those back to the kitchen if I were you,' Anna called over to her, clocking Jackson's untouched creation. 'Our chef won't be too pleased if his efforts have been spurned.' She raised her eyebrows as she took the wooden platter from Katrine and offered the lollipops to her and Harry instead.

'Ooh, don't mind if I do,' said Harry. 'These look delicious,' he said, holding his up to admire it in the chandelier light. 'Gaia doesn't know what she's missing,' he added in a low voice – with a brief glance back in the direction of the staircase, Katrine couldn't help but notice.

She picked up one of the rhubarb and rose orbs, too, glad of a distraction from trying to guess what was going on in Harry's head.

The candles glimmered as she bit into the perfectly balanced flavour bomb that seemed to burst on her tongue. 'I've never had anything like this,' she said, as the rich, fresh taste of the fruit fizzed in her mouth.

'Tastes like holidays,' said Harry, closing his eyes.

'In that case, we all need one,' said Anna, reaching for the last of the sweet-sour lollipops.

Harry laughed. 'Going to be a long three days, isn't it,' he said, shaking his head.

'I expect so,' said Anna with a nod. 'Goodness knows what tomorrow will bring. I think I might hide in the garden.'

'You never know,' said Harry. 'She might wake up on the right side of the bed.' He smiled, eyes gleaming in the chandelier light, but try as Katrine might, she couldn't read what was behind them – not tonight.

'Are you all right?' Katrine asked Harry as she turned the key in their front door. It was after one in the morning now, and the flat was bathed in liquid silver.

'Yeah, fine. Why?' Moonlight spilled in from the curtain-fringed window, illuminating her boyfriend's face. 'It's been a long day, hasn't it?'

Katrine nodded. 'Definitely.'

'Come here,' said Harry, pulling her into a hug. 'Cup of tea or crash into bed?'

Their usual rhythms wrapped around her like a well-worn blanket, and she felt a flood of relief. 'Bed, please,' she replied as she reached up to kiss him. Surely she didn't have anything to worry about – even she herself was half mesmerised by Gaia. She could hardly blame Harry for being so too. It was disorientating returning home, though, seeing everything just as it had been when they'd left that morning, but feeling as though somehow, their relationship had shifted since then. Katrine couldn't shake the sense that something unshared was coming to the surface, like a shell turned up on a shore, and half of her wanted to bury it again, but the other half wanted to know more.

Chapter 13

'I've brought you a drink,' said Jackson, and Anna looked up from where she was collecting nasturtium flowers in the kitchen garden. 'Does it have a double measure of rum in it?' she replied, smiling at him as he came to stand beside her.

Jackson shook his head. ''Fraid not,' he said as he handed her the cool glass.

'Ooh, it's not your ginger switchel?!' said Anna, straightening up as the gently spiced aroma of the cordial wafted towards her.

Jackson nodded.

'Well, that's even better.' She smiled. 'Just what I need.'

'Don't tell me you've had enough too,' said Jackson. 'You're out here hiding in the garden. You haven't even seen her so far this morning.'

'I'm not hiding, I'm harvesting these for the cashew and nasturtium pesto,' Anna replied with an arch of her eyebrow, holding up her wicker basket.

'Well, there's no need,' said Jackson with a sigh. 'Whole menu's changed overnight.' He picked a couple of the vermillion-coloured petals directly from the climbing plant, and crushed them between his fingers to release the mustard-pepper scent, then bent his head to inhale it like a refreshing tonic.

'Tell me?' said Anna, taking a sip of her drink. The zing-kick of the ginger hit the back of her throat, and her senses seemed to explode.

'Gaia doesn't want *any* of the things she's previously asked for. No hand-blended smoothie for breakfast. She wanted a coconut water bringing to her room. And not from a carton, from a *freshly picked coconut*. That common Cumbrian plant.'

Anna snorted at his quip and the ice cubes in her drink tinkled.

'So, I wish I could hide out here too, in all honesty.'

'I can take over if you need me to?' offered Anna. The fire of the cordial had made her feel more energised and awake. There was no reason why she couldn't help Jackson out in Moy for the next couple of days, just until Storm Gaia had passed through and they could get back to normal. It might be nice to be on the other side of the pass for a change.

Jackson shook his head. 'I'm not saying I can't cope.'

'I know,' Anna replied, as the warmth of the switchel spread through her body. 'But if you want a hand, then all you have to do is say. We're a team, okay?'

He nodded. 'I can manage,' he said. 'I promise.' But he gulped in the garden-fragranced air like it was much-needed medicine.

'Excuse me?' said a woman's voice, slicing though the still June morning like a pair of secateurs.

Both Jackson and Anna jolted.

But the figure walking towards them on the stone-pebbled path greeted them with a good-natured wave, giving away the fact that it wasn't Gaia. 'Good morning. Hi there,' she said with a smile.

Rachel, remembered Anna; their esteemed guest's assistant. She handed Jackson the basket of nasturtiums to signal she'd deal with whatever Gaia's messenger had been sent to say, and he gratefully retreated back to the relative shelter of the restaurant, with a parting whisper of 'Good luck,' over his shoulder.

'How may I help you?' said Anna, stepping away from the flower-entwined trellis and feeling the sunshine kiss her face.

'I'm looking for Harry. The guy who brought us across on the ferry last night?'

'Oh,' said Anna, trying to read the slight frown on Rachel's face, the twist of her mouth. 'Is everything all right?' She shaded her eyes against the bright light that bounced off the white hotel building beyond her.

Rachel nodded back at her, as though even her voice ultimately belonged to Gaia.

'He should be down by the jetty,' said Anna, extending an arm in the direction of the lake. 'I can show you if you like?' No doubt everything looked different for their visitors this morning, now night's black-silk curtains had been pulled back to reveal a brand-new day.

'That would be great, thanks,' Rachel replied.

The lake beckoned them with blue-gold waves, reflecting the fells in blazes of vibrant bronze-green. The boat was visible out in the water, halfway over to the island.

'There he is,' said Anna, with a nod.

But the view before them had rendered Rachel wordless.

'Pretty special, isn't it,' murmured Anna, gazing back at the panorama of mountains semi-mirrored by the lake. She woke to the same sight every day – so reassuringly constant yet always different, the sky playing with colours like an artist perfecting a canvas.

Still Rachel didn't speak.

'What was it you wanted Harry for?' enquired Anna, feeling a pinch of apprehension.

'Gaia wants to speak to him,' said Rachel, reluctantly tearing her eyes away from the scene in front of them.

Possible scenarios swirled through Anna's mind. Had Harry said something that had upset their guest? She suspected Gaia would revel in the opportunity to take a well-intended comment entirely the wrong way, wring some extra attention out of a moment in time.

'Oh, there's no problem – he's been amazing,' added Rachel with a smile.

Perhaps she was so used to predicting her boss's thought processes she could sense what was going on in her head, wondered Anna.

'So helpful and professional,' said Rachel.

'Excellent. I'm very pleased to hear it,' replied Anna, releasing the breath she'd been holding.

'There was something I needed to talk to you about, though.' Rachel grimaced, and a prickle of tension passed over Anna's skin. Rachel paused, lips trying to shape the sentence Gaia must have spoken into something softer. 'You know the boat trip that you very kindly organised for Federico coming?'

Anna nodded. Katrine had done all the work for the twilight cruise that had been planned for that evening, in honour of his arrival, but for the sake of speed she took the credit.

'Well Gaia's having a bit of a panic . . .'

Clearly code for class-A strop, judging by the way her assistant swallowed, mused Anna.

'She wanted it to be a wonderful welcome for him. Something to really showcase the Lakes and your *incredible* hotel . . .'

Anna recognised sugar coating when she saw it.

'She's rethinking it,' continued Rachel, 'seeing as Feddy will have had a very long journey, and probably doesn't want to get back on a boat again pretty much as soon as he's got here . . .'

'I see,' said Anna. The private launch was due to pick up the couple and their immediate party in only a few hours' time. The Derwentwater Cruise Company had been booked months before tonight, the musicians hired, the skipper briefed about the VIPs on board. 'So she wants to cancel it?' said Anna, picturing the musicians practising, the rows of champagne bottles ready to be popped.

'Oh no, she wants it to be moved to tomorrow instead,' Rachel clarified.

Anna rubbed her temple. 'Right.' She needed to speak to Katrine straight away.

Chapter 14

'If you'd like to come this way, I'll show you to your suite,' said Katrine, with a dip of her head.

'Thank you very much,' said Federico, before turning towards the dark-suited man beside him. 'I can take that, Si,' he said, reaching for his own suitcase. 'You get some rest.'

Katrine stared. She stood stock-still at the foot of the stairs, as she tried to reconcile the fact that *this* was Gaia's fiancé. The contrast was like comparing the Cumbrian night with the LA day.

Federico started to follow her towards the stairs and Katrine shook herself.

But just as her toe touched the first step, a screech from behind them both made her turn.

'*Baby!*' Gaia raced across the entrance hall to fling her arms around Federico's neck.

'I've missed you *soooo* much.'

A shaft of sunshine shone through one of the high windows, flooding the foyer like a spotlight, as though every second of Gaia's life could be from a film.

She reached up to kiss him, clutching at the collar of his pale-blue linen shirt.

Katrine looked away; caught sight of Harry, standing just inside the front door, his eyes on the embracing couple, and an expression on his face that she hadn't seen before.

'I can't wait to see the island,' said Federico, extricating himself from Gaia's grip but smiling at her broadly. 'It's wonderful to be here. What a beautiful place.'

She beamed back at him. 'Shall I show you our room?' She tugged at his hand. 'Wait till you see the view of Blencathra.'

Katrine tilted her head to one side. She didn't remember explaining that the suite was named after one of the mountains on the horizon. Had Harry told Gaia that when he'd dropped off her bags?

'I'll take it from here,' Gaia said with a glance at Katrine.

Katrine smiled back, feeling like she herself was the actress. Discomfort and confusion flurried inside her, like a foreign language was being whispered behind her back. She looked down at Harry again, but he was gone.

'So how exactly am I meant to turn it into a picnic?' said Jackson, crossing his arms.

Katrine bit her lip. 'Not sure.'

They looked at the kitchen counter in mute solidarity for a moment.

'Let me get this straight,' said Jackson with a sigh. 'She wants the same three-course meal that was designed to be eaten in the restaurant, serving on the other side of the island.'

'Yes. Still at a table, though, with the same crockery and everything.'

Jackson groaned. 'So why not just have it here?' He rested his elbows on the worktop and covered his eyes. 'She *must* be doing this on purpose.'

It was as though Gaia was delighting in altering the plans that had been painstakingly put together at her specific request, Katrine couldn't help but agree.

'I thought we had to postpone the boat cruise because it was too much on top of all the travelling, so why do they want to trek off to the far end of the island when they could just have dinner right here?'

'Knock, knock,' said a voice from the back door. Anna was standing there with a basket of just-picked new potatoes. 'Everything all right?' she asked, looking from Jackson, slumped over the counter, his *mise en place* on pause, to Katrine with her pale cheeks and clasped hands.

'How am I supposed to serve a perfect risotto – not only to a very high-profile guest but an *Italian* one at that – when I've got to transport it to some randomly selected location—'

'No need to worry,' said Anna, setting her basket down on the side. 'News just in: we're sticking to the first plan. The cruise is back on.'

'How come?' said Jackson, narrowing his eyes, needing further explanation before he believed it.

'Federico said he feels absolutely fine, and he's looking forward to it, so we're good to go ahead. Luckily the company's agreed to honour the original booking.'

'They'll regret that as soon as her majesty gets on board,' muttered Jackson.

'Oh, that reminds me,' said Anna, steering Katrine out of the kitchen and leaving Jackson to carry on with his prep.

'Gaia wanted to speak to Harry about something. Do you know if she found him?'

Katrine blinked. 'I don't know, actually,' she said. 'Did she give a reason?' she couldn't help asking.

Anna shook her head. 'No. Everything's always so hush-hush isn't it. In case a reporter's rowed across the water under cover of darkness . . .'

Katrine smiled, but in all seriousness, she couldn't begin to imagine what that was like. Always looking over your shoulder, worrying about how you were being made to come across in articles and candid photos. Despite herself, she felt a wave of empathy for their demanding visitor.

'Can't be an easy life,' she said kindly. She looked at her shoes, couldn't help comparing herself to shiny Gaia, and suddenly feeling inadequate.

'Are you okay?' Anna asked.

Had she noticed the way Harry gazed at Gaia too? Katrine wondered. 'Yeah. Just being silly,' she answered, smoothing a hand over her hair.

'If there's one thing you definitely aren't, it's silly,' countered Anna, gently steering her over to the sofa in the reception area.

Katrine pictured Gaia sitting on the very same cushions last night, her butterscotch curls swept back by a pair of jewel-encrusted sunglasses that sat on top of her head like a tiara.

'It's just . . . Harry seems to be under some sort of spell, ever since Gaia appeared . . .'

Anna took her stepdaughter's hand. 'Aren't we all a bit in her thrall at the moment?' she said.

Katrine nodded; she'd stared in wonder herself when Gaia had made her entrance, and turned her own head whenever she was in her presence – the woman's star power was indisputable. 'I suppose so.' She fiddled with the cuff of her jacket. 'He's just behaving differently – and he can't keep his eyes off her.'

'Well, *I* see how Harry looks at *you*,' replied Anna, nudging her fondly. 'All this will be over before you know it. In a few days, she'll be back in LA.'

'Until she comes again in twelve months' time,' murmured Katrine, as though Gaia was the fifth season of the year: as dazzling as a summer's day, and with all the warmth of winter.

Chapter 15

The June evening had gold-leafed the open deck of the boat, making the launch look even more magical, like something from a dream. The musicians were already seated in the cabin, playing a classical melody that soared out through the wide doors and windows to envelope the approaching party as they progressed along the pier.

Anna watched from the shore as the Lake Island passengers began to board their floating venue. The midsummer breeze was summer-sweet, infused with notes of sun-baked earth and full-bloom flowers – more inimitable and intoxicating than any designer perfume ever could be.

Meanwhile, Katrine guided Gaia along the slatted jetty, her stomach muscles tensing at the prospect of one of her VIP guest's stiletto heels slipping down each ink-dark gap. Federico followed behind his fiancée, his soft Italian accent melding with the string-instrument tune that drifted out from the boat.

'How does it compare to Lake Como?' asked Gaia, eyes wide as she dared him to choose between the two.

'*Bellissimo, amore mio.*'

Federico's murmured compliments matched the frequency of her complaints, but never quite cancelled them out, thought Katrine.

Next in the line slowly snaking along the landing stage was Rachel, who was drinking in the wraparound vista before them with wonder. 'Amazing, isn't it?' she whispered to Miles beside her, as they walked out across the water. He nodded back in agreement; no words could really do the landscape justice.

The security officers formed the last of their group.

Once everyone was safely delivered to the waiting vessel, Katrine allowed herself to breathe a sigh of relief – but then she glimpsed Harry waiting there on the deck ready to welcome the guests, his gaze so fixed on Gaia that his girl-friend could clearly tell he was hoping – no, *willing* – the star to look at him. Katrine moved aside to let the actress past, and felt goosepimples prickle her skin, as though she'd stepped into a swatch of shade.

'Thank you,' said Federico, turning towards her as he too strode onboard, but even his full-beam smile failed to soothe her.

The rest of the entourage filed past, too, blocking Harry from her view. When she next looked over in his direction, he'd merged with the rest of the crew, lost among the melange of white-shirted waiting staff offering round effervescent wine glasses and canapé platters.

'*Stop it,*' mouthed Anna, coming to stand beside her. 'I'm sure you'd be the same if George Clooney had come to stay.'

Katrine swallowed; she was absolutely certain that she wouldn't.

'Come on,' said Anna, placing a hand on her back. 'We've got at least sixty minutes of peace and quiet while they're gone – let's not squander it.'

By the time they'd reached the still-warm stones of the Lake Island's shore, the cruise had departed. They watched as it disappeared off into the lustrous lake – far from Katrine's sight but not her mind.

The guests on board were treated to a 360-degree view unlike anything they'd ever experienced before. Spun-sugar clouds met pink-tinged mountains. Dramatic and utterly beautiful – *just like Gaia*, thought Rachel. One of the servers held out a plate of exquisite-looking appetizers towards her – each one of them an identical, edible artwork.

'May I offer you a vegan courgette and red pepper rösti with chilli mayo?'

'The description is more of a mouthful than the food itself,' quipped Miles with a grin as he reached for one. He elbowed Rachel. 'Go on, Rach, have some. We're on holiday, remember.'

Rachel glanced over at her boss, unsure whether they were considered to be guests or staff this evening.

'She promised we could have a break as well, while we were here – she can let us have a bite to eat and a bit of fizz,' said Miles, already eyeing up a second rösti.

'I'm not sure we're meant to, though . . .' replied Rachel, angling her neck to see Chris and Si constantly scanning their surroundings, despite the fact they were in the centre of Derwentwater now.

'Bet they're just admiring the view behind their big dark sunglasses,' said Miles, before leaving in search of the circulating snacks.

Rachel tilted her head skywards to take it all in. Stunning scenery slid past the side of the boat, constantly changing like the backdrops used in a blockbuster. Glitter-rippled reflections of the undulating peaks glided by, and hidden bays unfolded before them as they made their way further along the lake. Out on the water was where you were truly wrapped up in the richness of Cumbria's ancient beauty, thought Rachel, hardly wanting to blink for fear of missing a single split second—

Miles presented a canapé to her on his napkin-cushioned palm. 'Amuse-bouche for madam,' he said in a low voice, just to make her laugh.

'Thank you,' she said, smiling back at him.

'Honestly, let's try to enjoy it,' he said as she placed the morsel on her tongue. 'We haven't been anywhere together for ages.'

Rachel felt the heat of the chilli-kick hit the back of her throat. But it wasn't the spice that brought tears to her eyes, it was being here with Miles, and feeling the fire still alive between them. She was about to reach up and kiss him, when a sudden movement made her jump. The security guards, Chris and Si, were ushering Gaia and Federico inside.

Chapter 16

'Get away from the window.' Chris signalled with a swift hand movement and Gaia ducked down beside one of the bench seats in the boat's cabin. The string quartet stopped playing, their bows paused while Si investigated whatever it was that had caused the two security officers concern.

'Not paparazzi here, of all places,' said Gaia with a sigh.

Federico crouched next to her and put an arm around her shoulders, as though he was personally culpable for the pests purely because the word was Italian.

'What if they find out this is where the wedding will be?' Gaia's eyes were wide.

Federico took her hand.

Rachel averted her gaze, feeling as voyeuristic as the photographers Gaia was always trying to escape. Not for the first time, she felt a burst of gratitude that she could go about her everyday life almost entirely under the radar. Being able to pop to the shops without anyone following her, wasn't something she'd counted as a blessing until now, but would she trade the luxury of total freedom for Gaia's privileged life? Not ever. She looked over at her boss squatting on the floor, her expensive clothes no armour at all against the constant invasion of privacy.

Rachel stood by the open window, half in order to shield Gaia from any long-lens cameras and half because she *could* – she herself wasn't of any interest to anyone. Miles bent to touch his lips to her forehead at that moment, as though to disagree.

She threaded her fingers through his as a gust of fresh night air swept in through the cabin as though making the point it could do just as it pleased.

'If there's a leak to the press all our plans will be ruined!' cried Gaia, claiming Rachel's attention once more. 'The whole point was to keep the rest of the world out for one single day. Get married like everyone else – with our friends and family and far away from prying eyes and other people's opinions—'

'Just a couple of canoeists,' announced Federico's bodyguard, coming back into the cabin and cutting into Gaia's tirade. 'Nothing to worry about,' he confirmed with a nod.

'Did they have cameras?' she asked in an uncharacteristically quavering voice.

Chris shook his head, once Si had given the all-clear. 'They weren't undercover photographers after all,' he said. 'But much better to be safe than sorry.'

'Think they were just interested in the cruise,' explained Si. 'Heard the music and wanted to enquire about booking tickets.'

'That's friendly Cumbrians for you,' muttered Gaia under her breath. She got to her feet with the kind of elegance that, considering the circumstances, made it obvious she was an award-winning actress.

'The best type of people,' said Federico, taking her hand. 'I love it here.'

Gaia beamed. 'I'm so glad. And sorry about that . . . thank goodness it was just two kayakers.'

'No problem,' said Federico with a bow of his head. 'It's different for me. No one really knows my name outside of the industry.'

'Modesty could be your middle name,' said Gaia, eyes wide. She entwined her arms around his neck.

Federico stroked her shoulders. 'It's not me that people wait for hours to see on the red carpet. My face isn't on the front cover of magazines.' The lowering sun streamed in through the glass and her hair gleamed as though to demonstrate it was *her* that belonged in the limelight.

Rachel watched as Gaia tilted her head up towards him, and Federico tipped his mouth towards hers in return, the ochre fells framing them beyond the window, in an image that could have been straight from a romance film. But was all the wealth and glamour really worth it? she mused. Being so instantly recognisable the world over, everyone clamouring for a piece of you, always having to fend off an unsatiable thirst for every last detail of your personal life.

Gaia eventually pulled back and took Federico's hand. She led him towards the door. 'There's something I want to show you.'

Miles made to follow them. 'Come on, let's go back outside,' he said to Rachel. 'We're missing the sights.'

'Maybe we should stay here,' she suggested, glancing over at the couple as they made their way back out on deck. 'Give them some time alone to enjoy it.'

'What, alone with two bodyguards, a ton of waiting staff and loads of crew?' Miles put his hands on his hips. 'We're just as entitled to see the view as they are, Rach. There's no red cordon we're not allowed to go through now. We can look at the scenery, for goodness sake. We'll stand on the other side of the boat. I've no desire whatsoever to eavesdrop on their conversation.' He mimicked Gaia and Federico talking to each other by opening and closing the fingers and thumbs of both hands like a pair of snapping beaks: 'You're so gorgeous; no *you're* so gorgeous . . .' he whispered in a high-pitched voice.

Rachel giggled despite herself.

Then Miles pointed at her. 'You're gorgeous, Rach. Don't ever forget it. And you deserve to see the place you've dreamed of coming to for so long. We're going outside.'

'The Jaws of Borrowdale,' they overheard Gaia declare with a sweep of her Pilates-toned arm as they walked out of the door and the wind carried her words towards them.

Rachel raised her eyebrows. Her boss must have done some research. Perhaps her job remit really was going to be more reasonable from now on. She thought of the contract she'd drawn up for the trip to the Lakes and the rules they'd agreed to. Enough downtime. No crazy middle-of-the-night errands. So far, Gaia seemed to be sticking to them, and was certainly treating her with more respect than she had done in the past. But how long would it last? She was only doing it to get her own way after all. Without her assistant, planning her wedding would be a whole lot harder . . .

Miles pressed his lips close to her ear. 'The Jaws of LA is my new nickname for Gaia,' he joked. 'She's far more terrifying than a great white shark.' He bared his teeth and pretended to bite a chunk out of Rachel's arm.

'Right, so they're due back in twenty-five minutes.' Katrine rested her head against the upright post of the stainless-steel pass as she watched Jackson at work in Moy's kitchen.

'Mmm.' He didn't glance up from prepping his micro-herbs.

'Is everything under control?' she asked, trying to catch his eye.

'I'm not sure I did enough dried hibiscus for the welcome-cocktail garnish,' he said, wiping his forehead with the sleeve of his chef's shirt and still not looking up.

He'd been perfecting the aperitif for days; tweaking the taste, improving the presentation. The finished result was an imbibable masterpiece named after the world-famous actress he'd created it for: the Gaia Martini. Just the right combination of sweet and sour flavours; fruity, with hints of pomegranate and cranberry.

'I thought I'd gauged it right, but if there are any mistakes there won't be enough . . .' He looked up at Katrine, eyes overly wild for someone discussing a pre-dinner drink. But she understood, had felt the same tight-rope tension of her own reputation hanging in the balance with such a high-profile guest sampling their hospitality.

'Honestly, we've practised it so many times, it'll be fine, I promise,' soothed Katrine, picturing the bar staff's focused faces during Jackson's multiple demonstrations.

'Do I need to go over it again, one last time?'

Katrine shook her head. She could see every step of the process in her mind – including the diagonal sprinkle of dehydrated petals that topped the drink with a deep-scarlet slash.

Jackson reached for the pestle and mortar. 'I'll crush some more, just in case.' He grabbed a container of the dried hibiscus flowers, almost tipped it over in his haste.

Katrine could sense his heart pulsing, she had the kind of sixth sense that working in close proximity cultivated, and was suddenly struck by a need to stop him. 'Hey, hey.' She put her hand on his arm. 'Jackson,' she said, forcing him to meet her gaze. 'It's going to be okay.'

Then Anna walked in through the swing doors. 'Everything all right?' she asked, noting the strained atmosphere and taut expressions of her two most senior members of staff.

Jackson gave a brisk nod. 'All under control.'

'I can do that for you, if you want?' Anna offered, coming to stand beside him.

Jackson's frame was rigid. 'All good.'

But Anna was unconvinced by his answer; she could see the muscles flexing in his jaw, the vein standing proud in his neck, as he concentrated with all his might, trying to keep on top of everything all at once.

'It's not an admission of defeat, you know,' Anna added, reaching for an apron. 'It'll take me two seconds, if there's something else you need to get on with.'

'Are you sure?' said Jackson, shoulders relaxing slightly.

'Positive,' said Anna, tipping a handful of tissue-paper-transparent petals into the stone bowl before her.

'Thanks.' Jackson smiled. 'I appreciate it.'

Anna nodded. 'No problem.' She told herself she was only stepping in to help Jackson out in a moment of intense pressure, but it felt strangely *good* to be back on this side of the pass, with the adrenalin rush of pre-service flooding her body and the buzz of her highly skilled team surrounding her. Above all, she felt *needed*.

She finished grinding the hibiscus. 'What next, chef?' she said gently to Jackson, expecting him to bristle and bark that he was able to manage just fine without her assistance. But when he grabbed the crushed garnish with a grateful nod and then asked her to check on the bread, she began to wonder whether it was just the fact she was there with him, that was making the difference. She strode over to the oven, saw the brioche buns were browning beautifully. 'They've got a gorgeous glaze on them,' she said with a grin.

Jackson turned towards her and a flicker of a smile crossed his face.

'Another five minutes on those, chef!' Anna shouted, feeling a flutter of exhilaration spread through her; the choreography of the kitchen was something she couldn't forget. A sense of excitement was stirring in her stomach as the rituals of service started to come back to her like the steps of a well-rehearsed dance.

'Reckon this was made with the blood of her victims?' Miles murmured to Rachel as he took a sip of his garnet-coloured Gaia martini.

Rachel silenced him with a tipsy kiss as the sharp-citrus taste of the cocktail tingled her tongue. 'Shhh.'

'Genuine question,' shot back her boyfriend, the setting sun turning his eyes a sparkling copper.

The drinks were being served out on the terrace overlooking the lake, and Derwentwater was delighting in their attention, shimmering a spectacular mixture of molten metallics as the light faded beyond the fells.

'I can't believe we're here,' Rachel said to Miles, gazing at the scene stretching out in front of them. The carved stone balustrade had been painted burnt orange by the June evening.

'Neither can I,' replied Miles with a glance in Gaia's direction as he took another gulp from his glass. 'If you'd have told me a month ago we'd be away with your gargoyle of a—'

'Gaia, hi,' said Rachel, spinning round. She had the ability to pick up on her boss's presence the way only an executive

PA could. 'Is everything all right?' she asked, her throat suddenly feeling parched.

Gaia's eyes were burning in the amber light. 'In the morning, can we run through some extra ideas for the wedding?' she asked, but Rachel could tell there was a blaze of underlying emotion that was barely concealed by her boss's bright tone, as though she was looking at an envelope held up to the light, not quite able to read the message inside.

'Of course,' said Rachel, registering the crack in Gaia's voice.

'Feddy has a Zoom at ten, so can we do then?'

Rachel heard Miles cough quietly.

'Please?' added Gaia, resting a hand against the solid stone of the balcony, as though reaching for something tangible in her world of falseness and fantasy.

Rachel nodded, noticing the way Gaia's gemstone necklace glittered as she turned to leave – a giant choker that looked constricting rather than covetable.

Miles took a step closer to his girlfriend, bent his head close to her ear. 'Maybe one day she'll realise that politeness is actually the best accessory.'

The restaurant staff were just as enamoured with their famous guest as Harry seemed to be, observed Katrine from over by Moy's entrance. She'd just witnessed two waiters almost collide with each other on their way back to the kitchen, their necks were so craned in the actress's direction, and although it made her job of ensuring everything in the hotel ran smoothly additionally difficult, she did feel somewhat reassured: no one was immune to Gaia's magnetism. It wasn't just Harry.

She left the dining-room doorway and walked back towards the reception desk, doing her regular loop of the hotel to check on each area. What would her dad think if he could see her now? she wondered, looking out through the high windows at the darkening sky. He'd be happy she and Anna had each other at least, she mused, her thoughts turning to her stepmother. It had been *years* since Anna had worked a full service in the heat and stress of the kitchen. Katrine wondered how she was faring. *I hope she and Jackson have everything under control*, she thought, feeling a twist of anxiety in her stomach. She had a sudden urge to leave behind the candle-scented, floral-decorated foyer and breathe a lungful of night-chilled air; the ideal antidote to Gaia's carefully constructed, rider-stipulated surroundings. Katrine crunched across the gravel, feeling the cool evening embrace her. She decided to do a lap of the grounds, have an invigorating blast about the garden to revive her before she headed back inside to see out the rest of her shift. She wondered whether Anna would want to see her for a debrief at the end of the night, as she wandered around the corner and began to cross the grass. She turned to look back at the captivating sight of the island illuminated at night. She felt a burst of pride as she gazed back at the building that Anna and her dad had brought to life. When the restaurant windows were ablaze like they were now, the hotel appeared even more alluring. A golden glow spread across the lake as though so much energy had been poured into the place, it couldn't help but overflow the four walls and spill out into the water.

The tranquillity of the landscape was a salve after the buzz and bustle of the hotel. Katrine could see the serving staff weaving between the guests with balletic grace. Gaia and Federico were visible through the glass, their table positioned to take in the view of Derwentwater, but their bodies angled towards each other instead. Gaia was leaning close to her fiancé, and from this perspective they looked to be an island all of their own.

Katrine turned away from the dining room, gazed out towards Keswick on the far side of the lake. Glimmers of normality were reflected back at her across the water: the lit-up houses and headlights like shining beacons of reason. She sought out the rough location of the little flat she and Harry rented – her haven. A far cry from the world Gaia and Federico inhabited. Suddenly she was hit by a craving for home. She thought of the life she and Harry shared – a stark contrast to the one the radiant couple sitting in the restaurant behind her led. Did he yearn for more? Wish he'd gone down a different path? She followed the contours of the fading Cumbrian fells, taking comfort from their familiarity, blinking as her eyes adjusted to the night. She was just about to head back inside when she saw the figure crouched beside the wall. Half-obscured by the dusk and semi-hidden by the branches of the espaliered trees, she almost hadn't spotted whoever was squatted there. Katrine froze, feeling her breath catch in her throat as she stifled a scream. She stood completely still, trying to steady her heartbeat with slow breaths. Where were the bodyguards? She could just make out the dark shape of a man as her vision adapted to the dimness. His back was facing her, as though he was hoping to escape her attention. *An intruder?* wondered Katrine. What was she supposed to do in this situation? Surely Chris and Si had been patrolling the grounds, would have made sure no one was able to get this close to—

He was moving, slowly getting to his feet.

Her blood was thudding in her ears. But how could she raise the alarm when there was no one else around? The grounds were deserted. What if this was a—

'*Goodness me*, you gave me a fright.' The man stumbled backwards on the grass, swore as a tumble of tiny objects scattered around his shoes.

'Oh, *damn it*, I dropped the basket.'

Will? Katrine frowned. 'What are you doing out here?' she asked, a hand pressed to her chest to try and persuade her pulse to slow.

'I thought I'd save Anna a job and pick the raspberries before the dew came.' He clambered upright, steadying himself against the kitchen-garden wall.

Katrine blew out a breath. 'I thought we had a trespasser for a second.'

Will grimaced. 'Oh no, I'm so sorry . . . I shouldn't have stayed out here so long. I was that engrossed in gardening, I didn't realise it was getting dark.'

'Does Anna know you're here?'

Will nodded. 'Oh, yes. She said to meet her after dinner was finished.'

Katrine could see his cheeks grow red even in the dwindling twilight.

'It's all right,' she murmured. 'No need to feel awkward around me. I want Anna to be happy.'

'But your dad—'

'He'd want that, too.' Katrine wiped away the teardrops that speaking of him always triggered, the same way the wind swept away the passing threat of summer rain.

The silence that fell between them was filled with the sounds of the island at night. They heard the call of an owl, haunting and beautiful. The noise made them both jump.

'Let me help pick these up,' she said, scrabbling to collect the fallen raspberries by the light of the hotel's glow.

'Oh no, you get back.' Will groaned as his bones moaned when he moved. 'I was just trying to help – Anna's so busy and I didn't have anything better to do.' He winced as he bent to collect the spilled berries.

Katrine smiled at him. 'She'll be really pleased to see you afterwards,' she said. 'Tonight's a big deal, and it's the first time she's done a full shift in *forever*.' She thought back to the opening night. The image of Anna rushing out of the kitchen and racing across the restaurant still seared into her mind. 'Will you just make sure she's all right?' she asked. 'It'll have been a lot for her this evening – emotionally as well as physically – and I know she always seems so strong but . . . I don't want the same thing to happen again.' She stopped herself before she pictured her dad slumped on the floor of Moy's dining room; that wasn't how he'd want them all to remember him. His story was so much more than that last-sentence ending.

Will nodded in the half-dark. 'Of course I will.'

'It's not that I think Anna can't cope or anything—'

'Oh, I know that.' Will chuckled. 'She's the most capable person I've ever met. Doesn't mean she doesn't need a bit of looking after once in a while. Everyone does.'

Katrine tipped her head up towards the clouds as though that would soak the dampness pooling at the corners of her eyes back into her body. 'I miss Dad,' she blurted out to the bruise-coloured canopy. Here on the island was where she could sense him most; in the hotel he and Anna had carefully restored, and in the garden he'd lovingly tended. Signs he'd walked the same pathways and worked the same soil surrounded her. She stretched out a hand and touched one of the cedar-wood structures that her dad had crafted to support the summer squash plants that would soon burst out into bright-yellow fruits. She suddenly felt vulnerable, exposed to the elements beneath the infinite sky, and before she could stop it a sob escaped her lips the same way the raspberries had sprung from their wicker container.

'I didn't mean to upset you . . .' said Will, clutching his basket.

Katrine sniffed. 'It's not your fault . . . I'm just being ridiculous.'

Will shook his head. 'No, you're not at all. I shouldn't have barged in here . . . busying about the place . . . and building the beehives,' he scraped a hand through his hair. 'I didn't think it through . . . I should have realised that you might want to keep things as they were. I hope you don't think I'm trying to—'

'I definitely don't,' interrupted Katrine, pulling her shoulders back to compose herself. Her dad was irreplaceable, she and Anna both knew that.

Will smiled. Kindness was carved into his wrinkled face like he'd been hewn from Cumbrian rock. 'Truth is, for the first time in ages I felt like I *belonged* out here . . . had a purpose again. I started out just wanting to lend Anna a hand, you know, after what happened, but I was made to be outdoors, feel the earth beneath my fingers . . . it was like I'd suddenly found my place in the world again.'

Katrine smiled as she saw his features soften as he spoke with such enthusiasm. She understood why people travelled so far to come to this place now. It wasn't just the fact that the hotel was on an island in the middle of the lake that offered its visitors a fresh outlook, it was the sensation of being part of a bigger picture. A vital puzzle piece that slotted into the rest of the intricate world, like the bees and the flowers and every other living thing that made up the Lake District landscape.

'I've so enjoyed getting stuck in with it all that I guess I got carried away . . .' Will glanced around at the raised beds beside them but the night had all but blotted them out. The animation left his face as though he'd awakened from a dream.

Katrine shook her head. 'I think Anna really appreciates having you here.'

His eyes widened in the floodlighting. 'Do you?'

Katrine nodded. 'A breath of fresh air among the madness,' she added, jerking her head in the direction of the hotel.

Will beamed. 'How's it going with the famous Gaia?'

Katrine grimaced. 'It's . . .' She searched for an appropriate word, but neither the Polish nor English languages seemed to offer up the right one. 'Interesting,' she settled on.

Will laughed. 'Very diplomatic.'

'I'd better get back to work,' said Katrine, turning to leave. 'But it's been nice to chat.' And as she made her way towards the beckoning bronze glow of the hotel, she realised she meant it.

Chapter 17

'I've burned the hispi cabbage,' said Jackson, not lifting his gaze from the tray of charred remains in front of them. 'I can't believe it,' he murmured. 'I've cooked it exactly right, over and over, these past few months . . . and when it comes to the moment when it really matters, I completely mess it up.' Dismay bled from every inch of him; sweat beaded his brow.

'No use beating yourself up about it now,' said Anna briskly, whisking the baking sheet out of his grasp. 'Won't solve anything.'

'But this was something *so* simple,' continued Jackson, still stationary. 'I should be able to do it in my *sleep*.'

'Maybe that's the issue. Not enough rest.' The dark shadows underneath his eyes evidenced the fact he laid awake for hours each night.

Jackson rubbed his temples. 'How could I have—'

'It's easily done,' said Anna. 'We've all been there. I once forgot to set the ice-cream maker off and ended up with custard soup.'

Jackson didn't smile.

'Do you need to take five minutes?' asked Anna.

'In the middle of service?' Jackson fixed her with reddened eyes. 'That would be insane?'

'I'm *concerned*,' corrected Anna.

'And I'm *fine*,' insisted Jackson. 'Just so behind with everything now. I really didn't need that.'

'And I don't need my head chef losing his mind over one misjudged main.' She put her hands on her hips. 'I don't care how famous the actress out there is –' she pointed a finger in the direction of the restaurant – '*nothing*'s worth that, okay?' she said.

Jackson gave a small nod.

'We're going to stay calm and start again,' said Anna, already arranging a row of sweetheart-cabbage halves beneath the grill. 'Let's get the next batch on, quickly. You do the chilli and garlic crumb.' She clapped her hands. 'Come on, Jackson, *focus*.'

'Yes, chef,' he yelled, reaching for a new set of ceramic plates from the shelf above his head and shooting her a grateful grin.

Rachel was trying to concentrate on the hot-sweet, crisp-crunch of the flavour-packed hispi cabbage creation she'd just cut into, but yet again her phone was vibrating, its persistent pulsing demanding her attention from the handbag she'd hung on the back of her chair. She was so accustomed to having to answer it, whatever the time of night or day, she'd almost developed an extrasensory ability to know when it was ringing. She'd taken the bold step of switching it to silent for the duration of dinner, reasoning that if Gaia was in the same room, she wouldn't actually need to call her, but then Rachel ought to have realised before now that when it came to her boss, 'want' was a much more powerful force than need for her behaviour.

But surely whatever Gaia desired could wait a few moments until she'd finished her main course?

'How do they make some *leaves* taste this good?' murmured Miles, marvelling at how such a humble vegetable could be transformed into something so sublime. 'It's quite amazing,' he added, taking another bite of his meal.

Rachel sliced off another mouthful of the smoky, succulent dish – but couldn't help but be distracted by the electronic buzzing still boring into her bones. It was no use; she'd have to answer it. She set down her knife and fork and reached for her phone. The number on the screen belonged to Gaia's father. She scraped back her chair and stood up with a sigh. 'Back in a sec,' she said to a scowling Miles.

'It'll go cold, Rach,' she heard him say as she made her way out of the dining room to answer it. By the time she got to the hallway, the call had gone to voicemail. As she clicked to listen to the message that had been left, she was struck again as to how strange it must be to have to call a PA if you wanted to speak to your own daughter. Rachel had spoken to Gaia's dad on several occasions, but only briefly, in order to direct a call or pass on a message. He always seemed ill at ease on the phone, as if he too found it awkward contacting Rachel rather than the child he actually wished to talk to.

Rachel gazed at a watercolour hanging on the wall opposite as she waited for the automated answerphone speech to segue into the message Gaia's father had left. It was a silver-blue hued depiction of Derwentwater, with the Lake Island Hotel visible in the distance. Simply done, with a mixture of short spiky brushstrokes and long, sweeping lines that created depth and dimension. It was small scale, but utterly enrapturing. The artists initials were inked in the corner, and Rachel wondered what the story behind the painting was. Something about it spoke of an affection for this place; it had a life and a dynamism that leapt off the paper and refused to be contained by the surrounding frame. She'd noticed the picture each time she'd walked along this corridor, but it was a delight to stop and take the chance to properly appreciate it. The way translucent layers of colour had been used to create a curious sense of light and shadow. She had the feeling that it wasn't a professional commission, but done by the hand of someone who had a personal attachment to the hotel—

She hadn't listened to the answerphone message at all, she realised as the robotic voice in her ear kicked in once again to ask how she wanted to proceed. She pressed to hear it for a second time, leaving behind the artwork and making her way over to the sofa in reception.

'Hello, Rachel . . . er, it's Thomas here . . . um . . . G-Gaia's father . . .' He always seemed to stumble over his daughter's name, realised Rachel; perhaps he struggled to square the superstar he saw on the big screen with the little girl she'd once been. 'Er . . . I was just wondering whether . . . um, we were going to see her while she was over . . .' he continued. 'So, if she could give either me or her mother a ring back . . . that would be great . . . I . . . um . . . thank you for passing this on . . . and I'll look forward to hopefully hearing from her soon . . . bye.'

Rachel sat back against the pile of tassel-corned cushions, wondering what Gaia's relationship with her family was like. She mentioned them so rarely, it was impossible to say. Probably fiercely protective of their privacy, reasoned Rachel – they hadn't chosen a high-profile profession themselves after all and maybe she wanted to save them from the constant media speculation she was so often trying to fend off. It was understandable she'd want to keep them out of the public eye, and the relentless scrutiny that came with it, thought Rachel, casting her mind back to the incident outside her and Miles's flat—

'Can I help you with anything?' asked Katrine, coming back into the foyer.

'Oh, no, I'm good, thanks,' replied Rachel with a nod at the hotel manager. She stood up and bent to plump the silk scatter cushions she'd been leaning against – that was her role, she realised: to ensure everything in Gaia's universe ran smoothly while remaining invisible at all times.

'There you are!' said Miles, appearing in the entrance hall at that moment. 'I've been looking for you. I asked them not to clear away your entrée . . .'

Rachel stopped rearranging the soft furnishings and smiled back at her boyfriend: the one person who truly appreciated her presence.

Katrine averted her gaze as the couple kissed in the arched doorway that led towards the restaurant. That had been her and Harry not so long ago, she couldn't help thinking. Not while they were at work, of course, but they'd made every minute together count, coinciding their spare time as much as they could, stitching their free moments together to weave a tapestry of shared memories. But recently they seemed to have let their relationship come second to their responsibilities at the hotel. All their energy and attention had been directed towards their celebrity guests. Once Gaia and Federico had departed, would they be able to get that closeness back? Or had holes started to appear in the fabric of *them*?

Rachel and Miles seemed to have got the balance right, thought Katrine, leaning her elbows on the oak top of the desk. How did Gaia's PA manage it? she wondered admiringly. She could look after the affairs of one of the most famous actresses in the world, fly around the globe, and *still* find time for her boyfriend.

What it must be like to travel the world with Gaia? she wondered as she watched Rachel and her partner disappear down the corridor towards the dining room. Alone in the foyer, Katrine found herself daydreaming about the world they inhabited on the other side of the Atlantic. What was it like to have a schedule full of glittering galas and parties and premieres? For work to consist of exclusive invitations and lavish dinners? It must be so different to being here, in the middle of Derwentwater, where the only stars were the ones in the ancient sky.

'Hey,' said Harry. He was standing in front of the desk; she'd been so distracted by comparing her world here to how she imagined life was like in Hollywood, that she hadn't seen him come in.

'How's your night been?' he asked, eyes crinkling at the corners with fondness for her. A distinct contrast to the infatuated expression that came over his face whenever Gaia was around, Katrine couldn't help thinking, but then she shook herself. She needed to speak to him. Make sure everything was okay. Rather than over-think like this, to no avail.

'Fine, thanks. So far, so good.' She reached across the desktop and his fingers curled around hers.

'I'm glad.' Harry tipped his head to one side. 'Sure everything's all right?' he added, noticing the way she bit her lip like there were words waiting to spill out of her mouth if she let them. 'Got something on your mind?' he asked.

'Just you know . . .' she trailed off.

He raised his eyebrows. 'No. I don't . . . tell me.' He squeezed her hand.

'The whole Gaia thing . . . it's getting to me a bit.'

'Tell me about it – I'll be glad when she's gone.'

'Will you?' Katrine asked.

131

'God, yes. She's rude and entitled.'

'And extremely beautiful,' murmured Katrine.

'That means nothing when you think you're better than everyone else.' Harry spat out the sentence.

There was a bitterness in his voice that Katrine hadn't heard before.

'Look . . . I probably should have told you this . . .' A blush pinked Harry's cheeks as though he'd been standing too close to a flame.

The entrance hall suddenly seemed several degrees chillier, despite the warm June evening, and Katrine clutched her suit jacket closer. '*What?*' she whispered; eyes wide.

'Well . . .' Harry coughed as though whatever confession was coming next refused to be kept inside him any longer.

But at that moment Gaia and Federico came into the room, arm in arm. The chandelier threw light at her in lieu of any crowds lining her path, and her diamond jewellery twinkled like it was its duty to distinguish her as otherworldly.

'Shall we go on a little after-dinner adventure?' she purred to her fiancé, and the Malteser-sized solitaire on her ring finger flashed in the absence of any cameras as though having no one there to capture how fabulous she was, was a waste.

'Where would you like to go, *cara*?' asked Federico, stopping at the foot of the stairs.

'Out on the boat,' replied Gaia, flicking her hair. 'Or should I say ferry,' she added with a glance at Harry. 'Can you take us for a quick lap of the lake?' She didn't wait for his response, had already turned back to her fiancé. 'I've heard the Northern Lights are in town.' Gaia grinned. 'It's like they knew you were coming.'

Federico raised his eyebrows. 'Really? I've always wanted to see them.'

Gaia beamed. 'Told you this was a very special place.'

Katrine's brow creased. Had Gaia been to the hotel *before*? Surely not. It had taken her dad and Anna ages to refurbish it. It hadn't been fit for anyone to stay, let alone someone as famous as Gaia, pretty much right up until she herself had started working here.

'They don't appear often, but Derwentwater has the dark skies you need to have a chance of catching them,' said Gaia, eyes glinting in the candlelight.

'*Wow*,' breathed Federico, but his gaze was still on his girlfriend, and the word could have been directed at her instead.

'And is that all right, going out on the water now?' Federico asked, turning to Harry.

'Are you worried about monsters?' said Gaia with a laugh, looping her arms around Feddy's neck.

Clearly not, thought Katrine, as Federico pulled his girlfriend towards him and planted a kiss on her lips.

'I thought it might be a little last minute, asking to be taken for a trip around the island this late.' Federico hitched up the cuff of his shirt so he could glimpse the sunburst dial of his Swiss-made watch.

The Northern Lights had their work cut out if they were going to shine brighter than the two of them, thought Katrine.

'Oh, come on,' protested Gaia. 'You can't *plan* to see them. It *has* to be a spur of the moment thing!'

Federico looked at Harry. 'What time are you meant to finish work?' he asked.

Harry gave a slight dip of his chin; the consideration wouldn't even have entered Gaia's head. 'Whenever my job is done. If you want to see whether the lights are visible, I'm happy to take you.' He directed his reply solely to Federico.

Gaia clapped in appreciation of her own idea. 'I can't wait to show you!'

'You can't just click your fingers and expect them to appear,' murmured Harry under his breath.

Nature was the one thing that wouldn't just bow to Gaia's will.

'Aurora Borealis,' enunciated Miles from where he lay on the bed. 'Sounds like it could be the name of one of Gaia's mates.'

Rachel laughed, catching his eye in the bathroom mirror as she brushed her teeth.

He began to read aloud from the webpage on his phone. 'Apparently you can download an app which tells you when the best chance of seeing them is,' he added, scrolling further down the screen.

Rachel glanced round at him. 'I'm surprised Gaia did that of her own accord.'

'Yeah, normally it's your job to do anything that involves lifting a finger,' replied Miles, propping himself up on one arm.

'Maybe she's learning to be a little more self-sufficient,' said Rachel, coming back into the bedroom.

'Hmmm,' said Miles, narrowing his eyes. 'I reckon there's more to it than that. I don't think it's for your benefit for one minute.'

Rachel's shoulders sagged.

Miles reached out his hand and pulled her close.

'Do you want to go and try and see the lights ourselves?' asked Rachel, her head resting on Miles's chest. The familiar sound of his heartbeat filled her ears like a favourite song.

'What, from the terrace or somewhere?' Miles shuffled upright and the soundtrack abruptly stopped. 'Happy to, if you'd like to. Some people wait a lifetime to see them.'

Rachel cast her gaze around the luxurious suite. 'You know what, I think us having this time away together is actually rarer than they are,' she said and tugged him back down onto the bed beside her.

She heard a gentle knocking noise as she kissed Miles's smile, and her eyes snapped open again.

'It's the wind,' said her boyfriend, but he already knew she would answer. 'Surely whatever it is can wait till the morning,' he muttered as Rachel made her way across the plush wool carpet to the door. The room was so huge he couldn't hear whatever was being said in the corridor, but it was only a couple of seconds before Rachel was pulling on her sneakers along with the sweater draped over the arm of the mahogany wing chair, and he couldn't help but sigh. *So much for the newfound agreement of work hours and boundaries.* He rested his head on his elbow. 'Don't tell me, Gaia wants a hot water bottle warmed by the souls of heaven's angels.'

Rachel reached for the room key.

'Or she and Federico can't possibly sleep in the same room twice, and we have to swap so it doesn't get samey,' continued Miles.

Rachel shoved her mobile in her pocket.

'I thought we agreed, Rach. There has to be a cut-off point where she can't contact you.'

Rachel spun round. 'It's the other way around this time, though – no one can get in touch with her.'

Miles sat upright. Stopped himself from quipping that surely that was a good thing when he saw Rachel's face, rumpled with concern.

'Gaia's gone missing.'

Chapter 18

Katrine yawned, the painted moon on the long-case clock face staring squarely at her from across the entrance hall, as if to ask: why are you still here at this hour?

But Harry hadn't returned yet.

She saw a flash of torchlight out of the window but when no one came through the front door shortly after, she assumed it had to be Rachel and Miles out for a late-night walk.

The silence of Reception only served to amplify the volume of the thoughts circulating in her head. She was just about to go outside and see if she could spot the boat arriving back at the jetty, when Anna and Jackson walked into the room.

'What a day!' said Jackson, scraping a hand through his hair. 'Thanks so much,' he said turning to Anna and blowing out a breath. 'You didn't have to do that, but it really made a difference. I honestly don't think I could have done it without you.'

Anna batted the air. 'Nonsense. You're perfectly capable. You just need to practise being *calmer.*'

Jackson grimaced.

136

'Or is that like telling the lake to stay flat in a storm?' asked Anna with a laugh.

'I'm trying, I promise. It's just the pressure . . .'

'I know. It gets to us all.'

'Thanks again for keeping me on the straight and narrow. As always.' Jackson touched the top of her arm.

Anna shrugged. 'You know what, I actually enjoyed it.'

Jackson opened his mouth. 'Does that mean it might not be a one-off?'

'Oh, don't worry,' said Anna, shaking her head. 'I'm definitely not after your head chef's hat.'

'We don't wear them,' he shot back.

'You know what I mean.' Anna put her hands on her hips. 'That chapter of my life has been and gone.'

'I don't see why it has to have done. No reason why you couldn't come back for the odd shift. Or on special occasions,' said Jackson.

'We'll see,' said Anna, using the universally understood two-word version of 'no' instead. 'Anyway, how has your night been?' she asked Katrine.

'Okay,' she added, covering her mouth to prevent another yawn from escaping.

'I'd better go,' interjected Jackson, his eyes flicking to the antique walnut clock. 'It'll almost be time for Rose to get up for milking by the time I get back.'

'Harry's still out I'm afraid,' said Katrine. 'Gaia wanted Federico to see the Northern Lights.'

'Oh God, she'll probably demand to stay there until they appear, knowing her.' Jackson flopped down on the sofa.

'You can stay in my spare room if you want,' offered Anna, taking the seat beside him. 'Be just like old times,' she joked, thinking back to when she'd first met him all those years ago,

137

before he'd even set foot in a professional kitchen other than the time he'd wreaked *havoc* at Hesta . . . She shook the memory from her head. It was hard to believe that he'd shed that chrysalis of recklessness to become the talented man he was today.

'You're all right. I want to see Rose, however briefly.' His face broke into a smile.

Katrine felt her heart swell at the sight.

'You've no idea when they'll be back, presumably?' Anna asked her.

Katrine shook her head. 'They've been gone since they finished dinner.'

'Oh dear,' said Anna with a frown. 'I think I might have an idea as to why she's so set on seeing the Aurora . . .'

'Go on,' said Jackson, leaning forward. 'What's the reason?'

'Well, she's been so intent on pulling out all the stops for Federico . . .' continued Anna. 'Constantly trying to please him, think up extra surprises to make sure this is the best trip ever . . .'

'Yeah, and it's driving me *mental*,' said Jackson, crossing his arms.

Katrine came to sit down in the chair opposite them, as a thought struck her: it surely must be difficult for the celebrity couple to try and trump the experiences they'd already had. When you were that rich and famous, what did it take to make a moment exciting and new?

'Come on then, tell us,' said Jackson.

Anna looked at Katrine.

Katrine was glad she'd sat down; what was it that had happened?

'Gaia wanted the painting.'

The sting in Katrine's eyes was immediate.

'The one in the—?' Jackson pointed towards the hallway that led to the dining room.

Anna nodded.

Katrine swept her fingertips over her face. 'What did you—?'

'I said no.' Anna slapped her hands on her knees.

Jackson sat up straight. 'I didn't know that was an option – I thought you said we had to do whatever Miss Gaia wants?'

'She can have anything she likes apart from that,' said Anna, standing up. 'I was very firm.'

'To her face?' asked Jackson. His lips formed a circle of surprise.

Anna nodded.

'I'd have liked to have seen that. Probably the first time she's not been allowed her own way.'

'She sent her PA to speak to me at first. Then came to see me herself. My answer was the same.'

Katrine released a breath. 'You don't have to say that because of—'

'It's not for sale,' said Anna. 'And I've made it clear that's our final word on the matter.'

'But what if it would mean—' Katrine could only imagine the sum of money Gaia would be willing to pay to acquire something she really wanted. It might secure the hotel's financial future—

'However much she offers, it's not enough,' replied Anna. 'And that's the end of it.'

'No offence, but why did Gaia want the painting?' asked Jackson, leaning forward on the sofa. 'Is it the rich person equivalent of buying a postcard?' He gave a laugh. 'They just pick a piece of art –' he clicked his fingers – 'like we'd collect a fridge magnet?'

'I guess so,' said Anna. 'She said she wanted it as a gift for Federico. A memento of their time here.'

'If she's enjoying it so much maybe she could tell her face that,' muttered Jackson. 'She could make it a bit more obvious for the rest of us, too. We're tearing our hair out trying to keep up with all her requests.'

'It's good to know she's pleased with her stay so far,' said Katrine, shoulders lowering a little.

'Indeed,' said Anna. 'And you're all doing an amazing job. You'll be getting a bonus once this is all behind us, as a thank-you from me for all your hard work.' She looked towards the window as the beam of a torch approached: probably Harry and their guests returning. 'You've really gone above and beyond,' said Anna, turning her attention back to Jackson and Katrine.

'Don't speak too soon,' muttered Jackson. 'Harry might've chucked her overboard by now.'

Katrine felt her back stiffen at the mention of her boyfriend and Gaia in the same sentence.

'Can't imagine she'll like it if the Northern Lights haven't put on a show,' said Jackson with a grimace. 'Not on top of being denied the painting.' He shot Anna a look.

'I think that's why she was so keen to try and see the display,' said their boss.

'*If* there is one,' interjected Jackson. 'You can't just press "on-demand".' He mimed using a remote control.

Anna folded her arms. 'God forbid she's disappointed.'

Katrine heard the doorhandle start to turn and jumped up from her seat.

But it was Rachel, Gaia's PA, who appeared in the foyer.

'We can't find Gaia anywhere.' She was out of breath, the flashlight in her hand still switched on, its beam flicking round the room as she spoke like it could sense Gaia belonged in the spotlight.

Miles appeared beside his girlfriend, put a supportive hand at the base of her back. 'We've been all over – right along the shore, everywhere,' he explained to the others.

A third figure followed them inside the entrance hall – Federico, his forehead more crumpled than his silk and wool suit. 'Si and Chris are still out looking for her.'

'You're telling me two of Hollywood's finest bodyguards can't locate her on an island of *this* size?' said Jackson, folding his arms.

'I think doing *treasure hunts* probably wasn't part of their job description,' said Miles.

'Would we class Gaia as—?' began Jackson, before Anna held up her hands.

'Hang on, can we go back to the start please. What's happened? And where's Harry?'

Katrine swallowed; she suspected she knew what the answer was before anyone else spoke.

'I think he's with Gaia,' said Federico. 'He went after her.'

'Then perhaps they don't want to be found,' said Katrine.

Chapter 19

'Can we just rewind for a minute?' asked Anna. The long-case clock chimed twice as though in agreement.

Two a.m. realised Katrine, the striking sound of the hammer and gong like a starting gun, signalling for her imagination to run wild.

'We went out on the boat,' began Federico. 'Gaia said Derwentwater is one of the best places in the country to see the Northern Lights.'

'How does she know that?' asked Jackson. 'I mean, it's true, but why's she suddenly such an expert?'

'Making a big effort to impress her Hollywood producer fiancé, obviously' replied Miles in a hushed voice. 'Shows she's capable of putting some effort in herself when she really wants to,' he said to Rachel.

She nudged him gently. 'Let Federico speak.'

'We were out on the lake, and it was beautiful.' Federico swallowed. 'But the sky was cloudy and the conditions were not ideal for seeing the Aurora. Gaia was so disappointed. I said it didn't matter. We'd had a nice day, and it was nice seeing the island at night. But Gaia's mood just –' he plunged his palm towards the floor. 'She wasn't happy so I suggested going back to the hotel. Still she wanted to stay.' He sighed. 'Sometimes she has such high expectations. It can be exhausting.' He rubbed his forehead. 'If you are always looking for something on the horizon, you will miss what is right there in front of your eyes.' He moved the fingers of one hand close to his face.

The room was quiet as the others contemplated his words. No one spoke while they waited for him to continue. 'Eventually I persuaded her we should turn back. We got to the – how do you say –' he mimed the landing stage like a flight attendant indicating the aisle of the aircraft.

'The jetty' offered Katrine.

Federico nodded gratefully. 'We are walking on the jetty and she still had the app open on her phone. She says it's the time with the best chance, the lights should definitely be visible.'

'I bet she wanted to go back out on the boat,' said Jackson.

'Probably,' agreed Miles.

'But she's so busy looking at the screen that she trips and drops her phone and it falls in the water,' continued Federico.

There was a collective intake of breath.

'Did she expect Harry to dive in and get it?' asked Jackson.

'I think so,' said Federico seriously.

Katrine flinched.

'Of course, he refused,' said Federico. 'Gaia was angry.' He raked a hand through his hair. 'A side to her I had not seen before . . .'

Shared looks spread around the room.

'I tried to take her hand. Said we would fix it tomorrow. Get a new phone.'

Miles noticed the way Rachel's lips twitched as she made a mental note to add it to her to-do list.

'I said to her, life is not perfect,' said Federico. 'She wants everything to be without problems, but that is not the world.' He shook his head. 'She walked off. Harry went after her. I thought she'd come back to the hotel. But she hasn't.'

'Is there anywhere we might have missed?' Rachel asked Anna. 'We've been round the grounds and right to the other side of the island.' Worry had worn furrows into her brow. 'What if she's not okay?'

'Surely she'll return when she wants something,' said Jackson. 'I imagine she's not an avid wild camper.'

'What do we do in the meantime?' asked Rachel.

'Just wait, I imagine,' said Miles.

'So much for getting home before the sun's up,' said Jackson with a sigh.

Rachel bowed her head.

All of a sudden Federico began to cry, covering his face with his hands.

'Hey, hey, it's okay,' said Katrine, steering him towards an armchair.

'I'll get you a glass of water,' offered Jackson, disappearing off towards the bar.

Anna fetched a box of tissues from the reception desk.

'Do you want us to give you a bit of space?' asked Rachel softly, crouching beside him.

Federico looked up at her with lake-like eyes. 'It's all right. I just thought it might be . . . different with . . . Gaia. The real thing.'

Katrine saw Miles shoot Rachel a disbelieving look.

He took a paper tissue. 'Please, get some rest,' he said to the others. 'I'll stay up in case she wants to talk.'

Sleep was the last thing Katrine felt capable of. 'Stay at mine,' said Anna, squeezing her hand. 'Jackson, there's a spare room here you can have.'

He nodded, resigned to the fact that he wouldn't be leaving the island that night. He took out his phone to text his wife.

'How does she manage to have such an impact on so many people's lives,' muttered Miles through gritted teeth. He looked up at the chandelier, sparkling above them, and was reminded of Gaia and how they all revolved around her.

'Gaia!' shouted Harry, as he stomped along the pebbled shore in search of her. The cooled stones perfumed the middle of the night air and the leaves on the nearby branches moved to camouflage any sign of movement; the island careful to keep the actress's secrets. He stopped still. Why was he even looking for her? There was no real tie between them, at least not anymore. 'Gaia!' he called again. Despite everything – all she'd put him through – he still wanted her to be all right. He sat down on a rock. Chucked a stone into the calm water and watched the mirror-surface shatter. Was everything just an illusion? he wondered as he watched the ripplets spread; a stark reminder of the impact one moment, one meeting, could have on the rest of your life—

He heard a sniffing sound; he was sure of it. Somewhere close by. He stood up, scanned the trees that seemed to reach towards the lake as though always ready to welcome people to the island. But there was no one there. He was about to turn back when he heard it again.

'Gaia?' he tried once more.

'Go away,' came her voice, from somewhere overhead.

Harry looked up, and there, almost concealed by the blanket of cloud, and huddled in the crook between two thick limbs of an old oak, like she was wrapped in a hug, was Gaia.

'What are you doing there?' he said, surprise rooting him to the spot. Entwined with the natural landscape, the branches of the tree curved around her protectively, Gaia looked so different to the person who'd been sending them all into a spin since she'd arrived at the hotel. Silver tears streaked her cheeks.

She didn't answer his question.

'Are you going to come down?' he asked instead.

Her pale skin was moon-like between the dark leaves. She shook her head.

'Right, okay.' Harry took a step towards the trunk. 'Budge up then.'

He gripped the rough bark and pulled himself up with a huff.

Gaia stayed put.

Harry heaved his body up another couple of branches till his face was level with her feet. *How apt*, he couldn't help but think, and purposefully climbed further. 'Shuffle up,' he said now he was alongside her, and Gaia made a half-hearted effort to slide along, if not to make space then to make it clear he could join her.

He didn't speak for a second. The perspective from up here was something else. Supported by the tree, he felt weightless, suspended, part of the nighttime canopy.

'Sorry you didn't get to see the Northern Lights,' he murmured, glancing upwards at the steel-wool sky.

Gaia didn't say anything.

'Hopefully you'll get another opportunity, be going somewhere else where they're easier to spot. I hear Iceland—'

'That's not the point,' mumbled Gaia.

'Right, well, I just wanted to . . . I don't know, make sure you were—'

They heard a scrunching sound from below; saw the body-guards striding along the stony shore.

Gaia put a finger to her lips.

Harry stayed silent.

When their footsteps had faded again, Gaia turned towards him. 'I'm hardly ever alone anymore . . .' she said.

Harry shifted position, preparing to descend from the tree. 'I'll leave you be.' He steadied himself against the solid trunk of the oak.

'You don't count,' muttered Gaia, a little too spikily for it to be a compliment.

Harry looked down at the ground; it seemed much higher up here than it had done down there. It was quite a fall if he was to suddenly lose his footing; perhaps that was how Gaia felt on a daily basis, he wondered: constantly worrying about crashing back down to earth from the pedestal she'd been put on.

He rested his cheek against the wrinkled skin of the ancient tree.

'Does Katrine know about me and you?' Gaia asked.

Harry shook his head. Guilt prickled the back of his neck. 'To be honest, it was a shock for me that—'

'Yeah,' agreed Gaia. 'Same. I never expected it.'

'Me neither.' Harry bit his lip. 'Does Federico know that—'

'*God*, no,' said Gaia, a touch too emphatically for Harry's liking.

'Right.'

Gaia sighed. 'Such a mess.'

Harry swallowed. 'Not necessarily. You should speak to him. Federico. He thinks the world of you.'

'Probably not anymore.'

'Why don't we go back?' suggested Harry.

'I don't want to – not just yet,' said Gaia. 'It's been so long since I've just been . . . *me*. Actual me. Not the one I think people want me to be.'

Harry felt an unexpected surge of compassion for her. 'And is this you now? You going to live in this tree?' he patted the puckered trunk.

Gaia let out a laugh, and the sound made him smile.

He traced a burl in the oak's bark, a beautiful irregularity rather than a flaw, thinking how people had their knots and imperfections too, just the same.

'You know what I mean,' said Gaia as her giggles dissipated. She put a hand on her tummy as if it had been so long since she'd genuinely belly laughed she'd forgotten what it felt like. 'I spend my life holding in my stomach,' she said suddenly. 'Worrying if I'm standing at the right angle.'

Harry looked at her: vulnerable and childlike once all the artifice and entourage were stripped away.

'Stressing that I'm not good enough, comparing myself to Victoria *bloody* Cole.' She scraped her gelled nails through her loose curls. 'Up here, no one's judging me, measuring me against some impossible standard.'

'I can't imagine,' said Harry. 'You have to ignore the critics,' he added softly.

'And how do you expect me to do that?' Gaia snapped. 'You make it sound so simple.'

Harry held up his palms. 'I'm just saying you could try concentrating on the people who care for you instead. Listen to what they say.'

Gaia sighed.

'Your parents must be proud,' said Harry with a half-smile.

'I haven't seen them in ages,' said Gaia. 'Not since I've been with Federico, actually.'

'Really?' Harry frowned. 'Are you not going to introduce them before the wedding?'

'*If* there is a wedding.' Gaia closed her eyes. 'They'll meet him on the day. That'll have to be enough.'

'For them or for you?' asked Harry.

'For everyone.' Gaia opened her eyes. 'Everything's always so tightly scheduled. Time is always accounted for – perpetually squeezed.' She made her manicured hands into claws that clutched invisible spheres of tension.

'Let's deal with one thing at a time.' Harry looked her straight in the eye, no longer as conscious of the distance between the branch he sat on and the ground below. Focusing on what was right in front of him, rather than the height he'd plummet from if the worst happened, lessened his fear. He wondered if the same principle applied to Gaia's situation. 'First of all, tune out the negative comments.'

'Difficult when it's the voice inside here.' Gaia tapped her temple.

'But how can that be the case?' Harry raised his eyebrows. 'Look at you!'

'That's all anyone ever does – reduce me to what I'm wearing on the red carpet or whatever.'

'I don't mean that.' Harry batted a hand through the air. 'I'm talking about how successful you are!'

'What even *is* success?' Gaia fixed him with her gaze.

'You tell me, I haven't achieved it.' Harry shook his head.

'You're kidding me. You live the dream – out on the lake all day.' Gaia swept an arm out in an arc in front of her. 'Surrounded by *this*.'

'You think it's *miserable* here. You said so yourself.'

'You know that's not true.'

Harry raised his eyebrows. 'Why did you say it, then?'

Gaia sighed again. 'I don't know . . . it sounds stupid saying it out loud, but I thought Feddy might think less of me if I—'

'Was honest with him?' Harry tipped his head to one side. 'Surely that's a basic requirement for going into a marriage.'

Gaia's shoulders sagged. 'I've just not made a big thing about—'

'Hang on a minute – are you ashamed of your background?' Harry sat up so suddenly he almost overbalanced.

'I just don't want Feddy to have second thoughts . . .'

'You can't have a wedding if he doesn't know the first thing about who you really are!'

'I don't even know who I really am,' murmured Gaia.

'Is this what this is all about? Trying to project some perfect image till you've got him down the aisle?'

'No, not at all . . . I intend to keep it up—'

'What, pretend to be someone you *think* he wants as opposed to who you really are?'

'Fake it till you make it and all that.' Gaia gave a humourless half-laugh.

'This is ridiculous.' Harry covered his face with the palm of one hand.

'You don't think I can do it?' asked Gaia. 'Be the woman fit to be Mrs Federico De Angelis?'

'I think you should be yourself.'

'And how far did that get me?' Gaia retorted.

'You're always so concerned with *distance*,' said Harry. 'When all you really crave is closeness.'

Gaia fell silent.

'Lying to someone isn't how you find love.'

'I *haven't*,' said Gaia.

'You mean the former or the latter?' Harry held her gaze.

Gaia's cheeks flushed. 'I've just kept some *mystery*, is what I meant. It's part of the persona. The key to Gaia's appeal.'

It was the first time she'd used the third person, her acknowledgement that Gaia was a *creation*. 'So, Federico's your fiancé, and yet you don't even know the first thing about each other?' said Harry.

'Of course we do,' shot back Gaia. 'But that's not all it's about, is it, in show business? Feddy and I . . . we were labelled the biggest names in Hollywood alive today . . . the press and the public, they were willing it to happen. Designers wanted to dress us; restaurants wanted us to be seen there – the papers reported we were dating before we'd even properly *met*. Plus everything's so accelerated because there's never any time – we're both so busy with work – but at the end of the day, our combined power is greater than either of us on our own.'

'Blimey. Is that really what it boils down to? 'Harry raised his eyebrows.

'It's the *brand*. You wouldn't understand.'

'Because I'm just a pleb, you mean.'

'I mean the speculation isn't something you have to deal with. The expectation.'

'Doesn't mean you can't be more open with him,' said Harry. 'In private at least. Let him in a little—'

'And shatter the illusion? You'd love that wouldn't you – to see me crash back down to earth. Reduced to *nothing* again.' Her eyes flicked to his before she looked away.

Harry winced. 'Wow. So that's how you see me.'

'I was talking about myself.' Gaia glanced down at the hard stones on the shore below.

Harry jutted out his chin. 'I'm proud to be me.'

Gaia opened her mouth. 'You should be.'

Harry gave a half-laugh. 'You don't need to humour me.' He looked out towards the speckled lights of Keswick on the far side of the lake. 'I'm happy with the path I'm on. I own the choices I've made – past mistakes and all.'

Gaia's head snapped round. 'Was I a mistake?' she asked.

Harry paused. 'You mean do I regret . . .'

Gaia nodded.

'Not for one minute.'

He thought he saw a flicker of relief twitch at the corner of her lips, but a smile from Gaia was more elusive than the Aurora.

Harry turned to face her. 'I wish you saw what I saw.'

'That girl doesn't exist anymore.'

'That's a shame, because she was pretty special.' He felt a stab of guilt in his stomach. Was it wrong to say that, when he loved Katrine? Suddenly the air seemed colder, as though the night air was trying to bring him to his senses. 'I really should go.' He studied the tree, trying to work out a relatively safe route down.

'Wait,' said Gaia. 'Was she?' Her eyes were wide.

Harry nodded. 'I thought the world of Grace Wilkins.'

Gaia flinched at the sound of Harry speaking her real name aloud; the syllables of it like a needle that pierced through her skin and found the soft flesh underneath.

'Why?' she whispered in a small voice.

Harry leaned back against the sturdy trunk of the oak tree and sighed.

'See, you can't think of a single answer.'

'No, she's just so far removed from the person sitting next to me, it's a struggle to recall,' said Harry pointedly.

Gaia opened her mouth, then closed it again.

152

The now-still night wrapped a cloak of quietness around them.

Gaia turned her head towards the time-old mountains. 'I'm sorry I've been so rude to you,' she said, and Harry nearly toppled off his bark-upholstered perch.

'It's okay.'

Gaia shook her head. 'No, it's not. It was wrong. I just . . . didn't know how to deal with it . . .'

'It was a shock for me too, to be honest. I didn't expect to see you again. Not in person anyway . . .'

She turned to look at him. 'Have you watched any of them?'

'You mean your globally successful blockbuster films? Yes, of course, I live in Keswick not under a rock.'

She laughed again; a generous, full peal that caused him to join in, too.

'I'm scared I'm going to get found out, Harry,' she said all of a sudden. 'People will see I'm just a phony and everything'll fall apart.'

'That's not the case. You're the most celebrated actress of our times. People don't get the awards you've won by chance, Grace.'

She pressed her hands to her cheeks. 'I'm worried one day everyone'll realise I'm just an ordinary girl from a tiny village no one's heard of.'

'I beg your pardon – Grange-in-Borrowdale was famous for being the home of the Bowder Stone long before you came along.'

She laughed once more, and it was as though a little of the old Grace had come back to life.

'In all seriousness, why does where you come from have any bearing on anything? Why would Federico be bothered about something like that?'

'Because he could have *anyone* he wants. He was with Victoria Cole for goodness sake!'

'Who cares? Why would you want to try and be a *copy* of someone else when you can be the original wonderful *you*?'

'*She* tries to copy *me*, actually,' retorted Gaia, thinking of the red-carpet dress her rival had worn at the premiere.

'Whatever, that's beside the point.' Harry batted the air; if he'd wanted to be party to those kinds of politics he'd have pursued a different career. 'Grace Wilkins is unique. In answer to your earlier question, she was *genuine*. That's what I liked about her.'

Gaia dipped her head. '*Ugh* . . . she was so naive and . . . *unsophisticated*.' She gave a shudder.

'No,' countered Harry. 'You were natural, in all senses of the word. You had this raw talent, that everyone could see, but coupled with a realness.' Their conversation was stirring long-buried memories, making them drift to the surface of his mind the same way the ferry propeller churned up silt from the lakebed.

'I hadn't learnt what it takes to get to the top.'

'And how is it up there?' asked Harry, grasping the oak's trunk like it was his anchor to the present. 'Are you happy?'

Gaia shivered as the breeze stirred once again, shaking the tree's branches, demanding an answer. 'I don't know,' she murmured. 'I should be. I have everything I could possibly need.'

'Do you?' probed Harry. 'Or is it all just *belongings*, rather than a sense of *belonging*?'

Gaia frowned. 'So you don't think I fit in, in Federico's world, either?'

'That's not what I said, and you know it.' Harry held her gaze.

'All right then, Mr Philosopher. What's the secret to happiness?'

Harry looked out across the water. 'I think it's different for everyone,' he demurred.

'Dodging the question,' said Gaia, nudging his arm. 'I meant what is it to *you*.'

Harry gave a laugh. 'We're the complete opposite, us two.'

Gaia seemed to slump slightly, sinking further into the oak's embrace.

'I think I used to think it was much more complex. But as I've got older, it all seems a bit clearer.'

'So, what is it, then?'

Harry shrugged. 'Simple stuff. Having meaningful connections. Feeling understood.'

'Is that how it is with Katrine?' murmured Gaia.

Harry nodded, didn't even need to think. 'Yeah.' A grin spread across his face as it always did when he pictured her face. 'Katrine makes me feel . . .' He struggled to distil their dynamic into a single word. 'Like I'm *enough* as I am. Totally accepted.'

'And I didn't,' whispered Gaia.

Harry shook his head. 'That's not what I meant. Back then, we were *kids*. We had so much growing to do, we didn't know *anything*, even though we thought we did.'

'I still don't,' said Gaia with a wistful smile. 'I've got all the trappings of success . . . but sometimes I just feel *trapped*,' she admitted. 'Suffocated by it all.'

'So that's why you're here, right?' Harry jerked his head to indicate the night-dark mountains. 'To get some air.'

'Yeah.' Gaia took a deep breath.

'It's not too late to redress the balance.'

'Isn't it?' she cocked her head to one side.

Harry's eyes met hers. 'No. Don't leave behind all the bits of you that make you *you*, Grace. Promise?'

She nodded.

'Otherwise it's such a *waste*.'

Her eyes glistened.

'And it won't lead to your happy-ever-after either. It's not worth having if it's false.'

'Is that how you see me and Feddy? As a sham?'

'I just know you crave something deeper. I'm not saying you can't have it with him. But you need to let him in.'

'You're right.' Her voice was thick with emotion. The wind had picked up, and he caught the scent of her perfume: unfamiliar now. 'Thank you,' she mumbled.

'Sorry, I didn't quite catch that?' quipped Harry.

Gaia jabbed him fondly in the ribs.

'Shall we get back?' he suggested.

'Good idea.' Gaia nodded.

He was about to twist round, attempt to find a foothold, when a glimmer of white light illuminated the now-clear sky.

'Did you see that?' he said.

Gaia nodded. 'Yeah, I did.'

Neither of them moved, their attention on the heavens above them.

A flash of pink flickered between the stars.

'Oh my god!' cried Gaia as a ribbon of iridescent green reflected across the lake.

'The Northern Lights,' mouthed Harry, watching the patterns of the Aurora shimmer in between the parted clouds.

Chapter 20

An arc of red and pink spread right overhead, seemingly exactly above the oak tree.

'Oh, *wow*!' breathed Gaia. 'I can't believe it!' A starburst of dazzling colours erupted at its centre like a giant flower.

'This is the best thing I've ever seen,' said Gaia, head tilted back to take in the lit-up sky.

'See, just when you stopped looking, you found them,' said Harry, his gaze fixed on the flutter and flare of the light display.

Gaia nodded, transfixed by the phenomenon flickering like a giant firework. 'Is that you telling me not to try so hard?' she asked, still staring up at the sky.

'Oh, only in some areas,' said Harry. 'You can definitely work on others – like being nice to boatmen.'

She batted his arm. They lapsed into companionable silence, absorbed by the vision in front of them. Then, all of a sudden, the grey-gauze cloud curtains started to close once again and obscured the rest of the Aurora, leaving them questioning whether it had really happened at all.

'Was that a dream?' murmured Gaia, eyes awash with wonder.

'No,' replied Harry. 'Though I'm currently sitting in a tree with a famous film-star, so it might be.'

Gaia threw her head back and laughed like she was releasing a lungful of long-held emotion.

Harry grinned. 'Happy now?'

Gaia sighed. 'I just wish Feddy could have seen them – it was so impressive.'

'You don't always have to be putting on a show, Grace.'

Gaia turned towards him. 'But he's used to dating models and travelling the world.'

'If he's half the person you deserve, he'd want to get to know the girl underneath all the glitz and glamour.'

Gaia blinked back at him.

'Why did you bring him here anyway?' asked Harry.

'Because it's the most beautiful place there is.' She smiled. 'I heard about the hotel and thought it would be perfect – completely private, a proper escape.'

'Didn't expect to bump into your first boyfriend then?'

'I nearly *died* when I realised it was you.'

'Yeah, you could definitely work on that charm . . .'

Gaia gave an involuntary snort. 'I forgot how funny you were,' she spluttered.

'*Are*,' corrected Harry. 'Really? Because I remember it all.'

'Do you?'

Harry nodded. 'Everything.'

'My awful haircut?' Gaia covered her face with her fingers.

'I thought that fringe suited you.' Harry shrugged. 'What happened to your Cumbrian accent, though?'

'Lost it somewhere along the way,' she replied, like it was nothing more than a pound coin dropped from a purse.

'Was I a nightmare?' asked Gaia, voice small now.

Harry was about to crack a joke, but he could see the seriousness in her eyes.

'We just weren't well suited,' he said. 'Wanted such different things.'

'D'you never wish you'd pursued acting?'

He shook his head. 'Not beyond wondering "what if?".'

'You were more talented than me.'

'Rubbish. You always got leading roles. But that's it: the competitiveness, the hustle – it wasn't the life for me.'

'I admire that – the fact you know your own mind.'

'Did you just give me a compliment?'

Gaia laughed.

'I liked drama school, and our course, but I didn't want to take it any further.'

'Bit like me and you?'

'That's unfair – it was mutual.'

'I'm only joking – we'd have killed each other.'

'But look at us now.' Harry smiled.

Gaia did the same.

'D'you think we should head back?' suggested Harry, and Gaia nodded. He started to scramble down from his branch seat, grazing his knee on the rough bark as he went. Once his feet were firmly on the ground again, he bent to brush flecks of timber from the scuffed fabric of his trousers, thinking that the scrape would be a reminder that their conversation had been real. He glanced up at the oak, its boughs like outstretched arms, and wondered what else it had seen in its hundred or so years on the island. 'Here, let me help you,' he said, looking at Gaia clambering down behind him. He reached up his hands, and Gaia took them both, leaping off a lower branch and landing with an ungainly thud and a loud giggle.

'Very graceful,' quipped Harry. 'See, the girl I knew is still in there somewhere.'

'Do you think so?' said Gaia.

Harry nodded. 'I hope so. I think Federico would like to meet her.'

Gaia bowed her head. 'He'll probably split up with me when he realises I'm an imposter. Just plain old Grace Wilkins.'

'Okay, stop it now.' He put his hands on his hips. 'I'm not going to flatter you anymore.' But when he saw her mouth tremble, he realised she was being sincere. 'Hey, hey,' he soothed. 'Do you need a hug?' He held his arms out. 'Seeing as we're friends.'

Gaia gave a small smile and took a step towards him.

Just as Katrine rounded the curve of the rocky shore and caught sight of her boyfriend wrapping his arms around another woman.

Chapter 21

So, it was true: her worst fears were confirmed. Katrine felt her cheeks flame hot. She stood there, as unmoving as the trees that lined the stony shore, trying to take in the scene in front of her. There was no two ways about it. If either Harry or Gaia tried to deny it, she'd seen it with her own eyes: the two of them as interlaced as the lakes and the fells. What about Federico? Did he know? She'd left him in the foyer, deflated on the silk-cushioned sofa, having sent the bodyguards off to bed. Si and Chris had returned to confirm what they'd both already suspected: his fiancée and her boyfriend, deliberately hiding on the other side of the island.

At first Katrine hadn't wanted to believe it. She'd waited for Harry to come back. Explain. But as midnight bled into morning, her resolve had begun to melt away. She'd had to find out what was going on for herself.

And now the first blush of dawn was just emerging beyond the hills. She started to make her way back to the hotel, head filling with a flurry of thoughts as she hurried along the woodland path. She wanted to leave, fly back home to Poland, get as far away from the island as possible. But Anna had become her family; the hotel was the place she felt her father's presence most. What a mixed-up tangle of threads life was.

She put one foot in front of the other, couldn't bear to look at the slash of daybreak spilling through the clouds, the colours too wound-like.

Would she have to be the one to tell Federico? Or would he guess by the look on her face? Surely Harry and Gaia would have to come clean at some stage. Couldn't continue their clandestine—

'Katrine?'

She glanced up and saw Rachel coming towards her down the hotel's lawn, cardigan hugged closely around herself, dew-damp grass sticking to her sneakers.

'I couldn't sleep either,' said Gaia's PA. 'I've got a new phone coming for Gaia this afternoon, so if someone could take me across to Keswick . . .'

Katrine wasn't concentrating. Out of the corner of her eye she could see two figures winding along the water's edge beyond the hotel's grounds. But before Harry could look up and notice her standing there, she turned and started to walk in the direction of Anna's annexe.

Her stepmother opened the door even before she'd lifted the brass knocker. 'I saw you from the kitchen window,' said Anna. 'Jackson's still asleep.'

'You were already awake?' asked Katrine, voice coming out as a croak.

Anna nodded. 'I was worried about you.'

Katine met her gaze. 'I thought everyone was busy wondering about Gaia.'

'Not all of us,' said Anna, filling the kettle. 'Come and sit down.' She jerked her head at a chair.

'How can your whole world turn upside down in only a couple of days?' murmured Katrine.

'We both know it can happen much quicker than that,' replied Anna as she reached for two mugs from the cupboard by her head.

Katrine sank down on a seat.

'Do you want to talk about it?' Anna asked over her shoulder.

Katrine sighed. She couldn't bring herself to describe what she'd seen down by the lake, despite the fact that Chris and Si had already availed them of the facts. 'I'm just sad . . . I thought Harry and I were . . .' she trailed off and Anna saw her press her palm to her chest as though her heart physically hurt. She knew that feeling.

'If you want to stay here . . .'

Katrine nodded, not quite ready to contemplate any next steps.

'It might not be what you think,' added Anna, picking up on it. She passed her stepdaughter a mug of hot tea.

'Thank you,' replied Katrine, cupping her hands around it for comfort.

There was a muffled creak, the sound of footsteps on stairs.

'I hope I haven't woken Jackson—' Katrine started to say, when Will appeared in the kitchen doorway.

Of course – he'd been meeting Anna after work, remembered Katrine. Must have been waiting around for ages while the whole Gaia saga unfurled—

'I don't want to disturb . . .' He looked from Anna to Katrine. 'I just heard about what happened last night –' he waggled a hand in the direction of the window to indicate the wild-goose chase of the previous evening – 'and wanted to make sure you were okay.' Concern crinkled his face.

Katrine felt an unexpected swell of solace at the fact he'd wanted to check. She remembered their conversation in the garden the night before, his worry that she might think he was trying to replace her father, and still he'd been compelled to come down and see if she was all right. 'Thank you,' she replied, a ripple of reassurance passing over her. 'I appreciate it,' she said, voice hoarse from a sleepless night. But the sensation was swiftly replaced with a stomach lurch of disbelief: Harry had obviously not given her a second thought. Had she even entered his head at any point last night? Or had he just thrown away their relationship as easily as if it were a pebble tossed to the bottom of the lake?

She pushed back her chair. She had to speak to him. It was no use hiding here – far better to confront the truth. He and Gaia might want to run away from reality but she lived in the actual world, and the sooner she came to terms with the situation the better. She took a gulp of tea to bolster her, in the absence of anything stronger. 'I'm going to see if I can find Harry . . .'

'I thought that had already been achieved,' replied Anna, her gaze full of sympathy.

'You know what I mean – get some sort of . . . an explanation,' said Katrine. 'It's just come as such a—' A great hiccupping sob burst from her mouth. She put a hand to her lips, trying to compose herself.

Will took a step towards the table. 'You've got us both by your side, just so you know . . .'

Katrine did her best to smile. She stood up, bracing herself for what she was about to encounter. Would Harry try to deny it? Offer her excuses for what she'd seen with her own eyes?

'You know where we are, if you need anything,' said Anna as she accompanied her to the door.

Katrine hugged her tightly, sensing her stepmother try to will some of her own strength into her as she squeezed her back.

'It'll be okay, whatever the outcome,' said Anna, still not letting go. 'Love you,' she added.

And Katrine felt a burst of courage, for it was the first time she'd ever said those words out loud to her.

Chapter 22

Katrine had walked through the front door of the hotel on numerous occasions, but now as she pushed it open, her pulse was thumping. The entrance hall was empty, no sign of anyone else. Her surroundings were all at once so familiar yet seemed foreign; the soft furnishings were the same but now everything was different—

A sound from the corridor that led to the dining room. Faint. Stifled.

Should she follow it? Stay here? She felt disorientated. No longer sure where she belonged, wanted answers but couldn't bear to hear them.

But she couldn't stay here, waiting in Reception like a guest in her own life. She walked towards the restaurant, ready to confront whatever she might find, rounded the corner—

And stopped still.

The picture on the wall had been swapped. The one signed in the lower-lefthand corner *D. Łaska* – it was gone. She pressed her fingers to her lips. Where once the landscape scene of the Lake Island Hotel had hung beside the door to welcome visitors to Moy, there was now a frame containing an oil painting of shell-pink roses. Katrine drew in a breath. Took a step closer in disbelief. *Replaced – just like that.* Was that how easy it had been for Harry to switch his feelings to someone else? She glanced back at the painting – it was as though the original had never been there at all.

But Anna had promised her it wouldn't leave the premises – at any price. She'd told Gaia to her face once and for all it wasn't for sale. What had happened since then? Did Gaia simply always get her own way? Just take what she wanted—

'Katrine.'

She jolted backwards at the sound of Harry's voice behind her. So, it wasn't him she'd heard ahead of her in the hall . . . But her shot of relief was short-lived – did he know about *this*?

'I've—' he began, reaching his arms out towards her.

'Don't say you've been looking for me when you haven't,' she whispered, holding up a palm to dam his speech. She felt a pinch of pain at the fact she could read him so well in some respects, yet other parts remained such an enigma.

His arms fell back to his sides.

'The painting . . .' she managed, before her words petered out. She pointed at the new picture on the wall.

Harry gave a good impression of being shocked by the substitution. 'Oh my g—'

'It's okay,' cut in Katrine. 'You don't need to act surprised. I have a good idea whose hands it's in now . . .'

'What do you mean?' Harry frowned.

'You know how important it is to me . . .' said Katrine.

He took a step towards her. 'Of course I do . . .'

'So please don't lie.'

'I wouldn't!' Harry flung out his arms. 'You *know* that!'

167

Katrine didn't reply.

'Don't you?' asked Harry, eyes wide.

Katrine swallowed. 'You said *yourself* that there was something you should have told me before . . .'

'Yeah, and that was stupid of me . . .'

'What, to admit there was something between you and Gaia or to keep it secret in the first place?' said Katrine, crossing her arms.

Harry's brow creased. 'I haven't done anything wrong, Katrine—'

She closed her eyes. 'Just tell me one thing: has Gaia taken the painting as well?'

Harry straightened. '*Taken?*'

Katrine nodded. 'Anna told her it wasn't for sale.'

'Of course – your dad painted it.'

'So you know how much it means to me.' Her eyes were huge in the hall light.

'Yes.'

'I *have* to get it back.' Her voice was thick.

'Okay, well, if you really think Gaia's gone off with it then I can try and speak to her . . .' offered Harry. He wasn't sure if what he said to Gaia would have any sway, but the two of them seemed to at least be on better terms than they were, after their tree-top tête-à-tête. He jutted out his chin. 'Whatever you think of her, Katrine, I know she wouldn't *steal.*'

Katrine bristled at the implied intimacy. 'You must know her *very* well.'

Harry sighed. 'Look, we were . . .' he trailed off, at a loss as to how to distil his and Gaia's relationship into a single sentence: two college kids who'd stuck together at acting school after discovering they'd grown up in practically the same area of Cumbria. Then they'd grown apart – like the boughs of the oak tree rooted in the island's soil – pursued their own directions. It was completely different to anything he shared with Katrine – or had thought he did.

'Doesn't matter,' said Katrine, making *her* the one who was lying. She felt a crushing sensation in her chest as she spoke the words.

'Can we just sit down a second?' asked Harry. 'My head is banging. I haven't got a clue what's happening.'

He was confused! thought Katrine. What about her? Questions scrolled through her mind like one of Rachel's endless emails. She pushed through the restaurant's door, seeking the quiet hush of Moy's deserted surroundings. But then through the enormous glass doors on the far side of the room she saw Gaia and Federico out on the terrace. They were standing facing each other, bathed in the bronze light of the early morning like they were a pair of exquisite statues carved by the same hand. And as Gaia reached up to cradle Federico's face, like a gilded goddess come to life, Katrine kept her gaze fixed forward, couldn't bear to witness any flicker of jealousy cross Harry's features as he watched the actress kiss her famous fiancé.

Chapter 23

'Come on,' muttered Harry. 'Let's leave them alone.' He turned to leave, and Katrine followed him back out into the hall. But one more look at where her beloved father's painting had once hung on the wall sparked a flare of defiance inside her. *No.* She'd been devoted to the hotel ever since she'd arrived, dedicated to catering to guests' needs and wants, but she couldn't let Gaia take something so dear to her for the sake of indulging her spoiled whim. She spun back around.

'Where are you going?' asked Harry, lines of worry furrowing his forehead.

'To speak to her,' answered Katrine.

'To who, *Grace*?'

Katrine froze at the use of a name so new to her, yet clearly not to Harry.

He appeared to have stunned himself, put a hand to his mouth.

Grace. The strange sound seemed to swirl round Katrine's mind. 'Is that what she's really called?'

But Harry didn't have time to reply. Katrine was making her way across the restaurant, weaving between the polished-wood tables, towards the terrace.

'Can we please just talk for a second . . .' he called after her, but Katrine didn't hear, his sentence drowned out by the name recurring in her head. She couldn't reconcile the gentleness of the word with the formidable diva visible beyond the panes of glass.

'Katrine . . . hello,' said Federico as she stepped out onto the flagstoned terrace.

She felt the fire within her falter. What was she doing? She was so used to behaving with deference towards the two of them, she momentarily lost her nerve. But her determination not to say goodbye to the one watercoloured link she had to her dad spurred her on.

'Where. Is. My. Painting?' she said levelly.

Gaia scowled. 'I've no idea what you're talking about.' Her eyes seemed to flame a warning.

Katrine stood tall. 'The one in the hall . . .' she pointed back through the glinting glass.

'We can discuss it another time,' Gaia replied through gritted teeth.

'I'd like to get to the bottom of it now,' countered Katrine with a jut of her chin.

Gaia glared. 'We're trying to have a serious conversation here . . .' She batted the air like she was dissipating dust motes.

Katrine didn't move. 'And I'm sorry to interrupt but—'

'Well then, can you not?' cut in Gaia with a dismissive flick of her wrist.

'What is this painting you talk about?' enquired Federico, turning to face Katrine. 'Can I help?'

171

Gaia held up a palm. 'It's *nothing*.'

Katrine recoiled. 'No, it's *not*—'

'Look, it was meant to be a secret—' Gaia hissed back to her.

'What, like you and Harry?' Katrine blurted out.

Federico took a step back. 'So it is true . . . you and the boatman?' he muttered, eyes flicking to his fiancée.

Gaia's cheeks flooded rage-red. 'What do you think you're doing?' she demanded, blue eyes boring into Katrine. 'You don't know *anything*.'

'I do now – Harry admitted as much,' she replied. 'And I saw you two together, with my own eyes. Down by the lake.' She put her hands on her hips. 'Federico deserves to know.'

'I think I'll go,' he murmured angrily, starting to stride towards the sliding glass doors.

'You're ruining *everything*!' screeched Gaia, clawing at her scalp.

'You can't just play pretend like they do in films,' said Katrine.

'But you haven't got a *clue* about *anything*!' shouted Gaia. 'Harry was *nothing*!' She stamped her foot on the paving slab to emphasise her point. 'And I don't even want your *stupid* picture! It was meant to be a wedding present for Feddy but I doubt I'll be needing that now, thanks to you!'

Katrine's stomach twisted. What had she done? If the wedding was off then Anna would lose the money and that meant the hotel's future – and her strongest connection to her father – might be left in jeopardy—'

'GET ME HARRY!' screamed Gaia all of a sudden, loudly enough to ricochet across the water and wake the whole of Keswick.

Chapter 24

The bodyguards burst out of the gigantic glass doors and raced across the terrace to the source of the disturbance. Chris bundled Gaia down the balustraded steps to solitary safety, while Si twisted this way and that, his back to the actress, searching for the supposed threat.

Katrine held her hands up.

'For god's sake, let me go!' Gaia shrieked from the grounds below.

Katrine gave Si an apologetic look. 'Sorry for the commotion. It's my fault she was shouting.'

Si scanned the expansive patio to make doubly sure there was no trouble. His shoulders dropped. 'Don't mention it.' He gave her a nod. 'All in a day's work.' He let out a sigh. 'Besides, there's always some sort of drama.' He rolled his eyes rebelliously. 'But we have to be on the safe side.' He bent his head conspiratorially. 'Though between you and me, if she got abducted I might not be in the biggest rush to find her.'

Katrine suppressed her smile as Gaia stomped back up the steps to the terrace.

'If you want to be *useful*, find Harry the boatman!' she yelled at Chris, who scurried off to fulfil his boss's orders.

'What on earth is going on?' asked Anna from behind Katrine, framed by the shimmering glass partition.

'The wedding is *OFF!*' cried Gaia at full volume, glaring at both of them, before storming across the terrace and back inside the restaurant.

Katrine bowed her head.

Anna blew out a breath.

Neither of them spoke for a few seconds, the actress's outburst having shaken the island like a hurricane.

Rachel sat bolt upright at the sound of Gaia bellowing; it would have been audible even if the bedroom window hadn't been wide open, but without the glazed barrier to deaden the noise, it was nerve-shredding.

'Who needs an alarm clock when you've got a boss with those lungs,' said Miles, clamping his goose-down pillow firmly over his head like a pair of luxury ear defenders.

Rachel wriggled out from under the duvet and went to draw the curtains, letting the fresh morning air filter into the room as an antidote. 'I suppose I'd better go and see what the issue is,' she said with a sigh. She drank in the vista before her, steeling herself for whatever she was about to walk into; the sunlight was dancing on Derwentwater, oblivious to the histrionics unfolding on the island. Her eyes roved over the hills, then their inverted reflections in the looking-glass lake – she hoped Gaia wasn't turning the hotel upside-down in a similar fashion.

Feeling only slightly fortified, she flung on some clothes. 'Right, back soon,' she said to Miles.

'Believe it when I see it,' he replied with a wry smile before resting his head back on the bed.

Rachel ran down the stairs and into Reception, and was almost out of the main doors before she saw Harry hunched over on the sofa. She walked towards him. 'What's happened?' she asked tentatively.

He looked up at her with reddened eyes. 'Long story.'

'Right.' Rachel grimaced.

'Maybe you can calm her down,' said Harry.

'Doubt it,' murmured Rachel, peering out of the front window with trepidation. A split-second slide show of instances where Gaia had completely blown up flipped through her mind. She bit her lip. 'So no advice for me going into the lion's den, then?' she asked, still not sure what the matter was.

'Actually, yeah – don't ask about the wedding,' muttered Harry, head back in his hands.

'Right.' Rachel's stomach dropped like she'd missed a step while descending the stairs. The situation was worse than she'd thought.

Chapter 25

'It's okay, I have the painting,' said Anna, putting her hands on Katrine's shoulders.

'Really?' Katrine's head jerked up. 'But how did you get it back?' she asked, pressing her palms to her cheeks.

'Gaia never had it to begin with,' explained Anna.

'What do you mean?'

'I did.'

Katrine frowned. Tiredness mixed with confusion had made her feel sapped of her usual strength. She reached for the stone balustrade, needing support. 'I don't understand.'

'It was me who replaced it, so she didn't get any ideas about taking it. I had this strange feeling that she might not be very used to being told no.' Anna raised her eyebrow.

'You mean it's not gone?' Katrine sank back against the railings.

'No, it's safe and sound at mine,' confirmed Anna.

'I'm so glad.' Katrine instinctively glanced in the direction of the annexe, even though it wasn't visible from where they stood. 'It's my one little piece of Dad.' Her face suddenly flushed crimson and she stood up straight. 'I mean it's *ours*.' She swallowed, feeling a rush of embarrassment – she'd been so possessive about a picture that was equally as precious to Anna as it was to her. And her stepmother had much more claim to it than she did: it was of her hotel after all.

'The watercolour belongs to *you*, don't worry,' corrected Anna.

Katrine's eyes welled. 'Thank you.'

Her stepmother smiled. 'Though, I'd like to keep it on the wall until such time as—'

'Stop,' whispered Katrine. 'Don't say it.' One day losing Anna in addition to her dad was something she didn't want to think about.

'I was going to say, until such time as you want to leave the island,' continued Anna. She dipped her head to denote the seriousness of the circumstances.

Katrine's lips twisted as the reality of her situation crashed back over her. *Harry and Gaia. Together.*

Rachel shielded her eyes against the blinding brightness of the glass-backdropped terrace as she ascended the flagstoned steps from the garden in hurried steps, slightly out of breath.

'Has anyone seen Gaia?' she asked, looking from the hotel manager to the owner.

'Not this again,' muttered Anna in a low voice. 'For someone so hard to miss, she seems to disappear extremely frequently,' she said to Katrine. 'I only *heard* her, I'm afraid,' she added with a nod at Gaia's PA. 'Might be best to give her some space, let her cool down for a bit first before you go after her,' she added. 'For your own sake.'

Rachel squinted back at her. 'I'm used to it,' she admitted. 'But I'll leave her a little while in case she wants to be alone.'

She looked out towards the lake and the fells again. The fact she was finally *here* was the only fitting payment for putting up with Gaia's antics. 'We weren't actually meant to be meeting till ten. So there's plenty of time.' She smiled. 'Oh, just a heads up in return: she wanted to discuss some "extra ideas" for the wedding with me this morning.' Rachel made speech marks with her fingers to quote Gaia's worry-inducing phrase. 'Not sure what that will entail exactly, or if she still does —' Rachel pulled a face in sympathy with the hotel staff — 'but I promise I'll try my absolute hardest to curb anything too ridiculously outlandish. Don't want to cause you too many problems.' She clasped her hands together and Anna and Katrine shared a glance, wondering when they ought to cut in and break the news.

But Rachel was already carrying on. 'It would be great to whiz through the running order for the big day with you both as well, when you have a minute,' continued Rachel, eyes flitting between the two of them. 'Most things are in place now — the helicopter rose-petal drop is confirmed; the drone display is all planned — oh, yes, that's what I wanted to mention, just while I remember —' she paused momentarily to gulp in a breath and Katrine could almost picture the to-do list rolling in the PA's head.

'*Pyrotechnics*,' announced Rachel. She splayed her fingers, mimicking a pair of synchronised fireworks.

'Do we need any more explosives when we've got Gaia?' interjected Anna before she could help herself.

But Rachel was mid-flow. 'We'll be launching a hundred heart-shaped rockets from the roof,' she flung out a hand in the direction of the delicate wooden eaves.

'Is that even *possible*?' asked Katrine.

'Oh, yeah, they're *super* impressive,' replied Rachel. 'I've seen them for real at a trial run – obviously Gaia was particular about having the ones with the sharpest love-heart shape—'

'I meant letting them off from up *there*,' said Katrine with a glance up at the centuries-old Georgian building behind her.

Rachel was nodding in response to her question but she didn't stop talking. 'It'll need to be cleared of any debris – leaves, branches et cetera –'

She was speaking like nature was an inconvenience, the island's attributes a bother not a blessing, thought Katrine and it rankled her.

'And we'll probably need to trim back a few trees.'

Anna crossed her arms. 'This is a national park! You can't just go about doing that – not even if you're *Gaia*.'

'But this is her *wedding* day,' Rachel countered. She just needed to hand over a full, finalised schedule for the best celebrations ever – and then she could leave this role. Have her freedom. Say goodbye to Gaia at last.

'Even so, Gaia can't always have her own way,' explained Anna.

'There must be a solution – some kind of scaffolding, a discreet platform – we can do it safely, I'm sure. I'll look into it. Think of something . . .'

Katrine tilted her head to one side; she'd imagined Rachel's job as a whirlwind of enviable events, her life crammed with countless perks and freebies. But she wouldn't swap places with her for *anything*. The strain of it all was painted on her face in a pallid palette. She needed a good dose of the outdoors, a better balance, that much was plain to see. Katrine wanted to put her out of her misery. She cleared her throat. 'I think you ought to know . . . the last we heard, the wedding wasn't going ahead.'

'*What*?' Rachel paled further. 'Is that why she was so upset?'

Katrine nodded.

Rachel pressed the back of her hand to her lips. 'Oh *no* . . . poor thing – no wonder she was screaming and shouting, she'll be *distraught*.' For all her gripes against Gaia, her stomach twisted with compassion. But was it actually true? She recalled the instances when Gaia had been totally convinced it was all over, yet each time it turned out not to be the case. Rachel knew only one thing: she had to find her. She was far too loyal to plan her exit while Gaia's life was in chaos.

Chapter 26

Gaia plonked down on the pebbled shore; she didn't need to pretend to be elegant, there were no newspaper reporters out here. She watched the water gleaming amber in front of her, saw a flock of geese soar towards the fells, totally free, and felt a twinge of if-only.

She lay back on the sun-soaked stones to look at the clear blue sky. What an overwhelming twelve hours it had been. She'd seen the Northern Lights, but more than likely lost Feddy forever. How life swung up and then down like a pendulum.

There was no sense in going back to the hotel. Federico didn't want to speak to her and she wasn't supposed to be meeting Rachel for another couple of hours – and it was pointless talking about the wedding any more anyway. She just needed to check in with her about a new phone.

Without her mobile to claim her attention, she was forced to look at her surroundings.

She twisted her head to the side, stared at the scaly bark of a tree-trunk nearby, as unique and captivating as crocodile skin. She saw a black-eyed bird studying her from a branch, its feathers like jet-coloured satin. The sound of the water caressing the shore filled her ears. If she closed her eyes she could be anywhere. But where would she choose? she wondered. A far-off beach? But, even then, she'd be conscious of her body in a bikini, fretting about the best angle for sunbathing in case she was spotted, or how best to get out of the sea. It would have to be an exotic island where she wouldn't be discovered. The June morning was warming her skin. The lake was starting to wake around her. She heard boats tinkling across the way in Keswick. She could be in an exclusive marina if she kept her eyelids shut. But then there'd be all the other yacht owners and their crews jostling for precedence, and curious tourists to deal with. Being on one of the super vessels was little better than being confined to a giant goldfish bowl in reality anyway. All those passers-by trying to peer in. If you so much as stepped out on deck you were asking to be papped.

She breathed in the pure Cumbrian air and watched a sheepskin cloud float into sight above her: the only spectator around. It was actually pretty perfect right here, she realised, surprising herself. She was finally on her own, yet not in the least bit lonely. Nature enveloped her on all sides. She felt an unfamiliar sensation stirring in her tummy. A small bubble of contentment.

Back in Hollywood she was always surrounded by people but constantly felt alone. Never quite sure who she could trust, who had her best interests at heart. Except for Rachel. She was different, Gaia mused. Her PA genuinely seemed to care, but she hadn't really treated her with a huge amount of respect. A pang of remorse replaced her feeling of happiness. Harry's words repeated in her head. It had stung when he'd said she could work on being nice. How long had that been the case?

A splashing sound broke her out of her thoughts and she sat up straight. She'd still never quite mastered being able to relax. Not since she'd made a name for herself. The risk of unwittingly putting a foot wrong and plunging from favour was crippling.

A shout.

From somewhere in front of her.

The hairs on the back of Gaia's neck prickled. She had no bodyguard to protect her out here. Nobody knew where she was. She shaded her eyes with her hand and scanned the horizon.

Movement.

In the water.

Fifty metres or so from the island's shingle beach.

Gaia scrambled upright, careful to get to her feet delicately just in case there was a camera lens somewhere that she hadn't yet spotted.

She cupped both her hands above her forehead, and looked out across the lake. There was definitely someone. A head bobbing above the surface. Wait, was that a second figure? She narrowed her eyes against the blazing glare of white light reflecting back from the water. Yes, two people clearly trying to make their way towards her. One of them was *waving*. Great. Her shoulders dropped. Fans trying to swim across to the island. This was what Chris and Si did their perimeter checks for. To make sure no one was trying to invade her privacy. At least they didn't look threatening, Gaia thought, her eyes darting towards to the swimmers once again. The extents people would go to to catch a glimpse of her never failed to amaze her. It was flattering, in a way, that fans would come up with such crazy ideas. They must be absolute freezing – there was no way she'd be doing that, she thought to herself, even if Feddy was standing across the way on Keswick's jetty.

Maybe she ought to at least wave back, she wondered. From what she could make out, they were just a couple of girls in bathing costumes. Besides, only one of them seemed bothered about seeing Gaia. And to her relief they didn't even appear any closer to the island than they had been before. They were still bobbing about in the same place they had been when she'd first noticed them, apparently content to make contact from afar rather than encroach on her space. Perhaps if she acknowledged the one trying to attract her attention then that would suffice, thought Gaia. Anyone with a grain of sense would realise she was on vacation and wanted to be left in peace.

She raised a hand – and a joyous cry rang out across the water. Another wave in return. Gaia smiled. If it was really that simple to make someone's day then perhaps she shouldn't be so churlish. Maybe Harry was right and she ought to show her softer side more often—

Another shout. Indistinct at this distance but Gaia had had enough now. A pinch of annoyance needled her chest. She felt irritated that her moment of quiet contemplation had been interrupted. She wasn't walking a red carpet or attending a press event now. She had a right to rest when she wasn't at work – it was so rare she couldn't remember the last time she'd had the opportunity to *try*. She turned away.

Another yell. But what more could she give them? Was she supposed to wade out and personally welcome the wild swimmers to the Lake Island Hotel? Was that what they wanted. A hot blast of anger roiled in her abdomen. It wasn't fair that she had every area of her life invaded. She started to march back along the shore in the direction from which she'd come. She'd notify Chris, he could deal with it. What else did they expect? It was their own fault for swimming all this way for nothing.

An animal-like groan, just as she was about to disappear around the corner into a patch of shaded woodland. Something about the tone – anguish muddled with desperation – made her look back one last time.

There was no waving now. Gaia stopped still. She'd lost sight of the swimmers all together in fact. She turned her head from side to side but she couldn't see any sign of them – just an endless expanse of lake. She ran back to the edge of the shore. Was that them? Floating flat on their backs like two human lilos? Why weren't they moving? She strained her eyes as she tried to piece together the situation. And all of a sudden it made sense. Gaia recognised that position – it was the same one she adopted if she failed an audition and felt like giving up.

Chapter 27

Gaia drew herself upright to her full height and projected her voice out across the water. 'Hello!' she called, her vocal training coming to the fore. But she immediately felt a hot flash of foolishness as the word left her lips and reverberated around the lake.

But then one of the swimmers stirred.

Gaia squinted at the person in the water, the same one who'd tried to get her attention to begin with: she recognised the pattern on the woman's bathing costume. Gaia watched as they tried but failed to lift an arm and wave. And suddenly she understood, the penny dropping at the same time as the figure flopped back against the water, overcome with fatigue. They didn't care who she was, how famous she happened to be. They just saw a fellow human being standing on the island and desperately needed their help.

She instinctively fumbled for her phone, trembling fingers patting down her empty pockets before she remembered. *Shit*. No mobile. *What now?*

There wasn't time to run to the hotel and scream for assistance – the bathers looked like they were in serious trouble as things stood. There was nothing else for it: she started scrambling out of her couture clothes before she could think twice, heart thudding. She sucked in a deep breath. At least her bespoke underwear could be passed off as a designer bikini at this distance. She kept her gaze on the swimmers as she crunched barefoot across the pebbles. 'Ouch,' she grumbled as a sharp-sided rock dug into her right sole, but then a shiver of shame flitted down her spine: *she* was complaining when there were two people who looked as though they could be fighting for their lives. She shook herself and continued towards the water's edge. '*Ohmigod*,' she said as the ice-like lake licked at her skin. Despite the warm day her calves stung as she waded out into the shallows. It was a lot colder than it looked. 'Come on, Grace, you can do this,' she told herself, holding her arms out for balance as she wobbled about wildly; the silt-covered stones on the lakebed were slick below her, and she was struggling not to slip in her haste.

'Get a grip, Grace,' she murmured, glancing once again at the motionless women. They needed her. She felt a swell of fear in her stomach. The scene that had looked so serene from the shore now seemed menacing. No wonder she preferred carefully managed movie sets to the great ungovernable outdoors. But the bathers were relying on her. The fact the gap between her and them was gradually beginning to narrow with every step she took bolstered her. 'You've got this, girl,' she mumbled to herself like she was trying to pep-talk a friend. She was submerged up to waist-height now. She took a last steady lungful of air and then launched herself towards the lifeless-looking shapes that lay unmoving on the surface of the lake.

Federico stopped when he noticed the stone folly in front of him. He'd been making his way methodically clockwise around the circumference of the island, figuring that if he stuck to a straightforward route he'd retain the head space for thinking, rather than navigating unruly undergrowth. Besides, he wasn't exactly dressed for walking through woodland. His hand-stitched Italian shoes were already scuffed, he noticed, though he'd picked his way carefully along the shore. He must be about halfway round, judging by the shift in landmarks. Almost at the other end of the island. His linen shirt was sticking to him. The morning was surprisingly hot considering they were in northern England. It looked much cooler inside the little octagonal temple that stood at the end of a flagged walkway. He wandered out onto the jetty-like construction that extended into the water. Gazed at the lake. Where was his fiancée now? he wondered. *Hopefully cooling off, too*, he thought as he stepped into the shade of the dome-roofed building and felt relief at being shielded from the sun. He decided to go to each of the small square windows in turn to take in the view. All three had an entirely different perspective, even though he was standing in the same spot at the centre of the temple each time. Perhaps that was how it was with people, too, he mused: maybe everyone saw a situation in their own unique way. He looked out of the second window in the sequence, leaning his forearms on the cold sill as he stared at the vista beyond the stone surround. This was the identical panorama he'd seen before, when he'd looked straight out at the folly from the shore – but now with the frame restricting it, it appeared different once again. He just needed to focus, think about things properly. They had problems but there had to be a way to get back on track.

Federico moved to the third and final window, its outlook taking in the curve of the island. From this angle he could see further along the shore, in the opposite direction to which he'd come. He followed the line of the beach a little way along – and couldn't believe his eyes. There, bent forward on the pebbles and soaked to the skin, was his partially bare, bedraggled-looking wife-to-be.

Gaia's muscles burned from exertion. She spluttered as she sank down on the pebbles, ragged breaths heaving in and out. She'd swallowed several mouthfuls of lake, and normally she didn't even drink *tap* water. But she'd done it. She couldn't quite believe it. Feeling the sun warm her half-frozen flesh again after being immersed in Derwentwater's cold depths felt like the greatest luxury she'd ever experienced. Droplets of water decorated her tingling skin with diamantes, and a heady rush of adrenalin mixed with endorphins flooded her system. Those sessions with the American Lifeguard Association had paid off in more ways than one, she thought to herself as she pushed her dripping-wet hair back from her face. She'd had a series of intensive lessons only the previous year for a lead role in a blockbuster thriller called *Beach Bodies*, where she'd played a crime-fighting coastguard on the hunt for a serial killer. She was nothing if not a perfectionist, and she'd been dedicated to preparing for the part. She'd aced the course, already having a brilliant base level of fitness thanks to her brutally demanding one-on-one PT programme, but before today, she'd only ever executed mock sea-rescues on fellow actors. Not actual swimmers in distress. Yet here she was, having performed two successful contact tows in a row. She felt a burst of pride that startled her. She'd managed to get the pair of them safely to the shore completely on her own. No mean feat in the circumstances: she'd had to calm them down first of all, and then wrangle one at a time into the correct horizontal position, careful to keep their heads above water, their airways unblocked, while swimming backwards herself. Four trips in total, beginning with the most vulnerable bather. She'd been surprised at her ability to summon the techniques she'd learned so quickly, and at her capacity to stay calm when it really mattered . . . But the stricken swimmers weren't out of the woods yet: Gaia leaned forward to check on the two young women, her gaze darting from one to the other. 'Stay with me,' she said to the weaker swimmer, scared the girl might lose consciousness and not wake up. She couldn't be more than about thirteen or fourteen. 'Keep those eyes open,' commanded Gaia. She patted the young girl's shoulder, then glanced at the slightly stronger swimmer, who looked to be about the same age, maybe a year older. 'You need to make sure she doesn't fall asleep, okay?' said Gaia. 'It's really important,' she explained. 'I'm going to have to run back to the hotel to get help, all right?'

The second swimmer gave a small nod, shuffling upright into a sitting position on the stones, taking what she'd said seriously.

Gaia gave a nod. 'I'll be as fast as I can,' she added as she pulled on her shoes.

'*Cara!*' came a shout from behind her.

Federico.

Gaia turned, his term of endearment automatically making her smile. Then she recalled their argument and it vanished from her lips. She searched his face for signs of how he felt about her. About *them*. It seemed an age since she'd seen him, with everything that had occurred in the interim.

'Are you okay?' he called as he reached her, concern creasing his handsome features.

She gave a brisk nod. There was no time to fill him in now. 'Can you look after them?' she asked, jerking her head at the pale-skinned pair shaking on the shore.

He stared back at her, eyes wide.

'You need to get them dry as quickly as possible.' Gaia remembered the instructor's grave warnings about the risks of afterdrop and the crucial need to warm up.

'Okay . . .' said Federico, crouching down.

'Use my clothes as a towel.' Gaia pointed at the crumpled pile of designer labels she'd left on the pebbles.

'*Sì*.' Federico was already balling a bundle of fabric in his fists.

'Keep them talking!' Gaia cried as she disappeared off in the direction of the hotel.

But once she was gone, Federico felt a tremor of fear. 'Here,' he said softly to the swimmer sitting beside him. He handed her the scrunched-up bottom half of the tailored trouser suit and she started to rub her body dry with the slip of satin.

Federico turned his attention to her companion, whose eyelids were drooping dangerously. 'What's her name?' he asked the other girl.

'S-sarah,' she replied, through chattering teeth. 'She's my little sister.' Her green eyes were rimmed red and filled with tears.

He grabbed Gaia's custom-made jacket and draped it around the younger girl, hoping the pure-silk material might help keep her warm. 'Come on, Sarah. Stay awake. Try to sit up.'

Her eyes were closing, staying shut longer in between each slow blink.

No. Panic began to build inside Federico. Gaia had been so calm, clearly managed to get both girls out of the lake single-handedly, but he felt sick with the pressure of keeping the two of them safe in her absence. 'Sarah, can you hear me?' he said, bending close to the younger girl's ear. She was little more than a child. He needed to do as his fiancée had done and pull himself together for her sake. 'Sarah! Open your eyes! Please!'

Nothing.

Her sister began to sob beside him.

Federico's mouth was sand-dry in cruel contrast to the sodden clothes surrounding them. *Please don't let her die*, he prayed. *Per favore, no . . .* 'Sarah!' he croaked, shaking her shoulder before realising he probably oughtn't to move her much in case she was injured somehow. *Oh, come back, Gaia!* he willed. *What do I do?* he wondered desperately. 'Sarah!' he rasped once again. She was only a kid—

The thump of footsteps pounding along pebbles made his head snap up.

Thank god.

He scrambled to his feet at the sight of Gaia sprinting towards them.

'I've called for help!' she cried, crashing down beside him on the pebbled beach.

'She won't open her eyes!' explained Federico, dropping back to his knees and pointing at Sarah lying still on the stones.

Gaia turned to the other girl. 'What does she like?' she asked hurriedly. 'What things is she interested in?' she asked, the lifesaving advice to keep speaking to a casualty still ringing in her ears as though she'd been on the course yesterday. 'Like does she have a favourite hobby or something?'

'Er . . .' the girl's exhausted sister struggled to compute the question.

'A song we can sing?' prompted Gaia. 'This is really important,' she explained. 'We need to get her attention.'

'Um . . . she likes the c-cinema . . .' her sister stuttered.

'And her name is Sarah,' added Federico.

'Right, well, Sarah, if you open your eyes for me, you've got a free trip to Hollywood, okay?'

Not a flicker of movement.

'For you and your family. And I'll take you all to a premiere.' Blood pulsed in Gaia's ears. *Open your eyes, please!* she begged silently. Never in her life had she wanted anything more. Suddenly nothing else in the entire world mattered. 'Sarah, you can see all of LA if you wake up, I promise.' Gaia could hear her own voice rising with urgency.

Still no response.

Gaia's mind raced. 'Who's her favourite film star?' she asked the girl's sister suddenly. She had connections after all; she'd be able to make pretty much any wish come true. 'Who is it her absolute dream to meet?'

'Gaia,' the girl replied without a second's pause. 'She wants to be just like her,' she said with a small smile. 'She's seen every one of her movies.'

Gaia swallowed the swell of emotion that rose up inside her.

'Sarah, open your eyes,' she said firmly. 'It's me, Gaia.'

And when the little girl finally did, it beat every single achievement in her idol's life to date: winning the Golden Globe, being presented with the Rising Star Award – the whole lot.

Chapter 28

Sarah blinked up at her in disbelief.

'It's me, Gaia,' she repeated. Granted, she probably didn't look like she usually did, Gaia thought as she looked down at her outfit – Federico's oversized jacket, that she'd seen discarded on the arm of the sofa in Reception and grabbed on her way back out to wear as a coverup, and precious little else – but she hoped she still resembled her pictures in some respect. She raised her eyebrows expectantly. 'The actress.'

Sarah blinked again.

But at least she was awake, thought Gaia with relief. 'You've seen all of my films . . .' she continued. 'Not sure which one was your favourite . . .' She knew she was rambling but it seemed to be working.

Sarah blinked again.

Federico marvelled at his fiancée; at the fact she'd succeeded where he himself had failed. She'd almost certainly saved this young girl's life, he thought, feeling an immense wave of gratitude that such a generous-hearted woman had agreed to be his wife.

'*Beach Bodies* was my last film,' Gaia said to Sarah, carrying on her one-sided conversation, all the promotional interviews she'd experienced in her time proving the perfect preparation for such an uneven interaction. 'But I'm not sure if you're quite old enough to have seen that one . . .?' With her wet hair plastered to her scalp and smooth, clear face the girl looked so childlike her precise age was hard to place.

Sarah frowned up at her.

'Keep talking,' encouraged Federico. 'You're doing such a great job.'

Gaia smiled at him. But she couldn't be complacent: she had no idea how long it would be until help arrived. She had to keep going—

'I'm fifteen,' murmured Sarah, with just enough umbrage to convince them she might be on the mend.

Gaia beamed back at her. 'Are you really?'

Sarah gave a small nod. 'Are you *really* Gaia?' she said in return, big brown eyes studying her. 'You don't look like her.'

'Yes, I am,' replied Gaia with a laugh. But then a thought began to niggle at the edges of her mind . . . Maybe there was something to be said for the low-key look: if no one recognised her when she didn't resemble her Hollywood image from movies and magazines, then maybe she'd be freer to roam around here than she'd first realised. Over in LA, people expected to encounter famous faces, it's what they went there for in the first place. But in Cumbria . . . She glanced up at the scenery that surrounded them on all sides: sweeping mountains, the sparkling lake. *Of course* . . . how had this never occurred to her until now? She recalled the way she'd initially assumed the swimmers were trying to get her attention because of who she was. She'd been so conceited . . . She'd spent all this time hiding out on the

195

island, but only because she'd drawn such attention to herself in the first place. She thought of the cavalcade of blacked-out four-by-fours. The besuited bodyguards. But, in actual fact, no one was looking for her, at least not like they were in California or London or New York. Cumbria's epic beauty provided the perfect distraction for her to fly under the radar. Everyone was far too busy looking at the magnificent sights that stretched as far as you could see in each direction, to care about what *she* was doing.

Well, except for a couple of people, she realised with a gut-punch of clarity. Two, to be precise. Reflexively, her gaze flitted across the water towards Borrowdale. She pictured them in her head, still living in the same shabby little house where she'd grown up. Mr and Mrs Wilkins. Her parents.

Chapter 29

'Where are your mum and dad?' asked Gaia, looking from one girl to the other.

Sarah turned to her older sister, waiting for her to speak, and for a second Gaia worried the girl's memory had been affected by spending so long in the water, but when the eldest of the two answered without a second thought it was clear it was just a habit.

'We live with our nanna.'

Gaia felt heat rise in her cheeks; she should know better than to make assumptions. She hated it when people did that about her. 'Sorry . . .' she murmured.

'It's okay,' said Sarah, but her older sister's features twisted.

'I'm meant to look after you . . . and it's my fault we're here,' she said, voice faltering.

Sarah reached for her sibling's hand. 'You always take care of me, Hannah.'

Hannah shook her head. 'We shouldn't have gone swimming. It was just so sunny, and it's Saturday, and I thought it would be something nice . . .'

'It was. It was a good idea. It was me who wanted to go to the island,' said Sarah.

'And I should have known better,' muttered Hannah. 'But we spend so much time stuck inside with Nanna . . .' The rest of the sentence was muffled as Sarah pulled her down for a hug.

Gaia felt for her, obviously trying to take care of Sarah while still figuring out the world for herself. She felt the unmistakeable gnaw of regret. Why had she taken for granted that her own parents would always just be there, in the same tiny house where they'd always been? Because one day, they certainly wouldn't.

People looked up to celebrities, regarded them as role models, yet here she was, learning some important life lessons from a pair of teenagers. Why wasn't she using her influence for the greater good? wondered Gaia. Suddenly she wanted to achieve something more meaningful than being voted best dressed in a glossy magazine, or beating Victoria Cole in the competition to wear the designer of the moment down the red carpet—

The roar of a motor getting louder.

The rescue boat.

Gaia glanced up to see a scarlet inflatable speeding towards them across the water.

Soon boots were splashing into the shallows and voices were echoing over the stones.

She and Federico scrambled backwards, standing up to let the professionals get close enough to assess the scene. And for once Gaia wasn't the centre of attention, and for the first time in her life she realised it wasn't actually always the best place to be.

Chapter 30

'Katrine?'

She didn't turn when Harry spoke her name, for the very first time. She rested her head against the jetty post, watched a teardrop fall from her cheek into the water. She sat on the last wooden slat, legs dangling above the lake. Derwentwater could have been a well filled entirely with her sadness.

'Katrine,' Harry said again, right behind her now.

'Can you just take me back to the flat, please?' she murmured, unable to mouth the word 'home'. The place that had once seemed like their shared refuge was now just a reminder of what she'd lost.

'Of course – but can you talk to me first?' Harry's feet were beside her. His outstretched hand visible in the corner of her eye. 'Please?'

She gripped the edge of the plank of wood beneath her palms, not quite prepared to hear any more about him and Gaia.

He waggled his fingers, and she almost took his hand, but a wink of light from the lakebed below caught her eye.

Katrine peered down into the water beyond the soles of her shoes, trying to see what it was that she'd spotted under the surface.

Another glint from among the rounded rocks.

An incongruous rectangle of manmade lines lay in between nature's ripples and curves.

Of course—

'That's Gaia's phone,' announced Harry.

So, he'd seen it too. Katrine felt her shoulders tense at the sound of him saying the actress's name. 'It'll be broken now, after a night down there,' she said, in case he was considering diving to retrieve it like an action hero from one of Gaia's movies—

Oh, he was, she realised, as Harry's T-shirt landed next to her left hand. Well he was certainly making his loyalties clear, she thought, as he launched himself into the water with a splash, showering her in the process. She clambered to her feet, feeling an uncharacteristic flash of anger.

'Got it,' declared Harry, his head appearing above the surface, a triumphant smile on his face.

'Are you doing this on purpose?' asked Katrine, her hands on her hips.

Harry frowned, treading water in front of her. 'What do you mean?'

'Making a show of . . . I don't know . . .' she wafted a hand, at a loss for words. 'You and Gaia.'

'What?' Harry swam towards her. 'I just asked if I could explain everything to you – I came down to the jetty for that reason only.' Harry reached up and slid the phone onto the wooden slats beside where she was standing. 'I'm not going to leave litter lying about in the lake, Katrine.' He pulled himself up out of the water. 'The hotel has a responsibility to keep it clean.' He smoothed his wet hair from his face. 'I've fished out four lots of sunglasses in the past few weeks. And a dropped wallet.'

Katrine lifted her chin. 'And you usually just jump in like that do you?'

'No, I have a fishing net I normally use.' He flicked some stray damp locks from his forehead. 'Keep it on the boat . . . But I had to get your attention somehow, didn't I?'

Gaia watched as the two girls were wrapped in foil blankets that had more than a passing resemblance to the silver-lamé ballgown she'd worn to the Met Gala the previous year.

'Promise we can come and visit?' called Sarah as she was ushered onto the rescue boat alongside her sister.

'Yes,' replied Gaia; she'd already given her PA's contact details to the paramedic. 'But only on the condition you stay within your depth in future.' She gave them both her best stern look, the one she'd used when interrogating suspects on the set of *Beach Bodies*.

They both nodded back at her solemnly.

'Good. All right. Keep safe,' she said, switching her expression to a smile as the rescue boat's motor began to rev in readiness for its return journey. And when they became just a blur of bright red on a vast canvas of blue, Federico dipped his head towards Gaia's ear and whispered the words 'I'm so proud of you.' And for once, Gaia actually felt the same about herself, too.

Chapter 31

'Come on,' said Harry to Katrine. 'Let's go back to the hotel.' He bent to pick up Gaia's phone and to their surprise the screen lit up.

'It's still working,' said Katrine.

How is that possible? thought Harry.

They both stared at Gaia's screensaver: a silhouette-shot of her and Feddy by a frond-leaved palm tree, surrounded by pure white sand.

My goodness, she is stunning, thought Katrine, still wondering what on earth Harry was going to tell her about him and Gaia . . . She glanced across at her boyfriend, who couldn't seem to tear his gaze away.

That phone case must be unreal, thought Harry, as he studied the protective cover: the mobile had spent all night underwater and survived!

'Maybe we should get it back to her,' suggested Katrine, seeing the stack of notifications that had already built up on the lock screen.

'Yeah, probably,' agreed Harry. 'Though if she isn't grateful . . .'

'What are you going to do?' asked Katrine, nudging him fondly before she could stop herself. 'You're not going to chuck it back where it came from.'

Harry brandished the phone in his hand. 'I'll . . . I'll send it off to a recycling site,' he said.

'Ooh, scary,' said Katrine with a mock shudder and they both burst out laughing.

She bent to scoop up his T-shirt and handed it to him.

'Thanks,' said Harry with a smile, and they started to walk along the jetty. 'So, after we've given this back to Gaia we'll sit down and talk?' he said, clutching the mobile.

Katrine nodded at him. She didn't have time to contemplate what he was going to tell her any further, because before they'd even reached the beach, they came face to face with the phone's owner and her fiancé, coming towards them from the northern side of the island.

Harry held it aloft. '*Grace!*' he shouted, before correcting himself. 'Gaia! We've got your phone!' he shouted.

Federico frowned in confusion, but before he could say anything, Gaia started running towards Harry.

'Oh my God, you've found it!' she cried, throwing her arms around his neck.

Katrine felt her face flame.

Harry stepped back, pulled on his T-shirt.

'I can't believe it!' babbled Gaia. 'I got sent this waterproof case when I was filming *Beach Bodies* but I never dreamt it would actually—'

'Sorry to interrupt,' cut in Katrine, holding up her palms. 'But while all four of us are here in one place, do you think we could get a few things straight?'

Gaia winced. 'Like what?'

'I saw you and Harry last night,' said Katrine.

Gaia batted the air. 'Yeah, I'm sorry about all that.'

Katrine bit her lip.

'He came to make sure I was okay.'

'Looked like a very thorough check,' muttered Katrine, as an unwanted flashback of their embrace appeared in her head.

Harry opened his mouth, but Gaia carried on speaking. She turned to Federico. 'I shouldn't have stormed off. I was just frustrated. Got upset that things hadn't gone to plan. I had such high hopes for this trip. I wanted it to live up to your others . . .' She trailed off, trying to dispel the image of Victoria Cole that involuntarily popped into her head. She knew Feddy and his ex had been to the Maldives together, remembered the long-lens yacht-deck photographs that had been published in the glossy magazines just as vividly as if they'd been printed across her own eyelids.

'And after all that, we ended up seeing the Northern Lights, just when we least expected it.' She looked at Harry.

'You watched the Aurora together?' murmured Katrine, glancing over at him.

'Not intentionally,' replied Harry.

'I wanted to make the holiday memorable,' continued Gaia, her gaze on Federico. 'And I've ended up doing that for all the wrong reasons.'

He wrapped an arm around her shoulders. 'You don't need to worry so much, *cara*. I am here to spend time with *you*.' He kissed the top of her head. 'The person you are in here is what matters.' He patted the left side of his chest. 'I saw what you did over there.' He pointed a finger in the direction from which they'd come. 'When you were alone, and there were no cameras; when you thought there were two little girls who needed you. The real Gaia is who I'm in love with.'

Harry coughed. 'Maybe now's a good time, Grace,' he said.

Federico's frown deepened. 'Why do you keep calling her that?' he asked.

Katrine glanced at her boyfriend, but it wasn't him who answered.

Gaia sighed. 'Because . . . it's my real name.'

Chapter 32

'I'm Grace Wilkins, from Grange-in-Borrowdale,' she said to the group.

Three pairs of eyes stared back at her and suddenly she felt more on show than she did when she was filming.

'It's no big deal.' She shrugged. 'Loads of people have stage names.'

'Grace Wilkins,' repeated Federico, trying out the syllables for the first time, like he was doing a line reading. 'But you told me you were from London,' he said.

'Well, I did live there for a year.' Gaia tucked a strand of hair behind her ear. Her people had tweaked her Wikipedia page and took care to keep any official biographies brief.

'So you've been pretending to be someone else this whole time?' Feddy's brow rumpled.

'Isn't that the nature of acting?' replied Gaia with a brittle laugh.

Federico bowed his head. 'I think I deserve to know who I'm dating . . .'

'Oh, so not *marrying* anymore,' shot back Gaia.

Federico sighed. 'It does sound like we need to . . . get to know each other first . . . before that.' He rubbed his right temple. 'You said your parents were actors, that they worked in the theatre.'

Harry's eyes widened as he listened, like he was being read a story.

'Is that a lie, too?' continued Federico. 'You told me your dad was in plays in the West End.'

'He was a cleaner and Mum was a dinner lady,' explained Gaia. 'At my secondary school.'

Our secondary school, thought Harry.

'But they were retired by the time I went to college,' she carried on, suddenly overcome by a need for Federico to know the truth about her, the woman underneath all the put-on personas and rehearsed roles. Once the floodgates had been opened, it was difficult to stop the outpouring of information. 'They had me quite late on. Their miracle baby, they said.' Gaia bit back a surge of emotion as she pictured them, Thomas and Mary, still in the same house she'd grown up in. Gaia thought of the two girls she'd rescued from Derwentwater, whose parents didn't appear to be on the scene. And yet hers were only a few miles away, at the other end of the lake.

'I don't understand,' said Federico. 'Why would you hide all that?'

Gaia shook her head. 'I was . . . embarrassed, I guess.' Her gaze dropped to the ground. 'My parents wouldn't accept any money off me to buy a better house, have newer, nicer clothes. They were old and unglamorous in my eyes. And I was young and immature. Ashamed of them for being the opposite of what I wanted them to be.'

'But they were so supportive of you . . .' said Harry.

'Wait,' said Katrine. 'How do you know that?'

Harry looked at Gaia and then back at his girlfriend.

'Go on,' said Gaia.

'Grace was my first ever relationship.'

'What?' whispered Katrine.

'You two were together?' said Federico, waving a hand between the two of them.

Gaia nodded. 'When we were practically kids, yeah.'

'Why didn't you tell me?' said Katrine to Harry.

'I should have done, in hindsight,' continued Harry. 'But when would have been the right time?'

He had a point, realised Katrine, wondering how she would have dealt with a similar situation. If she and Federico had once been an item, for example.

'When you and I were falling in love, it didn't seem relevant to bring up the very distant past,' said Harry. 'Then when Grace arrived on the island, it seemed too late. I ought to have said something then, but I didn't want you to doubt for one second how I felt about you.' He sighed. 'I should have handled it better; I just didn't know how.'

Katrine reached for his hand. 'I'm glad I know now,' she murmured.

'Me too,' said Harry. 'Grace is part of my history.' He glanced at her. 'We basically grew up together. She actually made me realise that this is where I belong.' He swirled a hand in the air to indicate the Lake District fells and the glimmering lake.

'Did I?' murmured Gaia.

'Yep,' said Harry. 'As much as I loved performing in the college plays and stuff, I like being outside more.' He breathed in the summer-scented air. 'This is happiness to me.'

'Well, you encouraged me to keep going with acting,' said Gaia with a smile. 'Told me to stick at it if it's what I really wanted. You said I'd get there eventually.'

'And you did,' said Harry with a grin. 'Not even eventually – pretty quickly.'

Gaia laughed.

'I'm glad you didn't give up the acting,' said Federico, pulling Gaia close to his side. 'Or we'd never have met.'

She grinned up at him, then turned to Katrine. 'You and Harry make a wonderful couple,' she said. 'I've never seen him so happy.'

Katrine lifted her chin. 'That's very kind.'

Gaia shook her head. 'No, it's just true.'

'Thank you,' said Katrine, still marvelling at the fact she'd spent so much time worrying about how she could ever compete with Gaia, when even Grace herself was doing the same. Perhaps they had more in common than she'd first realised, she thought with a smile, as Harry squeezed her hand.

Chapter 33

Jackson took his apron off. 'No one's coming for breakfast, are they?' he said to Anna, who was busy restocking the jars of fudge brownie for the guest bedrooms, slicing precise squares that were the perfect accompaniment to a cup of tea or coffee.

Anna straightened up. 'I don't think so, no.' She glanced at the clock. Just past eleven.

Jackson sighed. 'I spent ages getting the smoothie recipe just right. No one's even had one yet.'

Anna came to stand next to him, looked at the printout of the morning menu beside him. The jewel-coloured ingredients piled on the worktop: strawberries, kale, chia seeds.

'We'll make them into a Summer Glow salad for lunch,' she suggested.

Jackson smiled, forever in awe of Anna's ability to reframe disappointment as an opportunity.

'That sounds tasty, actually.'

'Good.' Anna gave a nod. She went back to the countertop where she'd been working, and tipped out Gaia's untouched brownies from their glass container to replace them with ones from the freshly baked batch.

'Same goes for these,' she said, holding up one of the actress's uneaten crispy-topped, gooey-edged chunks of chocolatey cake. 'Shame to waste them.' She popped the whole piece in her mouth and let out a moan of appreciation.

'See, even you don't want one of my smoothies,' said Jackson, crossing his arms.

Anna was too busy chewing to be able to protest otherwise.

Then there came a knock on the kitchen door.

Not one of the hotel staff, as they would just walk in, so it couldn't be Katrine.

And it wasn't Will, coming in from the garden, as he'd use the back door.

Anna quickly swallowed the last morsel of brownie.

Jackson stood up straight.

Was it one of the security guards, finally coming in search of something to eat after spending the whole night looking for Gaia?

Goodness me, thought Jackson and Anna simultaneously, as the woman herself appeared in the doorway.

'Hi,' said Gaia with a self-deprecating dip of her shoulders.

The chefs shared an undetectable glance. What was going on and where was the real Gaia? This had to be a doppelgänger. Should they be sounding the alarm to say she'd been kidnapped?

Jackson looped his apron over his head. 'What can we do for you?' he asked, masking his surprise with a smile.

'Please could we possibly have a late breakfast out on the terrace?'

Jackson struggled to keep his expression straight in the face of such a shift in attitude. Was she preparing for a role where she had to be polite and personable? There'd be a lot of hours of practise required for *that*, he thought, so maybe she was trying to get a head start—

'For two? For you and Mr De Angelis?' answered Anna, when Jackson remained too stunned to speak.

'For all of us,' clarified Gaia. 'My whole team. If that's not too much trouble,' she added.

'No problem,' replied Anna. 'We'll bring everything out to you as soon as it's ready.'

'Thanks,' said Gaia, disappearing out into the dining room again.

'Did I just hallucinate that?' spluttered Jackson.

'Well, I witnessed it too,' said Anna with an arch of her eyebrow.

'So it must have been real.' Jackson said, reaching for a bunch of kale. 'Dominik used to say this island was magical . . .'

'I don't think he meant it like that,' said Anna with a laugh. She always tended to think it was people, not places, that had that kind of power.

'What do you mean, we're invited to a *family breakfast on the terrace*?' repeated Miles in disbelief, sitting up on the swatch of sun-drenched grass where he'd been happily soaking up the peaceful atmosphere of a Gaia-free vicinity.

'That's just what she said,' replied Rachel.

'And since when has Gaia referred to us as "family"?' continued Miles. 'I thought we were just the minions who did her bidding.'

'You don't even work for her,' said Rachel, putting her hands on her hips.

'Exactly, so I don't need to go, do I?' said Miles, pursing his lips. 'She's just rebranding her specific line of servanthood.

Trying to make you feel valued by using some buzzwords. I don't buy it.' He lay back down on the ground.

'Well, I think we should go,' said Rachel. 'She's giving us a holiday after all.'

'You're falling for it already!' said Miles. 'A few falsely inclusive phrases like "family breakfast" don't make up for how she treats you, Rach.'

'We could give her a chance.'

'What's this now, the hundred millionth one?' said Miles. He shook his head. 'Na-ah. Not doing it.'

Rachel tilted her head to one side. 'I think it's different this time . . .'

'Oh, Rach, do your rose-tinted glasses ever come off?' asked Miles, sitting up again. 'I love that you see the best in people, I really do, but I'm not going to sit there and watch while she walks all over you.' He gave a huff. 'It'll just be some pretext to get us all on board with another completely over-the-top request for this upcoming wedding. She probably wants to swap the water in the lake for champagne, or rebuild the hotel as a replica of the Colosseum to surprise Feddy, or something equally as outrageous.'

Rachel stifled a laugh despite herself.

'Honestly, you might think it's funny but it upsets me, Rach. Giving you a couple of croissants and calling it a family breakfast doesn't make up for how she behaves towards you the rest of the time.'

'But we're changing that,' she said, touched by the fact he wanted to fight her corner so much. 'We drew up that contract, remember. She has to be more reasonable now.'

'I'll just believe it when I see it, okay?' said Miles, squinting up at her.

'But you have to be there in order to do that,' countered Rachel.

'*Ugh*, all right then,' Miles muttered as he scrambled to his feet. 'But it better not be green juice for breakfast. If there aren't pastries I'm going again.'

'God, you sound like Gaia,' quipped Rachel, giving him a good-natured dig in the ribs as they started to walk towards the terrace.

Chapter 34

Miles took the most minute sip of his smoothie: the half strawberry that sat jauntily on the rim of the glass was doing its best to distract him from the fact the drink was brilliant green, but it was an impossible task. He'd just have to swap his with Rachel's once hers was empty – which wouldn't be long by the looks of it – and hope that neither of the chefs at the far end of the table noticed—

But to his surprise, it was utterly delicious. Didn't even taste healthy. Or green. He took another slurp. A hint of honey; just the right amount. It was actually *moreish* . . . Miles shook himself. He wasn't going to be swayed by an exotic drink and a one-off show of cosiness: Gaia was an actress; she excelled at putting on a performance. He eyed her at the head of the table. Heard the tap of a spoon on a smoothie glass and the scrape of a chair being pushed back.

'Thanks for joining me this morning,' Gaia began.

Like we honestly had a choice! thought Miles. He felt Rachel squeeze his arm, able to read him like a menu.

'I just have a couple of things I'd like to discuss . . .'

Miles took another gulp of his drink, wondering what each of the poor people seated around the terrace was about to have dropped on them.

'. . . and then Federico and I will be leaving the island for the day, so we'll be out of your way and you'll be free to enjoy the rest of your day.'

Miles almost choked on his smoothie.

'Rachel, we were meant to have a ten o'clock meeting,' continued Gaia. 'Sorry for missing that.'

Rachel's jaw dropped open and she took a sip of her drink to disguise it.

'But in actual fact I've changed my mind since then.'

Ah, there's the Gaia we knew, thought Miles, his gaze flicking across to his girlfriend.

Rachel was flipping open a notebook, ready to write down whatever Gaia's latest wishes were.

Gaia wafted a hand. 'I'd just like to borrow your phone to ring my dad back after breakfast.'

'Right,' said Rachel, putting down her pen. 'What about the extra ideas you had for the wedding?'

'Won't be necessary.'

Was it still off? wondered Rachel, glancing over at Federico, but there he was, right by Gaia's side.

'Anna and Jackson,' continued Gaia, turning her attention to the hotel staff now. 'Could we possibly convert lunch into a picnic?'

Jackson pictured the meticulously planned menu, an assortment of salads such as braised golden beetroots with confit tomatoes and tahini dressing—

'No problem,' answered Anna. She gave Jackson a look that said *we'll sort it, don't worry.*

But how was he meant to pack up the dishes so they were transportable yet still resembled the plates of food he'd devoted untold hours to honing?

'A sandwich – anything,' said Gaia.

What? thought Jackson. Was sleep deprivation playing with his perception of reality? He was glad Anna was here to verify what he was hearing. 'Right . . .' he mumbled, mind whirling. What kind of sandwich did an A-list celebrity even eat?

'Harry,' said Gaia, turning her attention to him. 'And Katrine,' she added, including her with a nod. 'Would you be able to escort us across to Keswick?' She indicated herself, Federico and both bodyguards.'

Harry and Katrine bobbed their heads in unison.

Gaia continued working her way round the group. 'Chris and Si, once we're out of the town and up in the mountains, I reckon Feddy and I'll be fine. I know my way around the hills pretty well, I've climbed them since I was small.'

A ripple of stifled surprise circled the table.

'But if we could reconvene before returning here, that would be great,' she carried on. 'I'll figure out our route and we can arrange a time to meet. Oh, and we'd like to go to Grange-in-Borrowdale first of all, if you wouldn't mind taking us . . .'

Chris nodded. 'I'll be ready and waiting in the Land Rover whenever you need me.' He tilted his chin in the direction of the mainland.

A little humility wasn't half having the desired effect, thought Miles as he gazed around at everyone's faces. But he wouldn't be so easily fooled. Gaia had to be building up to something. This complete change in tack was probably a clever move to get them all back on side after she'd pushed every single one of them to breaking point. It couldn't possibly be a permanent improvement in her character. People didn't alter that much.

But then he thought about what she'd said: she'd walked these hills since she was young. What had that little girl been like? Maybe she hadn't always been so obnoxious. Perhaps she'd constructed this hard shell around herself to mask the insecurities that lay underneath. It was understandable behaviour, if not ideal for those who dealt with her day to day. It couldn't have been easy trying to break into Hollywood, he mused, coping with the inevitable rejection, and fear of failure, and he had to admire her determination. Couldn't imagine what it had taken. And as he looked at her now, fiddling with the pair of sunglasses clutched in her fingers, he wondered whether there was a different version of Gaia that had been buried deep inside long ago, but was gradually making its way back to the surface, like long-lost treasure—

He pushed away his smoothie glass and sat up straight in his chair, wondering what had come over him. Here he was making excuses for someone who had made both his and Rachel's lives *miserable*. No, it would take more than a green juice and a day off to win him round, he resolved with a frown.

Rachel was grinning at him. 'We've got the rest of the day free!' she said, eyes glittering in the sunshine. 'What shall we do?'

Miles beamed back at her despite himself. 'Be together,' he said, watching the assembled party disperse: the breakfast meeting was over.

'I couldn't think of anything better,' said Rachel. 'Unless you'd like to go on the hike with Gaia?' she asked.

Miles opened his mouth, aghast.

'Only joking,' she said before tipping her face towards the sky and letting the June day kiss her skin.

Chapter 35

'Just here is great,' said Gaia as the blacked-out Land Rover reached a narrow double-arched bridge across the river Derwent. 'We'll walk the rest of the way.'

'Are you sure?' asked Chris from the driver's seat. 'I can take you to the door.'

Gaia shook her head. 'I want to give Feddy the full tour.'

'Okay, well we won't be far away if you need us,' Chris replied, turning to Si sitting next to him on the passenger side: deep lines creased the other security guard's face as though in all his years of service, this was his most unsettling situation to date.

'And you definitely don't want us to come with you? Even at a distance?' he said.

'Everyone's here to see the Bowder Stone, not me,' said Gaia, opening the door. 'You'll see,' she added to a confused-looking Feddy.

'Right, well call us if you change your mind,' said Si, with a glance at his boss.

Feddy patted his trouser pocket. 'I have my phone.'

I don't, thought Gaia with a grin. She felt a sense of freedom she hadn't had since she was the little girl who had lived here.

They watched the four-by-four drive off, heard the babble and spill of the river fill the air instead.

'This place is beautiful,' said Federico, peering over the low stone wall at the clearest water he'd ever seen.

'I used to paddle here as a child,' said Gaia, almost as though she was reminding herself, rather than telling Feddy. 'Welcome to Grange-in-Borrowdale,' she murmured. 'Where I grew up.'

Federico met her gaze. 'It's amazing.'

Gaia smiled, not quite able to believe she was there with him.

But she knew there were two people who would be even more surprised by the fact.

'I don't think they're at home,' said Federico gently when Gaia had rung the bell for the third time.

'But they're always in . . .' muttered Gaia, going into the sliver of garden at the front of the house to see if anyone was visible through either the kitchen or living-room window. But she already knew the cottage was empty without investigating any closer; there was a still darkness behind the two panes of glass like they were a pair of life-less eyes.

She stepped back, suddenly cold, despite the day's warmth.

'Do you want your sweater?' offered Federico, taking the backpack they'd borrowed from Anna off his shoulder.

'Yes, please,' said Gaia, wrapping her arms around herself while she waited for him to retrieve her designer athleisure-wear.

'We could come back in a little while?' suggested Federico. 'Walk to the rock you were talking about?'

Even the way he spoke about the Bowder Stone didn't make her smile. 'I tried to ring them earlier but there wasn't any answer . . .' Worry began to flurry inside her, her thoughts flowing faster than the river.

But they hardly ever left the area. It was one of the things that had so frustrated her; the fact they were content to inhabit this little corner of Cumbria, that their world extended only as far as Keswick and its environs.

'Can I borrow your phone?' she said to Federico, sitting down on the bench that virtually filled the front garden.

'Here,' he said, handing it to her.

'I'll try them again.' The landline this time. But what was the point? She was sitting outside, she knew it would be fruitless, but she'd leave a voicemail anyway – hope they'd at least know she'd visited.

Feddy sat down beside her.

The village was so hushed Gaia could hear the ringing of the phone inside the house. She waited to hear her father's voice on the automated message. The sound of it made her chest tighten.

'Hi there, you've reached Thomas and Mary's phone. I'm sorry we can't answer at the moment but do leave a message and we'll get back to you . . .'

The familiar-sounding vowels that her childhood memories were made of. His words seemed to roll around her head.

She ended the call. Twisted the cuff of her sweatshirt between her fingers.

'We can wait?' said Federico.

But Gaia wasn't good at being left wondering.

'I'll try their mobiles again.' She stood up, a nervous energy spreading through her body. She paced the tiny patch of garden but the sheltered little area made her feel constricted.

With so much wide space surrounding them, she craved being out in the open.

'No answer,' she muttered. Her stomach dropped like she'd stepped off the end of a jetty without realising she'd got to the last wooden slat. She went back into the lane. Gazed up at the first-floor bedrooms. Should she be trying to break in?

'Grace?' said a voice from behind her.

Gaia turned to see a woman who'd been decorated with an extra decade of wrinkles since she'd last seen her.

'It *is* you!' she said, smiling.

Gaia stared at the two chestnut eyes that gleamed back at her, the lines surrounding them more beautiful than she'd read in any script: from a life filled with laughter and truly well lived.

Would she feel that way when she looked back at herself in ten years? she wondered fleetingly.

'I wasn't sure if it was you, at first, we're not used to film stars visiting . . .' She giggled.

Gaia knew Mrs Watson would have meant her words well, as a compliment, but in the circumstances they sparked a sickening sensation in her throat.

'And who's this?' she carried on, her gaze alighting on Federico, who was coming out of the garden gate across the road to join them.

'This is my fiancé, Feddy,' said Gaia, mind still eddying like an overrunning beck. 'Feddy, this is Mrs Watson, my old Geography teacher.'

'Not that old, I'm still at the school . . . we're all very proud of you.'

Gaia felt an ache in her stomach; she'd done nothing but run away from this place. But these were the people who were really behind her, had always had her best interests at heart. How had she got it all so wrong?

Federico held out his hand. '*Piacere di conoscerla*. Pleased to—'

'*Il piacere è mio*,' replied Mrs Watson. 'The pleasure is mine.'

Gaia raised her eyebrows.

'Just because I choose to live here doesn't mean I've never been anywhere else.' Mrs Watson's eyes twinkled. She spread her arms wide in a sweeping gesture. 'Best place in the world,' she said. 'Italy is second,' she added as an aside to Federico, and followed it up with another girlish laugh. 'Anyway, if you're looking for your parents, they've gone out walking. They were talking about doing Catbells today.' She jerked her head in the direction of the shapely ridge visible above them to the west of Derwentwater.

'The first mountain I ever climbed,' murmured Gaia to Federico, her brain instantly spooling back to a time when summer holidays were spent hiking the fells and camping by the lake.

'Well you ought to show Federico the view from up there,' said Mrs Watson. '*Magnifica*.'

'You think we can catch them up?' asked Federico, squinting at the steep ascent.

'Probably,' said Mrs Watson. 'At some point.' She looked at her watch. 'They walked that way about twenty minutes or so ago.' She pointed further up the narrow street, between the tea shop and the church. 'I was sitting outside here with a cup of coffee and they stopped to say hello as they went past.'

'I know the route,' said Gaia, glancing up at Catbells. The well-worn path was a pale spine along the hill's back. 'Are you definitely sure you're okay to do it, Feddy?'

He nodded. 'It's not one of the biggest ones, is it.'

A statement rather than a question. Gaia's mouth opened in surprise. He'd certainly done his Lake District research.

'My parents took us to Monte Tre Calle every year,' he explained.

'Ah the Amalfi coast,' murmured Mrs Watson, a dreamy expression coming over her face.

'Well, I'm not sure Catbells can beat *that* . . .' muttered Gaia, hands on her hips as she gazed up at the summit, framed against the cloud-mottled sky at almost one and a half thousand feet high above them.

'It's not always a competition,' said Mrs Watson. 'You can't compare a rose to a rainbow.'

Gaia tipped her head to one side as she took in Mrs Watson's wise words. She was right: they were both beautiful in their own way.

'We should get going if we want to try to meet up with your mother and father,' said Federico, adjusting the straps on his rucksack in preparation for the ascent.

'Yes,' replied Gaia. She turned to Mrs Watson. 'Nice to see you.'

'You too. Good luck.' She smiled back at them as they set off up the lane.

Gaia looked over her shoulder. 'If we don't manage to find them will you say that we—'

Mrs Watson nodded. 'Of course I will. But you've already gone after the stars, Grace. You're capable of anything.'

Chapter 36

'I'm looking forward to this,' said Federico. 'It will be the first walk we've done together.' He grinned at Gaia.

'Apart from the red carpet,' she replied. She looked ahead at the track that led up the slope in front of them, feeling her lungs fill with oxygen and her heart beat harder. But the realisation unsettled her: how were they about to get married, yet they hadn't done something as simple as go for a stroll on their own? She pushed the thought out of her mind and pressed on. She and Federico were the perfect match, everyone said so – all the papers and magazines had planned their union before they'd even been on a first date. Besides, if she messed this up and missed her chance to be Mrs De Angelis there would be a million others waiting to take her place. There was no time to waste. She strode out purposefully, pleased to see they were making quick progress up the side of the mountain. She was doing her best to keep up a consistently brisk pace, and even though they'd only been going for a few minutes, they'd already covered quite a bit of ground. She glanced behind her at Federico. She'd said she'd grown up hiking this landscape, so he'd expect her to conquer a modest hill like Catbells in no time—

'If we don't see your mum and dad today, we can come back tomorrow,' he called after her in between heavy breaths.

'Yes,' said Gaia without looking round. But the path was almost completely clear, there were far fewer people tackling the fell this way round, instead of the more popular option of starting from the north, nearer to Keswick. There was no reason why they couldn't make up some time, close the gap between them and her parents. She pulled down the peak of her baseball cap as a solo runner sprinted past, and pushed on.

'Do you want a drink?' called Federico after a little while longer.

She turned to see he was further behind than before. The backpack was by his feet and a bottle of water was in his hand.

She shook her head. 'I'm fine, thanks.' It took more effort to stand still and wait for him to finish what he was doing than it had to make all of the headway they'd achieved so far. If he didn't hurry up then her parents were just increasing their advantage. Every second he spent stationary was more chance for them to get further ahead. She sighed and scraped the ground with her trail shoe, like a horse pawing at grass.

'Is it a race?' said Federico, screwing the top back on his water bottle.

Gaia frowned. 'I thought we agreed it would be nice to try and meet up with—'

'I mean between you and me.' Federico picked up the rucksack again.

Gaia walked back towards him, stretched out a hand to take the bag. 'Of course not. Here, let me take that.'

'Then aren't we supposed to be admiring the view, too?' He looked out at the scene laid out before them, but Gaia was busy buckling the rucksack onto her back.

'We can see it when we're at the top.' She started off again.

She was always so concerned with the next thing, never paused to appreciate the moment, thought Federico to himself. But if you were always focused on what was coming afterwards, then you didn't ever experience the present. Was that what the wedding was, he wondered, just another future marker of supposed success that she wanted to tick off?

'Wait,' said Federico.

'What?' said Gaia without stopping.

He stared after her, marching up the parched-soil path. It was no use trying to speak to her when she was so intent on getting to the summit.

'I think you should drink something; it's getting warm,' he said instead.

'I'm fine, it isn't LA hot.' She laughed. She was used to bootcamp workouts in the blazing sunshine.

'Well, it's not far off,' said Federico. His phone said 24 degrees but he didn't need technology to tell him that it was the kind of weather where you could easily put your body under too much pressure; he'd grown up in the searing temperatures of Italian summers.

But Gaia wasn't listening.

Her determination was one of the traits he admired most about her, but sometimes he wished she'd hear him out, communicate properly as though they were a team, not two people on opposing sides.

He hurried after her, ignoring the splendidness of their vantage point in favour of closing the distance between them. Pearls of sweat beaded his forehead. This wasn't how he'd

227

felt on those blissful family holidays to Amalfi. He remembered those fondly, the constant animated conversations, the frequent stops to delight in the breathtaking sight of the Tyrrhenian Sea. To them, the journey had been far more important as the destination.

But this was different. It was unpleasant, to say the least. He'd rather have wandered to the Bowder Stone and back, then waited in the village for them to return.

'What are we doing, Grace?' he said, still not used to calling her a different name to the one she'd been introduced to him with. A multitude of questions started to bubble up inside him.

She spun round to face him, finally stopping.

'You and I,' clarified Federico, gazing up at her like he always seemed to have done ever since they'd met. 'This trip was supposed to be about spending time together. I feel like I've hardly seen you.'

Her shoulders sagged as though all of her fears and worries had suddenly been stuffed inside the rucksack on her back. 'You're having doubts about the wedding,' she said.

'See – always leaping ahead,' said Feddy, gesturing up the mountain with one hand. 'That's not what I said.'

'What do you mean, then?'

He strode further up the path so he was alongside her. 'Why are we rushing this?'

'The walk?'

He nodded.

'I want to see Mum and Dad . . .'

'I know, but why is it suddenly so urgent? I don't understand. When I asked if we were going to visit them when we were over here you said—'

'I know,' Gaia held up a hand. 'But that was before I spoke to Harry . . .'

228

'You seem to be able to talk to him much more easily than you can to me.' Federico gave a shrug.

Gaia felt as though the relationship was beginning to unravel right there on the mountain, her hopes and dreams in danger of roly-polying down the hillside before her eyes. 'That's not the case,' she protested. The stakes just felt so high with Federico. He was everything anyone could wish for, and now he'd discovered she was just ordinary Grace Wilkins from north Cumbria it was surely only a matter of time before he realised he could meet someone better. She thought of Victoria Cole – daughter of Hudson Cole, who'd won so many awards his nickname was Oscar – she had a whole dynasty of celebrated actors behind her. Credentials to back her up as a suitable partner for Federico.

Perhaps she ought to bow out now before things went any further, wondered Grace. Before he broke the news that he was reconsidering. It would be better if it came from her. She'd be the one in control. The spell was already wearing off anyway. He'd found out she was nothing like who she'd said she was. What sort of a foundation was that? He was probably just biding his time, waiting till they were back home to deal the blow. She'd put him out of his misery before he saw all her flaws and—

'Can we just sit down for a second?' said Federico.

She felt faint all of a sudden. Was it happening now?

She stepped off the track, sat down on the grassy ground. She gazed at the island at the opposite end of the lake, the hotel hardly visible now, just a disappearing white dot in the distance. Her wedding plans seemed to be fading from sight at a similar rate. She felt light-headed.

'I think I need to lie down,' she mumbled, leaning back against the lush green blanket that covered Catbells' slanted sides.

'Some water will help,' she heard Federico say from beside her.

She lifted her head to see him unfastening the lid of her drinks bottle.

'Thanks,' she muttered, taking a sip, then resting her head back on the grass. Now she'd stopped, she felt overwhelmingly exhausted. She closed her eyes, but a snapping sound caused her to open them again.

'For energy,' said Federico, handing her a piece of shortbread. 'Some biscotti would be better, of course,' he quipped, 'but this is all we've got.'

She smiled and sat up a little to take a bite. The buttery taste was balm for the heart, a burst of comfort in edible form.

They both looked out at the horizon in silence.

Gaia gazed across at Blencathra, the fell their suite had been named after. A majestic title that befitted the best room in the hotel. But would their accommodation have been equally as sumptuous had it been called something else? Just had a number on the door? She plucked at a tuft of grass. It would be exactly the same. Just as she was the identical person inside, whether she was known as Gaia or Grace.

She turned her head to take in Federico's profile. He had a scattering of copper freckles across his nose that she'd never really noticed, and his dark hair was longer than she'd seen it before and beginning to curl a little above his left temple. She propped herself up on her elbow. How much did she actually know about this man beside her? she wondered. The deep stuff, not only the physical.

'Feel any better?' he asked, tilting his face towards her.

She nodded.

'Good,' he turned back to the view of Derwentwater, a deep indigo below them. His eyes were hidden by his sunglasses, and she was struck by the need to know what was behind them.

'What are you thinking about?' she asked, tracing from his earlobe to the collar of his polo shirt with her gaze.

'Us,' he said. 'And you?'

'The same.'

'Something in common.' He smiled but he was still looking at the lake.

She lay back down, wanted to feel the firm earth supporting her when she asked the next question. 'Tell me honestly, Feddy, are you reconsidering our relationship?'

He gave a sigh, still staring at the verdant vista rather than her.

Gaia studied the white-cotton sky; the clouds were swabs waiting to cover a gaping wound.

Was halfway up Catbells where it would all come to an end?

But she felt a strange sense of comfort at the fact she was on home ground. She pressed the length of her body back into the turf – she couldn't fall if she was lying flat, after all. This is where she'd started, completely from scratch; built up her acting reputation from nothing. These folds of undulating land were as familiar to her as the features she saw when she looked in the mirror. She'd been to her very first show on that opposite shore: a festive pantomime her parents had taken her to when she was five. The production had been at the Theatre by the Lake, a location that was as idyllic as it sounded, where the extraordinary setting served to heighten the drama on the stage. She'd done her first ever audition over there at Keswick School, under the watch of Skiddaw which seemed to gaze down protectively at the town. She'd practised for the part of Juliet in that little cottage they'd passed earlier, in front of her two biggest fans, her mother and father, the first ones to be on their feet when the audience had given the performance a standing ovation.

So, if she and Feddy were over, and she had to start again, this surely had to be the place where it would feel most possible. She'd take the rejection the same way she would a professional one, and pick herself back up—

'I just think we need to rewind a few steps,' said Federico, pushing his sunglasses on top of his head.

'What does that mean?' she asked, looking up into his black-coffee eyes.

He took her hand. 'Get to know each other for who we really are, not who the rest of the world wants us to be.'

Gaia sat up. 'Sounds like a good idea,' she replied. 'Take the pressure off a bit.'

Federico smiled. 'Exactly. Enjoy the journey. Like today –' he jerked his head to indicate the steep track they'd been travelling along up the mountain'– what's the point of going on this walk together if we're miles apart. We might as well do it separately.'

Gaia nodded. Knew he was talking about the wedding, too.

'Let's slow down and see where it takes us,' he continued. 'Follow our own path at a pace we're both comfortable with.'

'I guess once I have a plan, I tend to just go for it . . .' she explained, slicing a palm through the air to demonstrate how there was no stopping her when her mind was set.

'Whereas I take my time more,' said Federico in return. 'There we go, we're learning about each other already.' He laughed.

Gaia tipped her head to one side. They'd been for dinners, attended premieres, and appeared at parties together, but they were activities she could do with pretty much anyone: looking picture-perfect and having surface-level chat didn't equate to love. It wasn't what a relationship was made up of. And when so much of her life involved putting on a show, at the end of the day she wanted to have something *real* to call her own.

'I'd like to find out more about Grace,' said Federico. 'After all, I only met her for the first time this morning . . .' he said, raising an eyebrow.

Gaia felt a rush of fondness for him, for the fact he was prepared to forgive her for keeping so much of herself from him and seemed keen to see the parts that she'd been too ashamed to show.

'I made a mistake and I'm sorry,' she said. 'I shouldn't have lied about my history to make you like me.'

'You know, it's actually the opposite,' said Federico. 'The times I've seen you be yourself have been the moments I could feel myself falling for you the most.'

Gaia's eyes widened.

'Like when you thought no one was watching and you went to help those girls.' Federico grinned. 'Or when you were getting ready this morning. No ball gown, just leggings and a T-shirt. Your beautiful face.'

Gaia touched her makeup-free cheek self-consciously. 'I thought it might mean no one would recognise me . . .'

'All the ones that matter would,' said Federico.

Gaia sighed. Suddenly all the pretence seemed foolish. How was she hoping to find a genuine connection with someone when she was being so fake?

'I'm not really called Federico, if that makes you feel better,' he said.

She frowned. '*What?*'

'Leonardo,' he said, holding out a hand as though they'd been introduced there and then on the hill.

Gaia took his fingers in hers; had an idea of how it had felt for him, finding out she wasn't who she said she was.

The fellside seemed to shift beneath her a little. She knew it was common for names to be changed in the showbiz industry, that agents often suggested alternatives in order to create a certain image, but it still astonished her too, made her question what it was that made up a person's identity.

'Federico is my middle name,' he explained. 'My management said I couldn't use the one I was born with. That it would cause confusion.'

'Leonardo De Angelis . . .' mouthed Gaia out loud.

'Sounds too much like Leonardo DiCaprio, apparently,' he said.

Gaia giggled. 'So you have to go your whole life being Federico now? Just because they've decided it?'

He shook his head. 'No, to my friends and family I'll always be Leo. Mamma and Papà never call me Federico. It's how I know I'm home.' He smiled.

Gaia pictured signore and signora De Angelis, standing on the rooftop terrace of the Palazzo Manfredi, the hotel where she and Feddy had stayed the last time they'd been in Rome. The four of them had met for dinner in the panoramic restaurant, with its unparalleled views of the ancient city centre, but she had been so preoccupied with trying to impress him and his parents, live up to the expectations she supposed they all had of her, she hadn't taken any of it in. She couldn't remember what the food tasted like, or how the fading light had fallen on the Colosseum behind them; she had been too keen to paint an image of herself she thought they'd find palatable, rather than appreciate being present with the people that were set to become her family . . .

'And my brothers all call me *topino*,' said Federico, with a chuckle.

'Is that a nickname?' asked Gaia.

He nodded. 'Little mouse. Because I was quiet – but only in comparison to the four of them! When we are together –' he splayed the fingers on both hands – 'it's *loud*.'

'I can't really imagine,' said Gaia with a shake of her head. 'It was only the three of us in our house.'

Federico looked at the grass. 'When I was young I used to hate all the noise and the –' he churned his hands in the air, searching for the right word. 'How do you say it . . .?'

'Hurly-burly?' suggested Gaia, smiling at the rhyming sound and wondering how to translate it – she needed Mrs Watson. 'I know what you mean,' she murmured. 'I used to wish for that when I was little.'

'It's *trambusto*, in Italian,' explained Federico.

Gaia giggled as she repeated it after him, wanting to remember it. 'I craved *trambusto*,' she said. 'That's what I wanted when I left here.' She gazed down at Grange-in-Borrowdale below them. 'But I think I was looking in all the wrong places.'

'I couldn't wait to get away too, but now, those are my favourite moments,' said Federico. 'Everyone round the table, talking over each other, passing food.' He beamed. 'The best times.'

Gaia tried to envisage it, but it was so far removed from the reserved dinners in luxurious surroundings that they'd scheduled with his parents and various configurations of his available siblings, it was difficult.

'Why do we always meet your family at the Palazzo Manfredi?' asked Gaia. 'Is it their favourite place in Rome?'

Federico laughed. 'None of them had ever been before that night we had dinner there with you.'

'What?' Gaia's mouth dropped open.

'They were meeting you for the first time,' explained Federico. 'A film star used to the finer things . . .'

Gaia frowned. 'That was for my benefit?'

Federico nodded. 'Otherwise you would have been squeezed in between my nonnas back in Esquilino.' He chuckled as though he was picturing the scene.

Gaia imagined a fragrant, chatter-filled dining room crammed with family and Italian food. She'd have *far* preferred that.

'Next time, can we go to your house?'

'Their apartment?' Federico raised his eyebrows.

She nodded.

'It's a tiny flat, in a run-down part of town, I'm not sure you'd—'

'Is it where you were born?'

'*Sì*. Not in the penthouse suite at the Palazzo, that's for sure . . .' He shook his head. 'I just rent that for them when they want to spend time in the centre of town, for a treat. They've done so much for me.' His eyes shone. 'Dad worked two jobs. Mum brought us five boys up in a space the size of our room at the Lake Island Hotel. It wasn't easy for them. Not that me and my brothers had any idea at the time. We ate wonderful meals together, lived in one of the most beautiful places in the world – what more could we have wished for?'

Gaia wiped her eyes beneath her peaked cap. 'I can't believe I've got everything so wrong. Run away from the things that matter, and tried to pretend I'm something I'm not to impress strangers.'

'Am I a stranger?' said Federico with a smile.

Gaia smiled back at him. 'No. I feel like I'm getting to know the real . . . Leonardo.'

'Good,' replied Federico. 'Because he likes Grace. Very much.'

Chapter 37

Federico pulled Gaia to her feet. 'So next time we see my family you want to swap Michelin-starred food for *lumache alla romana* at my house,' he murmured with a grin.

'Yes,' said Gaia beaming back at him. 'I can't wait to try it.'

'Really?' asked Federico, eyes sparkling at her in surprise. 'You know what it is?

'No.' She shook her head. 'But I bet it's delicious.'

'It is. Authentic Roman cuisine. Mamma's special recipe and my favourite.' Federico kissed his fingers like a chef. 'Snails in spicy tomato sauce.'

Gaia grimaced. 'Might stick to the Palazzo Manfredi after all . . .' she teased.

Federico laughed and pulled her in for a hug. 'Only joking, I don't actually like it much—'

'Grace?' said a breathless voice from behind them.

'Mum?' replied Gaia, spinning round to see her parents puffing up the hillside path that led up from the village. Her face broke into a rainbow-wide smile at the sight of them.

'I thought it was you, but then I thought it couldn't be . . .' said her mother through her fingers.

Gaia wrapped her arms around her, smelled the familiar scent of her coconut shampoo, the same aroma as the gorse blossom that flowered across the fells each spring.

Her dad stepped forward with an outstretched hand. 'You must be Federico,' he said. 'Lovely to finally meet you.'

Federico shook his fingers.

Thomas turned to his daughter. 'I didn't think we were going to get to see you – I left a message but—'

Gaia embraced him. 'We were coming to find you,' she said into the collar of his short-sleeved shirt. 'Mrs Watson said you were up Catbells. We were trying to catch up with you.'

'We stopped for a scone at the tea shop first,' said her mum with a glance at her dad.

'Pre-walk custom,' he added, and Gaia wondered whether she'd know that if she spoke to them more often. 'Jam and cream for essential energy.'

Federico laughed. 'Sounds like a good tradition to me.'

Gaia gazed up at him from beneath her baseball cap. Would the two of them make their own rituals as a couple?

'Welcome to Cumbria, Federico,' said her mum. 'Thanks for bringing the weather with you,' she added, casting her eyes across the lake below. 'What a magnificent day.'

'It is,' said her dad, but he was looking at their daughter instead. 'It's so good to see you, G-Gaia.' He grinned at her.

'*Grace*,' she said. 'And it's good to be home.'

'I can't believe we've bumped into you . . .' said her mum with a shake of her head.

'I know,' said Gaia. 'I thought you were in front.' She gestured in the direction of the summit. 'I was marching on as fast as I could—'

'She was.' Federico gave a nod. 'I was struggling to keep up.' He blew air into his cheeks.

'That's our Grace,' said her father with a shrug. 'Perseverance is her middle name.'

'Is it?' asked Federico, glancing at her.

'No!' replied Gaia with a giggle.

The others joined in with her laughter.

And as she looked around at their joy-filled faces, she felt her heart swell. There was something so freeing about being truly herself, in front of the people who loved her most. She'd striven for success all her professional life, chased after award-worthy parts, mastered impressive new skills to land lead roles, but right there and then on that mountain, she felt closer to the stars than ever before. Happiness wrapped round her shoulders like a shawl spun from sunshine, and a new favourite memory was minted in her mind. She finally felt sure of who she was, and from that moment on, she vowed never to forget it again.

'Shall we carry on to the top?' suggested Thomas, hands on his hips.

'Sounds good to me,' replied Federico.

Gaia nodded.

'You lead,' said her mum. 'You'll be faster than us.'

Gaia bent to pick up the rucksack and slung it on her back. 'Okay, but I'm not in a rush.'

Federico raised his eyebrows. 'Are you still feeling a little unwell?' he joked.

She nudged his arm. 'Ha ha. I'm fine now. Just needed to take five.'

Federico fell into step behind her as the four of them began to snake their way up the hillside. 'So what is your middle name?' he asked as continued along the path.

'Mabel,' said Gaia. 'After my grandma.'

'My mother,' explained her mum.

'That's nice,' said Federico. 'Meaningful. I can't wait to meet her.'

The rhythm of their footsteps filled the silence that followed.

'She exited the stage just as Grace was about to enter it,' said Mary.

'She died the day before I was born,' explained Gaia.

Federico saw her eyes fill momentarily.

'I never met her, but it's like she's part of me. A piece of my history,' added Gaia.

'And your other grandparents?' said Federico.

'No longer with us,' said Thomas as a tear slid down his daughter's face.

'I should have spent more time with them,' she cried all of a sudden. 'I thought they'd still be there . . .' she sobbed.

Her mum put a hand on her back. 'You were carving your own way in the world. That's what they would have wanted.'

Gaia shook her head. 'It's not an excuse. I was so self-absorbed . . .'

'You were doing your best,' said her dad.

'I missed everything that mattered, chasing things that weren't important,' muttered Gaia.

'They wanted you to be happy,' murmured her mum.

And was I? wondered Gaia. *Not really*. She had every material possession imaginable. A Hollywood mansion. A beach-side house in the Bahamas. A closet full of bags and shoes. Diamond jewellery. But if she was to disappear from one of those exclusive parties, would any of the other guests even notice? If she didn't leave her state-of-the-art apartment for several days, how long would it take for her to be missed?

What was it all for, if she ended up feeling isolated and lonely despite the crowds of people who surrounded her at every opportunity?

Her assistant Rachel was the closest thing to family she had over in LA and look how she'd treated her . . .

Sweat was making the skin beneath her T-shirt slick. From now on, she was going to live her life differently. She'd always felt like an imposter, but maybe that was because she herself was always pretending. Well, it was time to stop. As she touched the trig point that marked the top of Catbells, an idea crystallised in her mind: a small way of giving something back to the people and the community that had shaped her.

Chapter 38

'We brought lunch,' said Gaia, putting down the rucksack. 'There's plenty to go around if you'd like some,' she said to her parents.

'Oh, we've had cake, we're fine,' said her mum, sitting down on the smooth-surfaced rock-scape that crowned the summit of Catbells.

'Come on, we've got loads,' said Gaia, starting to unpack the beeswax paper-wrapped picnic the Lake Island Hotel had provided. 'Dad, you'll have some, won't you?'

Thomas tried to read the look in his daughter's eyes, wondered whether it wasn't about the food itself at all, but the fact of sharing a meal as a family, something they hadn't done for such a long while. 'Well, if you insist . . .'

Gaia's face broke into a childlike smile. The breeze at the top of the mountain was doing its best to rewild her hair, whipping strands of it round her cheeks. In that moment, she resembled the little girl she'd been the last time they'd come up here, many years ago now.

'Mum?' said Grace, twisting round to speak to her. 'Will you have a sandwich?'

'Okay, go on then,' she said, looking at the rich spread of gemstone-tones laid out before them. They didn't look like any sandwiches she'd seen before. 'What have we got?'

Jackson's neat labels described each dish as deliciously as if they were guests seated at one of the restaurant's dining tables, but today the summer-coloured countryside was the spectacular setting for their lunch.

'Carrot bacon?' said her dad with a frown, reading one of the typed titles to his wife. 'After you,' he said, leaning back.

Mary surveyed the options, taking her time to weigh up each of them, never one to dive into a decision.

'Feddy, are you going to help yourself?' said Gaia to her fiancé.

'Oh, yes,' he said, but up until that point he'd been content to just sit back and soak up the familiarity of the scene: the well-meant family banter, the abundant food. The simple things that conspired to make a pretty perfect time, in his opinion.

'Well, I'm going to try the coronation chickpea,' announced Gaia.

'Because it sounds fit for a princess?' quipped her dad, chuckling to himself.

'No!' replied Gaia batting his arm. 'I've had something similar back in America before, but it was called something different, and it was yum.'

'I'll take your word for it,' said her dad.

'Right, I'm going to be brave and have the "bacon"' he said as though he'd decided to do a skydive off the side of the mountain, not sample a new sandwich filling.

'That's actually incredible,' he declared, after taking a bite. 'It really does taste *smoky*.' He broke a morsel off to give to Mary. 'Honestly, have a bit of this.'

'Mmm,' she said, rereading the flavour notes underneath the description as she chewed. 'Maple syrup, soy and paprika . . . Well, I never.' She licked her lips.

'I'm going to go for the spinach falafel and pea hummus next,' said Thomas, reaching across for one of the origami-like wraps, and Gaia laughed at his distinct about-turn.

'What?' he said, with a grin, and his daughter giggled again, just like she had done when he and Mary had swung her by the arms as a toddler between the two of them. The sound seemed to echo in his ears, eclipsing the rest of the conversation.

'Come on, Federico, dig in,' said Mary, waving a hand at him.

Gaia touched his arm. 'Please can you just take a quick photo before we start?' she asked, feeling bereft without her own phone – but for the first time since they'd left the Lake Island Hotel that morning, she realised.

'Of course,' he replied, reaching into his pocket.

And as Gaia grinned into the camera, she wished she could save that very instant so she could relive it whenever she wanted, once she was back across the Atlantic. But when Federico beamed at her as he put his mobile away again, and then her mum offered him a pillowy pita bread brimming with citrus-and-chilli marinated Portobello mushrooms, and her dad suggested all going for ice cream at the café by the river later, she craved collecting memorable new ones too. She'd travelled to the other side of the world for work, stopped at nothing when it came to becoming a successful actress. Now it was time to do the reverse, and let nothing stand in the way of precious moments like this. After all, they were the jigsaw pieces that made up the real Grace.

Chapter 39

'I can't remember the last time I spent an entire day without looking at my phone,' said Gaia, taking a bite of her meadowsweet sorbet. Vanilla and almond flavours mingled on her tongue. 'I can't remember the last time I ate something like this, either.' But she wasn't conscious of sucking in her tummy or mentally punishing herself for consuming a treat. She didn't need a gruellingly intense workout to offset it. She'd been on a long walk in the countryside that had been as uplifting as it was active, and she felt strong and *energised* for once.

'I think this is the best ice cream I've ever had,' marvelled Federico, gaze still on his two-scoop cone of hazelnut-butter orbs.

'High praise indeed from an Italian,' said Mary, still deciding which of the selection to choose. 'It's made locally, up at Fell View Farm. When the café here started to stock it, it was a blessing and a curse – I could eat it every single day if I wasn't careful.'

'For breakfast, lunch and dinner,' added Thomas with a nod.

'I would be the same,' said Federico.

They devoured the last of their waffle cones and a contented quiet settled over them as they sat at one of the café's picnic tables beside the river. Its glassy surface danced with every shade on the spectrum, the rounded rocks below glistened rose gold and russet.

'What now?' asked Gaia, so used to having every section of her day meticulously planned out that it was a novelty to be as free as the flock of geese she'd seen flying through the sky earlier that morning.

'Well, I imagine you have somewhere exciting to be . . .' said her dad, looking at his old digital watch, the one he'd worn ever since he'd held her hand when she was small; not the one she'd sent him for his big birthday – no doubt that would still be in the oblong red-leather box, unopened, saved for best.

'We don't actually,' answered Gaia. 'Not tonight.'

'Really?' said her mum, eyes lighting up, her mouth opening as if she'd been about to say something more, but then thought better of it.

Federico nodded. 'We don't want to intrude, though . . .'

'Oh no, you wouldn't be,' said Mary with a waft of her hand. 'It's just . . . it wouldn't be what you're used to, if we invited you back to our house.' She looked at her husband as though apologising for their humbleness in comparison to his high-flying lifestyle.

'I'm used to my family being so loud I leave the house with a headache,' said Federico. 'And to saying *sono sazio* about ten times while my aunt tries to give me yet another plate of *tagliatelle ai funghi*,' he added with a laugh. 'So this is not a bad thing.'

'I meant, you know, in Los Angeles,' said Mary.

'Oh.' Federico put a palm to his chest. 'I see. I always think of myself as a Roman first, then an Italian second.' He smiled. 'Have you heard of *campanilismo*?'

'Is that a new restaurant?' asked Gaia.

'No.' Federico chuckled. 'It is like a sense of pride for your hometown. Our identity, it is tied to the place we come from.' He patted his heart for emphasis.

Gaia gave a mute nod.

Mary glanced at her. 'We do understand why you wanted to leave here,' she murmured to her daughter. 'Expand your horizons. Explore the wider world.'

'I didn't need to run away completely, though, did I?' Gaia replied.

'We're so proud of you for striking out on your own and going after what you want,' said her mum. 'That's all parents can hope for, for their kids to be happy.'

'*Good* parents,' corrected Federico.

Mary dabbed a finger at the corner of her eye. 'We tried our best.'

'You were wonderful,' said Gaia, reaching across the table to grasp both of their hands in each of hers. 'I couldn't have asked for more.'

'It's okay to want more,' said Thomas. 'As long as you were out there doing what you loved, that was all we could wish for.'

'I should have come back more often, though,' said Gaia, feeling a stab of guilt for being ashamed of her origins when Federico wore his as a badge of honour.

'It's a very special place,' said her fiancé with a smile. 'I will certainly be returning in the future.'

'You'll always be welcome,' said Mary.

'And you in Rome,' he replied. 'And America.' He grinned. 'Have you not been to visit?'

Nobody spoke for a second or so, and he noted the atmosphere of tension as keenly as he could sense the faintest trace of truffle in the air of any kitchen.

'Mum and Dad did come once,' murmured Gaia. She swallowed. 'But I wasn't very . . . accommodating.'

Federico frowned. 'They didn't stay with you?'

'Oh, no, we did,' said Thomas.

'In LA?' Federico looked at each of their faces.

Mary nodded. 'We probably got in the way . . .' she muttered, studying the knots in the table's wooden top.

Gaia opened her mouth to say that wasn't the case, but if she was truthful that's how it had seemed. Having them around had felt like a hindrance, not a gift to be appreciated; a parcel of time that not everyone was given.

'What happened?' asked Federico, unable to help himself.

'It was quite early on, not long after Grace moved out there,' explained Mary. 'I think we were just eager to know she was all right.'

Gaia bit her lip. She thought of the sacrifices they'd made for her when she was growing up. The unwavering support. And how had she repaid them?

'It was more for our benefit,' said Thomas, as though he could tell what she was thinking, making the point she didn't owe them anything. 'We wanted to know she was safe. You hear so many stories . . .'

She'd been so young, thought Gaia. Eighteen. Never travelled beyond the boundaries of the county before she'd been accepted into LAMDA. She remembered the day she'd got the news, how they'd celebrated with a bottle of champagne bought from Booths, the first she'd ever tasted. Toasted to her future with fizzing glasses and full smiles. She felt her stomach clench as she recalled it. How she'd reread that acceptance letter more times than she'd read through any lines before. *BA course in Professional Acting.* So much had been ahead of her, but she'd failed to see what was right in front of her.

Her parents had been endlessly patient with the ups and downs of the process, the constant trips to auditions, the subsequent cheering or consoling, the stress of the application procedure and the anxious wait that followed. Until she'd finally set off to London in pursuit of a place on the next ones-to-watch list, excited to meet her fellow students, and suss out the competition, with a suitcase bigger than she was and ambitions that were more sizable still.

But then when the tables had been turned, and her parents had required a little tolerance in return, she'd been nothing but irritable and short-tempered. She remembered her mum snapping photos and filming videos on her iPad that first day of their visit, tablet held up with outstretched arms, but instead of being touched by the evident enthusiasm, Gaia had cringed at the uncoolness. She'd winced at her dad wearing his best suit when the restaurant dress code said smart casual. She couldn't wait for her parents to leave so she could re-polish her image and pretend none of it had ever happened. But the problem was with her and not them. Since when had an overtly loving family been something to shy away from? She felt extremely sheepish about how she'd been.

'We ended up coming home early,' explained Thomas to Federico. 'It just wasn't the best timing.'

The melodic tinkle of the river Derwent did its best to distract from the awkwardness.

Gaia cleared her throat. 'It wasn't just that.' She put her palms flat on the table. 'I was a brat. Too big for my boots.'

She bit her lip. 'But in my defence – and this is not me condoning how I acted at all – I was dealing with so many doubts about myself, always thinking that I couldn't do it, that I wasn't good enough, that I didn't deserve to be there, in Hollywood with all those A-listers.' She brushed her fingers over her eyelids. 'It was horrible of me to be how I was, but I constantly felt like a fraud. I was trying to put on a certain front. Make people believe I was a big deal, because I didn't believe it myself.'

Her mum reached for her hand. 'Hey, hey, it's okay, love.'

'You are a big deal,' said her dad softly. 'Not because you've got a gilded trophy at a fancy ceremony. Or because some critic says so. But because no one else can be you, Grace Wilkins.'

She gave a sniff. 'I'm so sorry . . .' Life was a single-take shot and she'd ruined that holiday whether her parents admitted it now or not. She hung her head. What could she do about it now? Second chances were for rom-coms and sequels were always worse than the original.

'How about if you come again,' Federico suggested all of a sudden, looking from her mum to her dad.

'Now circumstances are different,' he added. 'There are two of us to host and show you round.'

'Oh, no, you'll be busy with the wedding and everything,' said Mary, batting the air.

Gaia's head snapped up. 'Well, we've actually been discussing that.' Her gaze flicked to Federico. 'The plans got a bit out of hand to be honest. We're taking a step back and getting to know each other properly without that pressure.'

'Oh, good idea,' said her mother.

'We have been a bit worried,' confessed her dad.

'And you didn't say anything?' asked Gaia, looking from one to the other.

'It's not our place,' said Thomas.

'It's hard being a parent,' declared Mary.

'It's difficult being a *person*,' said Federico.

It was all she'd wanted, to be famous, thought Gaia; to have scores of adoring fans and worldwide acclaim – but what for? To prove she was someone? Yet the only person questioning her worth was *her*. Perhaps it wasn't too late to start channelling some of her hard-won star power towards a different direction, for a greater purpose. And again, the idea she'd had earlier gained a little more colour in her mind.

Chapter 40

'I was planning to take some time off after the wedding,' said Gaia to her parents. 'It's already blanked out and set aside.'

'Oh, of course,' said Mary, swallowing the term honeymoon before it could slip off her tongue.

Gaia sensed the word hovering in the air nevertheless, sweet-sounding and crammed with expectation. But it only really denoted a much-anticipated holiday, just with double the pressure to be perfect. 'I was thinking, we could come back here instead.'

Federico looked at her. 'Good idea.'

'But I guess we don't really have to wait till then,' said Gaia, thinking aloud. 'I've still got some promotional commitments I'm contracted to do for my last film, but there's no reason I couldn't come back for . . .'

Mary's eyes shone like twinkling lights. 'Christmas?' she whispered, the syllables out of her mouth before she could stop herself.

Gaia looked at her dad. *Don't say it if you don't mean it*, said Thomas's pursed lips. He kept promises, when others tended to drop them as carelessly as lost loose change.

Gaia nodded. 'I'm serious.'

'I thought you said LA was amazing in the holidays,' said Mary. 'That there were so many parties it was important to be there.'

'For my career, maybe, but not for me personally,' said Gaia. Besides, the definition of 'important' seemed to have shifted in her internal dictionary lately.

Mary pressed her palms together. 'We haven't had Christmas together since . . .'

'Yes, I know,' interjected Gaia.

They all recalled it, except for Federico.

'When?' he asked, wondering what festive remembrances were about to be described. He pictured his own mother making chocolate and fruit panettoni in her kitchen, enough to give to every friend and relative in Rome.

'I was home from drama school and Dad had booked to take us to a play as a Christmas treat.' She could still see him holding three fanned-out tickets in the foyer of the Theatre by the Lake.

'What was the show?' asked Federico.

'*Tom's Midnight Garden*,' murmured Gaia.

'And it was good?'

Gaia nodded. 'The reviews all said it was brilliant, but I didn't even give it a chance at the time. Said I was far too old for something like that.'

'It was meant to be for all ages,' explained Thomas.

'I thought it was magical,' said Mary.

'But I was so ungrateful,' continued Gaia. 'Spoiled it for everyone.'

'There was a lot of sighing,' recalled Mary.

'And scowling,' said Thomas.

The memory was clearly still as raw for them as if it had happened the day before.

'I kept talking about how a girl off my course was going to the Radio City Spectacular in New York and how much better a show on Broadway would be.' Gaia blushed. 'I can't believe it when I look back now.'

'I think the place by the lake sounds *bellissimo*,' said Federico.

'I'll take you,' said Gaia, including the four of them in her gaze. 'We'll all go.'

'And what about your next film?' asked Mary, managing her expectations; she wasn't entirely full of faith that her daughter would be back in six months' time.

'Still in pre-production,' said Gaia.

'What is it, this one?' asked Thomas, taking the opportunity to ask his daughter the questions he usually dreamed of doing on the phone calls that she never returned.

'A period drama. The script is still being tweaked but it's a Regency romance.'

'Ooh,' said Mary.

'I play a character called Arabella Thornthwaite . . .' She trailed off as a thought struck her. 'This would be the perfect place to really get to grips with the role.' The Lake District countryside was a much more suitable location for fully immersing herself in Arabella's world: far away from LA's sprawl of high-rise buildings and heavy traffic. 'It's so unspoilt here,' Gaia mused. The Lake Island Hotel was the kind of house she imagined Arabella and her family calling home. In all seriousness, there couldn't be a better spot to rehearse.

'You think we still live in the eighteen-hundreds anyway,' joked Thomas. 'Just because we don't have a Starbucks on every street.'

Federico chortled. 'I don't know why people always want everything to be the same. Each coffee shop to be the identical experience. We are afraid of different.'

Gaia looked around at the rushes and reeds that fringed the river as she contemplated his statement. Nature was full of variety, no one would expect each plant or flower to be alike. Yet humans were obsessed with trying to fit in, not do their own thing. Individuality was positive, part of the richness of life.

'Is the movie set in the UK?' asked Mary, leaning forward, and Gaia saw her dad put his hand on her mum's knee, a protective salve: he was trying to prevent her getting her hopes up.

'Yes,' said Gaia. 'So, I'll be back again for filming, all being well.' It was a departure from the types of protagonist she'd been cast as previously, and she was more than a little trepidatious about gauging it right, bringing her own distinct personality to the part but being on point with the appropriate period mannerisms.

'So we might be seeing quite a bit more of you,' murmured Mary. She turned to Federico. 'You're very welcome to come for Christmas, or at any other time,' she added with a smile.

'*Grazie mille*,' said Federico with a grin. 'It has been wonderful to meet you.'

And as Gaia looked at her parents sitting opposite, beaming back at him, she felt as though a weighted training vest had been lifted off her shoulders. Her lungs filled with the perfume of June: a medley of plants mixed with mid-afternoon warmth. No one spoke for a few moments, and she drank in the scene that surrounded them: the river Derwent was dazzling in the afternoon light, the trees that lined its banks embroidered with a lace-like lattice of leaves. One skittered onto the table-top, sun-crisped and fractal-patterned; as intricate as human skin.

255

So much beauty in every direction, though she'd never really noticed any of it before.

Federico's phone began to ring, piercing the peace with the subtlety of a popped balloon, the electronic tone so at odds with their organic environment.

Mary jumped.

Thomas gripped the tabletop.

Gaia gave a laugh. She couldn't remember the last time she'd gone so long without looking at her own mobile. But in the absence of its distraction, she was truly seeing the tiny details of the landscape she'd always taken for granted, and it was mesmerising. Like she was watching a wildlife documentary on a giant 4K TV in 3D – yet it was all real. Everything was here to touch and to feel.

'It's Si,' said Federico, looking at his phone screen.

'His security guard,' explained Gaia to her mum and dad as he answered.

'Oh, of course,' mouthed Mary.

He was probably wondering where they were, thought Gaia, glancing at her watch. But as she got up from their table to go and pay the bill, she saw Chris sitting at the next bench, head bent behind a copy of the *Westmorland Gazette*.

'Quite a good read, this,' he muttered as she passed his table. 'You'll be pleased to know they've described that new thriller *Beach Bodies* as "the smash hit of the summer".'

Gaia flashed him a smile, then remembered there was something she wanted to ask.

'Please can we make a stop in Keswick on the way back, if that's okay?' she said.

And Chris was so thrown by receiving such a politely phrased request from his boss that all he could do was nod.

Chapter 41

The wind toyed with Katrine's hair, as though vying for her attention as she waited for Harry at the end of the jetty. Look up, it seemed to whisper, see the light on the hills, their molten mirror-image reflected in the water. She lifted her eyes, gazed out across the lake. But she couldn't help her thoughts circling round to Gaia once again. So, she had been born over there, in Grange-in-Borrowdale. Been Harry's first girlfriend. Katrine couldn't quite believe it. The well-known actress, from all those big-budget films. Growing up here, hiking the Cumbrian mountains, thousands of miles away from the Hollywood Walk of Fame. Who would have ever imagined that? Perhaps none of us was really that different underneath after all.

She thought of her own first relationship. *Aleksey*. The son of their nearest neighbour back in Zakopane and her brother's best friend. They'd been so young, the two of them, barely sixteen. Spent their days out in the fields filled with pink-fronded rosebay willowherb, walking and talking and working out the world around them. They'd broken up when she went off to university. He'd stayed in Zakopane, wanted to pursue being a ski jumper. And he'd done it, according to social media. The details of their split were hazy now, it was so long ago, but it had seemed obvious they were destined to explore different paths. She hadn't thought of him in ages, his features were even hard to picture precisely in her mind, but time had sieved the pain from the positives, and now when she thought of him it was a faded fondness. Like recalling a favourite book from childhood, where the exact story was fuzzy but there was a lingering sense of affection for it. They'd more or less lost touch, but Mateusz had mentioned Aleksey was married now; her brother had attended the wedding at some point while she was travelling a few years ago. She'd seen on Facebook that he had two small kids and a smiling wife called Nina. They'd broken each other's hearts as teenagers, yet taught each other so much in the process. They'd gradually mended, of course, and morphed into a sequence of adult versions of themselves that still carried faint scars and fierce truths from the period they'd shared together. He'd encouraged her to be more adventurous. She'd taught him the importance of considering another. They'd both learned two people could have differing perceptions, without either being wrong.

What if hers and Harry's situations had been reversed? Katrine wondered now, and Aleksey had been the one to come and stay on the island. Her first boyfriend had been the piece of the past to so suddenly appear in the present, instead of Gaia? Would seeing him now, as the world-class athlete he'd always wanted to become, change anything? She'd almost be glad to have the chance to say well done to him, she realised, to her surprise. Perhaps even be a little proud that the boy from the next farm along had succeeded in his long-held dream. He was a part of her, in a way. Had pushed her to chase the things she wanted out of life. Told her to believe in herself. Maybe without knowing him, she'd never have taken the plunge and left Poland. Might have had an entirely different perspective on love. He'd shown her that partners didn't hold each other back. Helped her believe that things not working out wasn't always a bad thing. An end was simultaneously a beginning.

Perhaps Harry's time with Gaia had been similarly valuable, she thought, understanding their connection a little more now, and that it didn't have to diminish what he and Katrine had now. Life was a complex patchwork of experiences that people sewed together as best they could. Some made superhero capes from scraps, others stitched comfort blankets from segments of time spent with family and friends. But everyone was just doing their utmost to stitch together these moments, make something meaningful from the mess of being human.

Where was Harry? she wondered, looking over her shoulder. She wrapped her arms around herself as the heat left the day.

'Katrine,' she heard him call just as she'd turned back round, his voice couriered to her by the wind.

She smiled at the sight of him coming towards her.

'Sorry, I went to see if Will wanted a lift back to Keswick,' he explained in between panting breaths. 'But he's staying.'

'Again?' Katrine raised an eyebrow. Things seemed to be going smoothly with him and Anna, at least, she thought with a grin. She'd seen them sharing a gentle kiss when they thought no one was looking on more than one occasion.

'He's helping in the garden. The squash plants have collapsed or something,' said Harry with a shrug.

'Sounds like the perfect excuse to spend time together,' said Katrine as she climbed aboard the boat. 'Remember when we used to do that?'

Harry glanced up from untethering the rope. 'I don't remember us making pyramid supports for courgettes on any of our date nights,' he joked.

Katrine laughed. 'You know what I mean: think up reasons to see each other,' she said.

'I always want to see you.' Harry leaped onto the wooden deck of the ferry. 'If I'm honest, I'm quite glad Will isn't here too. It feels ages since it's just been us.' He leaned down to give her a kiss.

It really did, thought Katrine, feeling the crossing over Derwentwater transform as they spoke, from an essential journey to pick up guests to a romantic trip for two. 'I love you,' she said, as they left behind the landing stage and glided out into the lake. The familiar commute became an exciting excursion. They were encircled by the full scope of Cumbrian colours, from the emerald-bladed fields below Blencathra to the vivid purple pigment of the wildflowers growing on the opposite shore, and with Harry by her side, Katrine felt completely cloaked in happiness.

Chapter 42

'We've had twelve whole Gaia-free hours,' said Miles with a glance at his watch and a grin at Rachel. 'Who would have ever thought it?' He nodded at the neat white box on the bed, its sterile newness and straight lines the opposite of everything else on the island. 'Do we have to give her that new phone?' he said to Rachel.

She laughed. 'Yes.'

He sighed wistfully. 'Shame. It's been *wonderful*.' He flopped onto the bed beside her to savour the last moments of no contact with her boss. No doubt as soon as she was back, they'd know about it. 'Where have her and Federico been this evening, anyway?' he asked. 'It's almost eleven.'

'They went to the theatre,' said Rachel.

'Really?' Miles propped himself on one elbow.

'That's what Chris's text said.'

'I didn't think there'd be one near here. Thought we were in the middle of nowhere.'

'It's the Lake District, not Jurassic Park,' replied Rachel.

'Are you sure?' Miles tilted his head to the side. 'Gaia reminds me of a velociraptor: same screech.'

'Don't be ridiculous,' said Rachel with a giggle.

'No, you're right, I think they had feathers, so they'd have been *far* softer,' said Miles with a shake of his head. 'I'll Google it.'

Rachel smiled as she watched his eyes scan a web page.

'Paleontologists think they never actually made it to England,' he said, glancing up at her. 'So I guess you're right.'

She batted him with a pillow. 'Dinosaurs are extinct.'

'We'll, let's hope the old version of Gaia is, too.' Miles ducked out of the way of another playful pillow-blow. 'I just don't believe it'll last, do you?'

'I hope so. And I think we need to give her a chance to change. Not expect the worst before it's happened.'

'Some things are too good to be true though.'

'Not everything.' She dropped the pillow and kissed him. 'Anyway, I know what you're doing: delay tactics.'

Miles pulled her close again. 'It's just been so nice to have some us-time. No distractions.'

'It has. Special.' If she'd carried on neglecting their relationship, relentlessly prioritising Gaia instead, would it have died out, too? Rachel wondered.

She saw Miles's lip tremble in the bedside lamplight. 'I just felt like I was on the wrong side of some one-way glass, desperately trying to get your attention but nothing was working.'

'Except working is all I was doing,' murmured Rachel.

He gave a small laugh: shared humour had always been the glue that drew them together, formed the spine of their story, the same way pages were bound in a book.

'I put work above you, above everything,' she said.

'Most worryingly, above yourself,' said Miles. He took her hand. 'That's what was the worst part about it. Seeing the Rach I fell in love with disappear. That happy, full-of-life woman that everyone who knows you adores.'

Rachel looked at their fingers clasped in such a fragile lock. How close had she come to losing him? To losing herself?

'I just felt like we'd drifted so far apart, I was more of a fixture in some strangers' lives than I was in yours. Honestly, when I'd had a longer chat with the man at the gas station than I'd had with my own girlfriend in the last month, it was a wake-up call.'

'Was that really the case?' whispered Rachel.

Miles squeezed her hand. 'I just missed you. Us. Obviously, things alter. Life gets stressful, of course, but I thought we'd always be in it together. I felt shut out. Like you'd almost be relieved if I wasn't there anymore, because I was just another thing on your to-do list.'

'That was never the case.' He hadn't even made it onto that, thought Rachel with prickle of guilt.

Neither of them spoke as the truth crackled in the air.

'Am I holding you back?' asked Miles, his voice breaking.

She squeezed his hand tighter, as though willing herself not to let go, rather than really believing she wouldn't. 'No.'

'Because I would hate that.'

She leaned her head on his shoulder. 'I'll do better.' The promise felt flimsy even as it was made. Too woolly and undefined, like a cloud she'd be trying to keep intact.

'I don't want *us* to need some kind of contract, like the one you wrote for Gaia,' said Miles, sensing her train of thought. 'Rules we try to stick to. I'm not sure it should be this difficult, Rach.'

Things would have disintegrated far sooner if Miles had been less forgiving, that was for sure.

This time, the silence that ensued wasn't followed with some kind of joke, swiftly filled with laughter. Their minds swirled separately with thoughts that stayed stuck in their skulls, couldn't quite make it out of their lips, and although their skin was still touching, their fingers tightly gripped together, they could both feel their connection slipping through their fingers, but had absolutely no idea how to stop it.

Chapter 43

A ray of sunlight was just beginning to tiptoe across the carpet from the window. Anna had crept out of the bedroom just as quietly earlier, and now Will could hear her footsteps crossing the gravel outside. Something was on her mind; he knew that much. The garden was her sanctuary, the place where she weeded out her worries, worked over her thoughts, and pruned back her fears, all while her fingers were busy tending the plants.

Even though she'd been lying on her side, facing away from him, he'd been able to tell she wasn't asleep a long while before she'd eventually slipped out of bed: the butterfly-like flutter of her eyelids against the pillowcase had given it away, but he'd sensed it too. Like he couldn't rest if she was tense. That's how he knew his feelings were growing like seedlings, taking root with every hour with her he spent.

He sat up, unsure whether to follow her, or leave her among the fruit trees and fresh air to feel more like herself again, enjoy the solitude of first light.

Was she all right? he wondered, trying to think of what could be wrong. He sifted through the events of the previous evening in his head, like a beachcomber searching for clues. They'd sat up late talking, had eventually fallen asleep after midnight, melded around each other like mountain ridges, the start of one indistinguishable from another. The last thing he remembered was the slope of her slumbering back, the way it had resembled the outline of Blencathra.

He closed his eyes now, but it was no use. He needed to know if she was okay. Whether there was anything he could do to help ease whatever it was whirling in her head.

He got up and went downstairs, found her sitting on the bench outside near the beehives.

She smiled at him and his chest felt summer-warmed, though the morning air was still cool.

'Sorry, did I wake you up?' she said.

He shook his head. Sat down beside her. She turned to face him and he studied the speckles of amber in her irises that he'd never noticed before.

The birds twittered and chirped as though trying to encourage them to talk.

'What is it?' asked Will.

'Oh, nothing.' She smiled again but the glint was gone from her eyes.

'Nothing shouldn't really be a word,' Will replied. 'It never actually *means* nothing.'

Anna turned to look at him. 'Okay, nothing for you to worry about, then.'

'You can't help it when you care about someone,' he said, turning towards her, her silvered hair streaked with sunshine highlights.

'Is there anything I can do?' he asked.

She shook her head. 'I don't think so.'

'Are you concerned about something?' he asked.

'Only the hotel in general.'

He felt a glimmer of relief that she hadn't mentioned him. But there was no 'only' about it, he knew how much this place meant to her. 'You can talk to me about it, if you want to.'

'Thank you.' She gazed up at the building's white walls; it had once looked so different, back when she and Dominik had bought it, crumbling and unloved, and she was constantly trying to stop it sliding backwards into a state of disrepair. It wouldn't be long before the outside needed another coat of paint, the roof was in want of repair, and the rooms would need updating to guests' ever-increasing standards. Maybe the time for it to become someone else's was closer than she'd once thought. No one truly owned anything, not really. That was one lesson the Lake District often taught.

'I understand if you don't want to tell me, though,' added Will. 'I'll be here for you whatever. Just want to share the load if I can. And you want me to.'

She looked at him sitting beside her. Not that long ago, she would have laughed in disbelief if someone had described this scenario: her and Will. In a relationship. They hadn't seen eye to eye in the past, now they spoke heart to heart. Life could surprise you in ways you least expected, the important thing was to keep your mind open.

'Two heads might be better than one, I suppose,' she said with a sigh. 'I'm just trying to make the numbers stack up.'

Will nodded. 'I understand. It was like that when I had the farm. As much as I wanted it to work, I couldn't seem to figure out a way to make a profit.'

'We're bringing in money, but not really enough. Not to cover future expenses as well. There's always something that needs doing.'

Will scanned the kitchen garden that surrounded them, bursting with herbs and vegetables, at its summer best. 'I can do more. If you'd like. I enjoy it.' He swallowed, wondered how honest to be, trying to gauge whether their bond was built to take the weight of total truth, like the plant supports he'd helped her construct the previous night. He lifted his chin. Decided to take the risk. 'Being here has given me a new lease of life. Something to look forward to each day.'

Anna frowned, glanced round at the raised beds. The chard needed picking while it was still young and tender. There was always so much to do.

Will followed her line of sight. 'Look at the stems. Like a rainbow.' He chuckled.

He was right. The vegetable had straight stalks in shades of orange, yellow and purple which brought a splash of colour to the garden. All she could see when she looked at any area of the hotel were its problems. 'I don't want it to be a burden,' she said. She paused, didn't know whether to elaborate further. There was more to it than that. The finances. She couldn't afford to employ him permanently, even if there were enough jobs to keep him busy for every season twice over.

'Even with the restaurant full each night and all seven rooms booked out, it's not enough.' She frowned.

'It must have helped a bit having someone pay for exclusive hire,' said Will, thinking of Gaia. For all her painful demands, she'd paid a premium to have the place to herself. 'Hmm. So we just need a few more famous guests to come and stay.'

'Yes, simple!' said Anna with a laugh. 'I'll put an order in for some celebrities when I ring my suppliers later.'

Will bit his lip. He was trying to help but he didn't know what to suggest. Rose had been the one to come up with a solution for the farm. To start making ice cream and take their business in a new direction. He needed to follow his daughter's example and think outside the box.

Anna's expression turned serious again. 'All jokes aside. I need to think of something.'

'*We* will think of something,' said Will. He racked his brain. There was always a way, a choice that could be made to better a situation. His strong, capable daughter had shown him that. 'More events?' he proposed. 'Having a high-profile wedding is a good start.'

'But no one is supposed to know about that, so we can't really publicise it.'

That was a point. He put a finger to his chin. 'Well, I'm sure lots of other people would like to tie the knot here . . .' He pictured the wide terrace full of chattering guests. Or there was that pretty stone folly down by the water for smaller ceremonies. There were plenty of options. It was the perfect venue: enchanting but adaptable. 'We just need to spread the word without disclosing the details of Gaia and Federico's special day.'

'Easier said than done.'

'Not like you to be negative.'

'I know,' she said. 'Sorry, it's just overwhelming sometimes. So many plates to spin. Running a hotel isn't something I ever imagined doing on my own.'

He wanted to take her hand and say she didn't have to. That he was in it with her. But it was probably too soon, he reminded himself. 'What about your staff?' he said instead.

'Yes, they're amazing,' murmured Anna. 'I couldn't ask for a better team.' She mustered a smile. 'Sometimes you just want someone else to take the reins though, don't you?'

'I know what you mean, but that's not always straightforward either.' He thought of Rose's plans to diversify the farm, and how he'd resisted her input at first. 'Tell you what, I'll make you your lemon tea and we can think of some more ideas to bring in extra income.' He stood up. 'Sound good?'

Anna got to her feet, too.

'No, you try and switch off for a second,' said Will, kissing the top of her head. 'Stay there and enjoy the sunshine.'

She opened her mouth to protest, unused to sitting around, accustomed to being constantly busy.

'It's okay,' he added over his shoulder. 'You can lean on those around you when you need to, it's not an admission of weakness,' he said. 'It's a sign of strength. Think like a plant,' he added with a grin, pointing a finger at the squash vines they'd resurrected together, carefully entwining the growing tendrils around a pole so it would thrive. And once again Anna wondered how much more the garden had to teach her.

Chapter 44

'Can't believe it's our last day,' said Gaia as Jackson set down her spinach and apple smoothie, made to the specific recipe approved by both her and her personal trainer slash nutritionist.

He was so busy wondering what the point of travelling to anywhere new was if you were just going to stick to eating the exact same meal plan as you always did back home, that he didn't realise she was addressing him at first. He did his best to arrange his facial features in a fitting expression of surprise, but wasn't quite able to form a sentence to match. To him, it had been the longest stay imaginable.

Gaia and Federico were seated in the restaurant, as the Lake District had resumed its traditional weather of drizzle mixed with wind. Derwentwater's surface was puckered with peaks and troughs, made rough like tree bark by the morning's blustery gusts.

'It's just gone sooo quickly,' Gaia added as she took a sip of her breakfast drink.

'I hope you've enjoyed it, though,' said Jackson, desperate to retreat to the kitchen.

'Oh, yes, I can't wait to come back,' replied Gaia with a grin.

'The time will fly by, I'm sure,' said Jackson, heart heavy at the truth in his response. She'd be here again all too soon, a recurring nightmare. He just hoped that beyond that, the only time he'd see her was on a poster outside Keswick's cinema.

'Before you go,' said Gaia, putting down her glass.

What did she want now? he wondered.

'There was just one thing I wanted to ask . . .'

Jackson clutched the circular drinks tray like it could transform into a shield.

'I don't want you to be offended,' she continued, adding a grimace to give the impression she cared the slightest bit about his feelings.

Jackson pondered what she was about to say in the fleeting moment before she carried on speaking. He'd put together every meal according to her precise dietary requirements, run all of his ideas past her in the first place, there surely couldn't be a problem with anything he'd cooked, could there? Perhaps she wanted to increase the numbers for the wedding breakfast. Make a change to the banquet that had already been agreed. Maybe that was it—

'Why don't you sit down?' said Gaia, indicating the chair beside her.

Jackson could think of a million reasons. He didn't want anything less.

Then Rachel appeared, clasping her notebook and pen. So, it was serious if her PA was here to mediate.

Federico gave him a smile, but it failed to reassure him.

Jackson took a seat. He'd survived their stay so far, he could see it through to the end, he told himself. Though what on earth for, he really didn't know. He couldn't even put any of this on his CV, thanks to the fact he'd had to sign that stupid NDA. But then he thought of the man he'd once been, the way he'd have thrown in the towel long before now, and felt proud of his perseverance. Despite all of the obstacles she'd thrown his way, Gaia had said it herself: she'd really enjoyed her stay. That was a triumph against all the odds that nobody could take away. Yet still, in the second or so it took for her to continue talking, the upholstery beneath him felt as comfortable as if it had been woven from stinging nettles.

'Firstly, thank you for all your hard work,' she said. 'From both of us.' She glanced at Federico beside her. 'You've gone above and beyond and we're very grateful.'

Jackson got the distinct feeling he was about to be served a compliment sandwich. He clutched the sides of the chair.

'But with regard to the wedding,' began Gaia.

They weren't cancelling, were they? Suddenly the only thing worse than welcoming Gaia and her retinue back again in the near future was them reneging on the whole thing altogether. What would that say about Moy? About him? If they called off the current plans and took their business elsewhere. As much as he'd dreaded these last few days, they'd formed the pinnacle of his professional achievements to date. And to have been chosen out of all the other fabulous hotels and restaurants there were, not just locally but worldwide, to host such a prestigious event was a career highlight without doubt. Now it was probably going to be taken off the table, he didn't want it to be—

'We know you've put so much effort into the preparations so far . . .' said Federico, picking up where Gaia had left off. 'And we really appreciate it . . .'

'Was there an issue with the food, is that it?' cut in Jackson, unable to help it. He was desperate to know the cause of their change in heart. Otherwise he'd torture himself for the foreseeable—

Gaia paused, which did nothing for his stress levels. 'No, not at all,' she said, voice lilting with astonishment as though that had never actually been the case before.

'We've left a tip at Reception for each member of staff,' explained Federico.

'Oh,' said Jackson. 'Thank you . . .'

'Don't mention it.' Gaia batted the air. 'Just a small token of our appreciation, for looking after us so well.'

She was buttering him up now. Getting ready to deal her final blow.

'Now, I hope this doesn't cause too much upset.' She shifted in her seat.

At least she had the decency to act as though she was uncomfortable, thought Jackson.

'But the wedding isn't happening anymore.'

'Right.' Jackson couldn't help slumping a little in his chair. 'I'm sorry about that . . .' he mumbled, managing to remember that it couldn't have been the easiest decision for the two of them.

'I know you've already gone to so much trouble, put a lot of work in . . .' Gaia continued, but Jackson had tuned out. All those hours he'd spent practising and perfecting – totally wasted.

'Better for everyone all round, I would have thought,' said Rachel with a nod. She raised her eyebrows at him, as though hoping that might prompt him so speak.

Jackson blinked. He hadn't heard a word of what they'd just said, his mind had been so busy spinning like a spiraliser.

'So let me get this straight,' said Jackson. 'We're not doing anything that we'd planned.'

Gaia pouted like she was genuinely apologetic.

Federico was frowning with concern.

Rachel tapped her pen on her notepad. 'Well, it should take the pressure off you and the other chefs in all honesty, as an informal buffet-style meal would be something you could prepare in advance.' She looked up. 'I did run it past Anna on the way here and she seemed to think you'd be happy for it to be converted into something more relaxed.'

So the dinner was going ahead, but the wedding wasn't, realised Jackson.

'If it's okay with you, we'd like to pare the whole thing down and make it as simple as possible.' Gaia reached for Federico's hand, and they both smiled back at him.

'Sounds good to me,' murmured Jackson, hardly able to believe his own ears.

'*Eccellente*,' said Federico.

'Maybe the party can be out on the terrace if it happens to be a fine night,' suggested Gaia.

The wind rattled the glass doors that led to the patio, as if to say, don't count on it in Cumbria.

'A party,' repeated Jackson, still digesting the developments.

'Yes, for our friends and family,' confirmed Federico.

'All the people who have been there for us,' added Gaia.

'Great – that's sorted then,' said Rachel, snapping shut her notebook and popping the lid on her pen. It was moments like this that reminded her why she'd wanted to be a PA in the first place. The satisfaction of plans coming together. But she couldn't escape the fact that her job seemed to be pulling her and Miles apart at the same time.

Chapter 45

Once she was absolutely sure the guests were out of sight and the boat was reduced to a toy-size miniature on its journey back over to Keswick, Katrine blew out a breath. Her fringe flittered away from her eyes as she exhaled, and for the first time since Gaia and her entourage had arrived three nights ago, she felt calm again.

'Thank goodness for that,' said Jackson beside her. He dropped the hand that had been waving a little too enthusiastically as the visitors left the island.

Anna raised her eyebrows as though she couldn't believe they'd finally gone. 'Well done, everyone,' she said with a nod. 'That was a long few days.'

'Can't wait till they come back next summer,' said Jackson with a big false grin.

'I hate to break the news but I think it'll be before then,' said Katrine as they turned towards the hotel's doorway.

'I hope that's a joke,' said Jackson, with a shake of his head.

'Afraid not,' replied Anna. 'Rachel came to speak to us earlier.' She glanced at Katrine. 'Apparently Gaia's going to be coming a lot more often.'

'You can't be serious,' murmured Jackson, stopping still in the entrance hall.

Katrine made a face. 'Yes . . . She and Federico have both fallen in love with the place, her PA said.' She sat down in front of her computer.

Jackson groaned. 'Ugh, why didn't I think of this? I've been so busy trying to make sure everything's perfect, but it's only going to come back and bite me in the future.'

'Hey, hey,' said Anna. 'I think you'll find we *need* guests to return, Jackson.'

'Yeah, just not those ones,' he muttered, folding his arms to make a pillow for his head on top of the reception desk and sighing dramatically.

'We've had enough diva behaviour these last few days,' said Anna with a roll of her eyes.

'Er, Jackson, I think you might be about to change your tune . . .' said Katrine, peering into the brown paper envelope that had been left beside her keyboard by Rachel at check-out time.

'I doubt that very much,' mumbled Jackson without moving his head. 'Unless you've got written confirmation they just want bowls of chips for this party they're having, and nothing else. I can't survive another experience like this.' Neither of the other two responded to his histrionics, so he carried on. 'I hope they're paying the same fee as they agreed for the wedding,' he muttered. 'We already spent god-knows-how-long chopping and changing everything according to Gaia's latest whim. So. Much. Wasted. Effort,' he huffed. When still no one spoke he stood upright, almost wondering if they'd crept off and left him to vent on his own.

But Katrine and Anna were both standing there looking stunned.

His eyes darted over to the window as he wondered whether Gaia had forgotten something and was on her way back to collect it. But there was no boat anywhere near the landing stage. He turned back to Anna and Katrine. 'Okay, what is it?' he asked.

Katrine tipped the contents of the envelope onto the reception countertop.

'Oh great, a bunch of business cards,' said Jackson, throwing his hands in the air. 'What are they for? In case we miss having some theatrics about the place and want to get in touch? No thanks.'

Katrine held one up to his face between her finger and thumb. 'Flight gift vouchers, Jackson. One for each of us. With five hundred pounds on, to use with any airline.'

He plucked the rectangle of plastic from her grip to inspect it for himself. Flipped it over to see a small Post-it with his name on.

Katrine spread the others out on the oak surface. One for every member of staff.

'There's also a cheque of the same value,' she added, fanning out a bundle of white slips and selecting the one that was his.

Jackson squinted at it. 'They've left us each a tip of a thousand pounds?'

Katrine nodded.

'Well, my opinions can't just be bought.' He folded his arms.

'There's also a thank-you letter,' said Anna.

'Bet the PA wrote it,' he muttered, still processing the unexpected gift.

Anna pointed at the card Katrine had stood up on the oak desk. 'Look inside and see for yourself.'

'All this must have been Federico's idea,' Jackson mumbled as he picked up the greetings card.

But it was signed by Gaia and written in the same looping hand. He started at the top.

To all the staff of the Lake Island Hotel,

Thank you for going out of your way to make our stay so wonderful. We've had delicious food, the most attentive service, and I am grateful for everything you've done, so please enjoy a mini break of your own. You probably all need a holiday now!

Gaia x

Jackson flicked his wrist to look at the picture on the front of the card. It was of a modern impressionist painting of Derwentwater on the front. She'd put some thought into this, he had to admit. He turned the notelet over to look at the back, find out where she'd got it from. An art gallery in Keswick. But there was a further line from the actress too.

Ps. Katrine, when I saw this card, I was reminded of your dad's beautiful watercolour painting. It would make an amazing image for our party invitations! If you didn't mind us using it, I'd be happy to agree a price, but totally understand if you're not keen. It would just make such a lovely souvenir for guests, and mean they have a little piece of the Lake Island Hotel to take away with them! x

'That's actually quite a good idea,' said Jackson showing the secondary message to Katrine. 'Not sure if you've seen this.'

Katrine frowned and started to read the words for herself.

'We could print some to sell at the hotel, too.' He gave a shrug. 'Extra revenue stream.'

Katrine passed the card to Anna. 'Take quite a few greetings card to make a dent in the hotel's debts.'

'Oh god, are things that dire?' asked Jackson.

Anna wafted a hand. 'That's not your concern,' she said with a smile. 'You concentrate on cheffing.'

'As long as the kitchen's still going to be here – I love this job—'

'Didn't sound like it earlier,' shot back Anna.

Jackson shut his mouth and mimed zipping his lips closed.

Anna turned to Katrine. 'What about letting Gaia use the picture for her invitations, how do you feel about that?' she asked.

'Well, it was on the wall for guests to see anyway. There's no sense in keeping it squirrelled away.'

'It belongs to you, you can do what you want with it,' said Anna.

'I'd like you to be able to share it, too. I think it should go back on display outside the dining room,' said Katrine, 'so there's some of Dad here.'

'There always is,' said Anna with a smile at her step-daughter.

Chapter 46

'Good afternoon, madam,' said the flight attendant with a dip of his head, and Rachel grinned back at him as she stepped onto the aircraft after Gaia and Federico. She still felt the thrill of turning left rather than right, glanced round to share the moment with Miles, but his shoulders were hunched as though he'd suddenly found himself in hostile territory rather than surrounded by luxury.

'Are you all right?' she asked in a low tone as they made their way down the aisle towards their pod-style seats.

'Yeah, fine,' he said, but the frown on his brow said otherwise.

'Sure?' Rachel whispered. 'Because we're in first class and you look like we're at a funeral!'

Miles didn't laugh at her quip. 'It's so hushed, we could be.'

'Don't tell me you'd prefer to be back there in economy?' she asked as they reached their allocated areas.

'Yes, I'd be more comfortable,' replied Miles.

'What?' Rachel laid a hand on the butter-smooth leather of the flat-bed seat she was standing beside. 'That's not possible!'

'It really is,' mumbled Miles as he slid into his solitary compartment, looking about as relaxed as someone who'd inadvertently boarded a rocket bound for a space mission.

'I thought you liked it on the way here?' asked Rachel, taking her place opposite.

'I did. In a bucket-list kind of way. But once was enough for me.'

'Not really how it works with a return ticket, is it?' Rachel retorted.

Miles replied with something but the seats were so spaciously arranged it made it quite difficult to have a conversation.

'Glass of champagne?' offered another flight attendant, and as Rachel reached for the chilled flute in front of her, her tongue fizzed with anticipation of the sparkling first sip. She glimpsed the label on the bottle. The good stuff. Vintage. Freshly poured and complimentary. She leaned back against the head rest. If she could just keep Gaia in check, maintain this new balance, then the job really wasn't so bad. People paid *thousands* to have this kind of treatment just once in their lives, and here she was travelling the world completely free—

'Are you going to tell me what Gaia was speaking to you about earlier in the lounge?' said Miles, head peeking around the corner of his pod.

'When we can sit down together and talk properly, yes,' said Rachel, peering over the top of hers. She wafted a hand between them to indicate that it was hard to conduct an in-depth chat in their current circumstances. 'I don't want to have an argument across the aisle . . .'

Miles raised his eyebrows at her choice of phrase.

Rachel opened her mouth as though she was about to correct what she'd said, but closed it again.

'Right,' said Miles, disappearing back out of sight. He closed his eyes against all the accoutrements that came with possessing a premium plane ticket. Although he was ensconced in possibly the most sumptuous seat imaginable, that exchange with Rachel had left him in absolutely no doubt as to where he stood.

Miles looked out of the cab window at the bumper-to-bumper cars inching along the road either side of them as they crossed West Century Boulevard, and couldn't help thinking that downtown LA was like an artist's depiction of the exact opposite of the Lake District. Gone were the lush greens and blues of nature's landscape paintings, and in their place hung vast digital portraits of manmade things: advertising billboards filled with all the stuff humans didn't really need.

He turned to Rachel on the backseat beside him, but she was tapping away on her phone, engrossed in catching up on the emails she'd received in the time it had taken them to pass through security and baggage reclaim.

She must have sensed his gaze on her, as she glanced up. 'Can't wait to get home,' she said, more out of habit rather than because she meant it, thought Miles, going by the way she didn't even take a moment to meet his eye. Her focus was entirely on the touchscreen device clutched in her hands.

So, their normal routine had resumed. Back to being three of them in the relationship. He sank back in the taxi's rear seat. But then a realisation struck him as forcibly as if it had flashed up on one of the brightly lit billboards. There was definitely an unbreakable couple in this situation, but neither of the two people involved were him.

Chapter 47

'You're not going over to Gaia's now, are you?' said Miles, looking up from bundling laundry into the washing machine. It felt strange being back in the apartment; he knew where everything was, but it all felt unfamiliar at the same time. The foundations of their life together had shifted since they'd last been here.

'Only for an hour,' said Rachel, already ordering a cab bound for the Hollywood Hills on her phone.

In that precise split second, Miles realised that Rachel was equally responsible for maintaining the electronic umbilical cord that connected her to Gaia as her boss was.

'We both know that means you'll be home at bedtime, then,' he mumbled. It was almost 7 p.m.

'We didn't have any other plans, though, did we?' she asked, still not glancing up. It was a statement, not a question: Rachel could probably memorise a month's worth of upcoming engagements, it was that kind of diligence that made her the best in the business.

'No,' he replied, wondering if he ought to schedule a slot to spend time with her on a calendar app.

'It's an idea she just had. If it happened, it would be so exciting,' replied Rachel still not looking up. 'I'll tell you all about it when I'm back and I've got all the details.' She finally glanced at him. 'Gaia's being so different, you know – almost unrecognisable from the person she was before.'

Miles bit his lip, thinking the same could be said about her.

'How about Rome?' suggested Harry, spinning the gift card between his fingers. 'Federico was talking about it on the ferry, and it sounds fascinating.'

'I've always wanted to go there,' said Katrine, leaning forward to select one of the canapés they'd plated up from the cluster of cardboard boxes that Jackson had bundled them off with when they'd left the hotel, declaring that he didn't want to look at anything that reminded him of Gaia's stay for a single second longer. Harry had spread the surplus hors d'oeuvres out on the coffee table, and as they'd sat cross-legged on the floor either side of it, toasting each other with mugs of tea, the living room of their little flat transformed into a private dining space, and their dinner of leftovers became an unparalleled feast.

Harry reached for one of the artichoke arancini. 'Ooh,' he said as he popped it into his mouth. 'Ah.' He waggled a hand in front of his lips as the pesto centre burst on his tongue.

'Very hot,' interpreted Katrine.

'Why, thank you,' said Harry, pulling a pose like she'd complimented him.

Katrine laughed, primarily at the smudge of sauce on his chin. She passed him a kitchen-roll napkin.

'So, is that our destination decided, then?' said Harry.

'Sounds wonderful to me,' said Katrine. She pictured the two of them gazing out over the city from a wrought-iron balcony at a boutique hotel. Imagined the sites she'd seen in guidebooks brought to life, seeing ruins that made time rewind, for real. 'Shall we book it?'

'Now?' said Harry, offering her the last leek and sun-dried tomato bite.

Katrine cut the little roundel in half, took her share as she spoke. 'Why not?'

'Don't want to mull it over anymore?' he said, picked up his portion of canapé.

'Well, sometimes you can overthink things, can't you?' She gave him a wry smile.

'I suppose so,' he said, sensing the inference. He leaned forward to kiss her. 'I'll go and get my laptop.' He scrambled to his feet. 'Oof,' he said, clutching his stomach. 'Too much famous-person food,' he added, as though it was a recognised cuisine. He heard Katrine's laughter follow him down the corridor as he went into the next room. His laptop wasn't in the kitchen, but there was something else he needed to do first. He opened a cupboard door.

'You can't be looking for biscuits, surely?' shouted Katrine with a giggle. 'I couldn't eat another thing!'

'Just fancied something sweet to finish,' he called, savouring the moment. He could taste metallic nervousness on his tongue, the kind he'd once felt when he was just about to go on stage.

He took out the cereal box from the shelf beside his head. Reached in to take out the half-empty packet from inside and placed it on the counter.

'Oh, go on, bring me one too, then!' called Katrine, hearing the tell-tale rustle of cellophane. 'Don't just gobble the whole lot in the kitchen. Especially if it's those chocolate ones . . .'

'Okay!' Harry stifled a boyish laugh as he reached into the cardboard container to take out the duck-egg blue box concealed beneath. It had been there for weeks. Katrine had stood next to it every morning as she made her toast.

He felt a frisson of risk, the kind where life presented a forked choice of two paths. He considered stuffing the little leather-clad square back where it had come from and waiting till they were somewhere more far-flung and photogenic. A flight away from here, at least. Rome would be perfect.

He heard Katrine start to clear away the plates from the coffee table. Shortly she would come in here, wondering where the laptop and the biscuits were. What was taking so long?

But the question *he* wanted to ask had been brewing inside him for months now. He listened to the clatter of cutlery on crockery, felt his stomach clench involuntarily. It wasn't very fitting to do it here, in a superficial sense, but what was the point of saving it for a time in the future that was supposedly more special yet so much less personal? Nowhere felt as fully theirs as this little flat with their odd selection of furniture and a thousand tiny reminders of their time together. Like the ticket from their trip to the pencil museum, that stayed tucked inside the paperback on her bedside table, always used as a bookmark, like he was part of every bit of her story.

He heard her footsteps. She was seconds away.

'Katrine?' he called, voice quavering like it had last done in auditions long ago. 'Can you please wait there?'

'Why? What's happened?' she replied and he pictured the furrow on her forehead, half-hidden by her fringe.

'Nothing,' he replied truthfully, for it hadn't yet. 'It's about to,' he shouted back, and took a deep breath.

Miles switched off the TV. He hadn't a clue what was happening on the screen, his mind hadn't been on the programme. He put the remote down, could hear the hustle and hurry of the city outside now, a far cry from the calm and quiet of the Lake Island Hotel. He looked round the apartment, at the objects he and Rachel had accumulated, all the markers of a shared a life. But yet he felt alone. The picture frame with a photograph taken at a friend's party felt like an unkind reminder that things had once felt different. Rachel had her arms flung around him. He remembered how his face had hurt from grinning so much. She'd left a lipstick mark on his cheek, without even meaning to. That was how it had been back then, unintentional, inescapable. Far harder to stay apart than to be pulled back together. He touched the exact patch of skin on the side of his neck where she'd first kissed him, before they were even a proper couple, when potential had shimmered in the air like a mirage. But perhaps they were holding on when they shouldn't. Clinging to a firecracker that was about to explode.

He heard the front door of the apartment open and close.

He wondered if now was the right time to speak to her, then realised such a moment didn't really exist.

He stood up from the sofa, then sat down again. Didn't know what to do with his hands.

'Hi,' said Rachel as she came into the room, as though she'd found a stranger there instead of him. 'You're still up!' She smiled as she put her handbag down on the dining table.

'I thought we were going to talk,' replied Miles.

'Now?' she glanced at the clock as though he'd been the one to just walk in.

'Well, I wasn't sure when else,' Miles said honestly.

She came to sit beside him on the sofa. 'What about?' she said, smile fading with the last of the day.

'You said you were going to tell me about Gaia's idea.'

'Oh, yes.' Rachel gave a yawn as she nodded, as though it wasn't physically possible for her to do only one thing at once. 'She had a whole bunch actually. It's really exciting,' she continued, eyes glittering beneath the living-room spotlights despite her evident tiredness. 'She wants to move into theatre. Do a play.'

'Oh, okay.' Miles watched her as she spoke. Her skin shone, and her hair shivered about her shoulders as she described Gaia's wishes: she wanted to do a short-run show to begin with, somewhere less intimidating than Broadway . . .

Rachel was in her element, he realised, already planning, determined to make meetings happen, put wheels in motion.

Encouraging a change in the dynamic in hers and Gaia's relationship had been the best thing he could have done. It had indeed made her happier. She was more appreciated. Had proved to her boss she was indispensable. And that's what you cared about when you loved someone. She was more in control of her life, less at Gaia's beck and call. But maybe it was time for him to create some more space for her to flourish too. He was reminded of the plants that spilled over one another in the grounds of the Lake Island Hotel. The pink-flowered rhododendrons, that he hadn't known the name of, that the owner had told him could poison the soil for other shrubs trying to grow nearby.

'So we might get another holiday,' finished Rachel. 'I hadn't taken any annual leave up till now so I've still got loads.'

No break for just the two of them, then, thought Miles, feeling the roots of his realisation start to spread.

'And the new film – the historical one – that sounds incredible,' Rachel continued. 'It's all top secret at the moment so I can't say much but the cast –' she quivered with delight – 'the crème de la crème of the acting world.'

'Oh, wow,' said Miles. It was a strange sensation, feeling such sadness that their romance had turned out to be only a novella, but a distinct surge of joy at the fact he could practically see her wings unfurling in front of his eyes.

'Sounds like quite a bit of travel,' she added with a grimace. 'So I'm sorry about that in advance.'

'You honestly don't need to be.' She shouldn't have to apologise for something that she found so fulfilling.

'Oh, thank you, for understanding.'

'Don't mention it.' He reached for her hand, and as their fingers touched he felt her jolt. 'Sorry, I almost forgot – how was your night?'

He nodded. 'Okay.' What had he really done apart from wait for her to come home? Since when had he lost sight of his own contentment completely? He fidgeted, as though the thought was a circling fly that could be shooed away. 'Did some chores.' He jerked his head in the direction of the washing machine. More often than not it was his brain that felt like it was on spin mode.

'Thank you,' said Rachel, squeezing his palm.

This was it now, thought Miles. He'd lit the touchpaper; there was no extinguishing the fuse now it had sparked into flame inside his mind. This was the last few seconds of togetherness before the eruption. The brief lull before the bang.

'Is everything all right?' Rachel asked, angling her body further towards his on the sofa.

He could feel his own pulse thumping in his palm.

Rachel clasped his fingers tighter as though she too knew this was the last time their skin would touch, that it was the moment they were both about to finally let go.

Chapter 48

'I feel silly in this, and scruffy in a jumper,' said Will, tugging at the cuffs of his tailored jacket as he stood in front of the full-length mirror in the bedroom. He looked over at Anna, wondering whether she hadn't heard him beneath her towel turban.

But when he opened his mouth to express the same sentiment in a different linguistic format, Anna held up her palms. 'I honestly don't think anyone will be looking at us,' she said. She'd never seen anyone appear less comfortable than he did now. Even chefs in the middle of service weren't as flushed about the face. 'You're absolutely fine in a shirt.'

'Really?' Will huffed a sigh of relief, started pulling the woollen sweater back over his head.

'It's too hot for this,' he mumbled through the fabric.

'Why don't you get some fresh air,' Anna suggested, tilting her head in the direction of the window. She knew the cool of the late-afternoon garden would soothe him.

'Good idea. I'll wait for you outside,' said Will, smoothing his hair in the mirror before disappearing down the landing.

They'd lived together for almost a year, discovered the foibles that took four seasons to bloom. After Dominik had died, she never imagined weaving the strands of her life with someone else's, let alone Will's, but once again the garden had whispered its ancient wisdom. She'd been adamant she had everything she needed. What she lacked after Dominik had gone wasn't replaceable. The space he'd occupied in her heart couldn't simply be replanted. She had her friends and family to nourish her soul. Wanted nothing more. But like leaves stretched towards the sun, she'd found herself content to be in Will's company. She'd witnessed the time-old lesson of natural balance in the great outdoors so often, yet still, their relationship had come as a surprise. They were so different, in all sorts of ways, yet they'd found a harmony she usually saw among the plants and herbs they spent their days tending.

She'd only really realised what was happening when they'd sown the leeks and carrots side by side in the soil. As she and Will had sat on the bench afterwards, sipping ice-cold cordial in the spring-scented garden, they'd discussed the benefits of putting certain vegetables in close proximity. Companion planting. And it had occurred to her there and then that people could bring out the best in each other, too.

She looked at herself in the mirror, smoothed the dress she'd last worn several summers ago. She was accessorising it with a few more wrinkles now, and a slightly longer, softer hairstyle now she wasn't working in the steam and sizzle of the commercial kitchen on a daily basis. Ageing wasn't as straightforward as ticking boxes off on a calendar or seconds on a clock. She swept on a slick of mascara. Blinked at herself in the mirror. Another incarnation of Anna. One that had wedge heels on and was off to the theatre.

The clouds had gathered above Keswick as though they too wanted to watch the play. The chatter from the queue waiting outside the building by the lake shore echoed out across the water. Anna had been able to see and hear the crowd accumulating as they crossed on the boat.

'Have the best time,' Harry said as they reached the jetty on the other side.

'Enjoy going into town,' she replied, as he moored the boat with her stepdaughter by his side. 'We're going to try that new Italian place for dinner,' Katrine added. 'Relive being in Rome.' She clasped her hands together, and the solitaire stone on her left one winked star-like against the grey canvas of the Cumbrian sky. 'See you tomorrow, though.'

'Looking forward to it,' said Will.

It had come around so quickly, Gaia and Federico's summer party for their friends and family, thought Anna. What had once been twelve months in the future was now less than twenty-four hours away.

'The longest day of the year . . .' she said aloud. It couldn't have been a more fitting date for the event, she thought to herself; of course, Gaia would want the maximum amount of sunshine, it was nature's spotlight.

'Sorry, I should have let you do this, skipper,' said Harry to Will as he finished winding the length of rope around the landing stage. 'Force of habit.' He stood up and handed Will the keys with a grin. 'All yours. But call me if you have any problems.'

'Aye aye, Captain,' replied Will with a nod. 'You can relax, though. I can remember everything.' He'd trained on the boat in preparation for deputising during Harry and Katrine's trip away, but once they'd come back, he found he'd yearned for the exhilaration he'd felt out on the lake, the sense of liberation, the luxury of being surrounded by incomparable views in every direction. So now he did the odd shift when Harry wanted to be spelled off. Harry got a break, and he got his fix of feeling the breeze brush his face, ruffle his hair, remind him he was *alive*, part of this incredible landscape he was lucky enough to call home. The perspective out on the water was like nothing else. It was why Anna loved her wild swimming; he understood that now. He came back to the hotel after a full day of ferrying guests to and from Keswick revitalised, not only full of conversation from the people he'd met, but refreshed from being right at the beating heart of the most beautiful place imaginable, in his opinion.

'Right, we'd better get going,' said Harry. 'Our booking's at seven.'

Katrine looped her arm through his. 'I'll be in early to do the last-minute prep for the party,' she said to Anna, before the pair of them set off along the lakeside path.

Will raised his hand in a wave, then turned back towards the theatre's entrance. 'Ooh, people are starting to go in,' he said excitedly, indicating the moving line of ticketholders.

'Come on, then,' said Anna, and as she took his hand, she twisted her head sideways to look at the Lake Island Hotel opposite before they passed through the doors into the foyer. She'd stood not so far away from this spot, over there in Crow Park, where Katrine and Harry were walking alongside now, all those years ago, could never have pictured being in this position, but at that very moment, the present felt like just as much of a gift.

Chapter 49

Anna had been here before in the past, but this evening there was palpable suspense in the atmosphere. The auditorium had a collective energy unlike anything she'd ever experienced. The eagerness of an audience keen to see a show was mixed with something more tonight. The unmistakable allure of a once-in-a-lifetime opportunity. As the lights dimmed and a hush descended, four hundred pairs of eyes were fixed on the stage, waiting for the crimson drapes to be raised. But before they were given their first glimpse of the person they were really all here to see, a woman wearing a black T-shirt and a microphone headset strode out into the centre of the platform to address the rapt spectators.

'Ladies and gentlemen, it is my utmost privilege to welcome you here to the Theatre by the Lake tonight, for the final performance of an unbelievably special production that quite frankly we are still pinching ourselves about having the pleasure of putting on,' she began. 'It came as no surprise to anyone that this was a sell-out run, but the level of interest has been unprecedented. We couldn't have anticipated the dramatically positive effect it's had in terms of support for the arts. The uplift in funds and sales for future productions has been extraordinary, but most importantly, the renewed enthusiasm amongst young people is what's truly remarkable. Storytelling has always been an important part of our heritage, and championing local voices and new talent is at the heart of what we do, so we are over the moon to announce that our guest of honour is in fact now a patron of our theatre.'

A hum of wonder rippled around the room.

'I'd like to take this opportunity to show our deep appreciation. So please join me in putting your hands together for . . .'

But the rest of the stage manager's sentence was drowned out by the spontaneous applause that erupted around the auditorium.

'Gaia?' said the stage director. 'Curtain up.'

She nodded back, and drew a long, controlled breath into her body using her diaphragm. It wasn't like when she was filming, all the lines had to be ready in her head. She exhaled slowly, tried to push the negative thoughts from her mind, quiet the voice that told her she couldn't do it. She walked out onto the darkened stage, and in the seconds before the lights went up and the play started, she saw the enthralled faces of Sarah and her sister Hannah, the girls she'd rescued from Derwentwater, sitting on the front row with their nanna. This was why she was doing this. She stood up tall. Sucked in another deep breath. Remembered how it had felt when she'd been a kid, watching from the rows of seats she was now staring out at. The escape of being whisked off to another world for an hour and a half, far away from her everyday existence, and sinking into a captivating story. And who knew, she might even inspire someone from the next generation.

The stage manager gave her her cue, and she felt a rush of adrenalin flood her system. This was it. The play had begun.

Rachel settled down in her seat. Tried to still her racing brain. It was rare that she had the chance to sit back and be entertained, and she wondered whether she had the ability anymore. It had been a while, and Miles had always teased her for her lack of chill. A memory flashed through her mind like a movie trailer: the time they'd caught a show together in New York. She squashed it, attempted to focus on the tale unfolding on the stage. But before long her attention slipped to the list of tasks jotted in the notebook jutting out of her handbag by her feet. She was excited about the meeting they'd just scheduled with Anna for the day after tomorrow . . . She blinked, tried to concentrate on what the characters were saying, but wondered whether she ought to have stayed at the hotel and cracked on with work like she had done the previous nights. She repositioned herself in the seat, accidentally nudged Sarah's elbow in the process, making the poor girl jump, yanking her from the action and catapulting her back to the present.

'Sorry,' she murmured.

Perhaps Sarah would have minded more if Rachel hadn't just given her and the two other members of her family tickets to a Hollywood premiere plus flights and spending money, but she smiled and turned back to the play.

Rachel trained her gaze on Gaia again. She was good. Really good. It didn't take more than a couple of minutes to discern that much, whatever the material she'd been given. Anyone could appreciate that. The nuanced mannerisms and natural delivery of her lines was what transported her viewers to an alternate universe, where the protagonist in front of them was a living, breathing person just like anyone else—

A blueish bright light was visible in the corner of her eye, distracting her once more: Federico's mobile, illuminated further along the row. He'd obviously pulled it from his pocket and been paralysed with surprise, for he failed to shield the screen for several seconds despite the performance being in full flow. And so the sheer size of the latest iPhone model combined with his delayed response conspired to mean the screen was clearly within Rachel's sight. She couldn't quite read the name that was displayed, but the accompanying picture was clear as day. Victoria Cole was calling. The face in the photograph was as instantly recognisable as Gaia's. But why was she ringing Federico? Rachel leaned over to get one last look, make absolutely certain it wasn't a hallucination, just as a disgruntled murmur of disapproval started to rise up at that end of the row and Federico swiftly put the offending electronic away.

Chapter 50

The applause was deafening. For all the high-profile films she'd done, there was nothing that compared to the exuberance of a live audience, seeing the lit-up expressions on people's faces, their heads thrown back in reverence, arms raised to clap. A thunderous wave of foot-stamping made the auditorium vibrate. People were turning to each other to exclaim how brilliant the performance had been. She'd raised the roof, finished the run with a bang. She took her final bow, soaking in the sound of the crowd, revelling in the fact it had been a resounding success. As she made her way backstage, she couldn't resist looking over to where her mum and dad were standing, in the centre of the ongoing ovation, just like they had been when she was at school in her first lead role. There was something immensely gratifying about coming full circle, being back where it had all begun. That five-year-old girl who was mesmerised by the Christmas pantomime would be proud. She no longer felt like an imposter. Dared to believe that she'd *made it*. And not because she'd moved to America, starred in globally successful films – but because, despite all the rehearsals and line-learning, the costume and the makeup, deep down she knew she was no longer pretending to be someone she wasn't. At last she was at peace with herself, comfortable in her own skin. Surrounded by people who cared about her, and in the place that had always been her home.

The rapturous reception she'd received was still ringing in her ears as she reached her dressing room, and she relished the silent solitude awaiting her inside. She sat down on the armchair, wanting to bask in the elation she felt. Everything was finally falling into place. She'd given the performance of her life, remembered every word of the script, impressed herself as well as everyone else with the amount of emotion she'd imbued in the role. And to top it all off, she'd found Federico, her utterly perfect fiancé. She pressed her hands to her cheeks. She was glad she'd found a sense of peace at last, had the confidence to drop the façade she'd spent so long constructing over in LA, at least around those who really loved her. She thought of her parents and the people who'd known her all along. They cherished the real Grace. The girl who'd had a childhood wish to tread the boards at the Theatre by the Lake and had gone and done it. She pictured Mrs Watson, beaming at her from her seat on night one. The sincerity of their support was more precious than any promotional partnership or publicity campaign. Genuine connections were the riches to chase. Strong relationships were the assets that truly mattered. And that had to start by being comfortable with yourself. Why hadn't she realised that till now?

She stood up, suddenly wanting to wriggle free of her stage outfit and brush the firm-hold spray from her hair. She gently pulled off her frock, was about to put it back on a hanger for the costume department rather than leave it in a crumpled pile for them to deal with like she once would have, when a knock on the door interrupted her thoughts. She pictured her parents patiently waiting for her to finish getting changed on the other side and quickly threw on her dressing gown. She opened the door a crack, just in case: the ingrained fear of a crazed fan finding her was something she wouldn't be able to shake, unlike other elements of her persona. She could feel her heartrate increase in the instant before she saw who was standing there in the corridor. She clutched her robe tighter – but it was Federico, with a huge bunch of ruby roses and a radiant smile.

Chapter 51

Rachel didn't know whether to say anything about what she'd seen. It seemed a shame to spoil her boss's high spirits when it was probably nothing. Just a nuisance call from an ex that Federico had clearly had to fend off. And even if Victoria was still trying to get him back, it wasn't something Gaia needed to worry about right now, not before the party later. It would ruin it. As her PA, Rachel saw it as her job to protect her from unnecessary problems like this. She wanted to make sure the celebrations tonight went as well as possible, and until there was something properly concerning to report, she'd shield Gaia from any extra stress, as she always did. In the meantime, she'd do her best to ascertain the reason why Victoria Cole was still trying to contact him.

She lay diagonally across the king-size bed in the Latrigg room. She'd asked Katrine if she could swap from Bleaberry, the one she and Miles had shared last time. Didn't see the sense in needlessly bringing up thoughts of being here with him, on this stay. But memories couldn't be confined to rooms, and recollections from her previous trip to the Lake

Island Hotel seemed to steal under the door and seep into her head.

She sat up. She told herself life was far simpler now. She could concentrate on work without always feeling that she was failing as a girlfriend. Unless you were a fairytale pair like Gaia and Federico, made for each other, then it was easier to be single.

She walked into the bathroom, began to run warm water into the tub. She had an hour and a half before she wanted to be downstairs doing her last checks with Katrine. But since the party had been streamlined, turned into a small, sophisticated occasion for Gaia's nearest and dearest, she had a much-reduced remit. She poured lemon verbena bubbles into the bath and the citrussy fragrance filled the room. She was looking forward to the party, she thought, as she swirled her fingers through the froth. She had her duties, of course, couldn't entirely switch off, but it was a definite perk, being back here in the exquisite surroundings of the Lake Island Hotel.

As she sank back in the roll-topped tub, she briefly wondered whether Miles ever thought of their holiday here. If his mind ever flitted to her, to them. Their break to the Lakes had been a dreamlike interlude in their latterly fraught relationship. Maybe if they'd lived in permanent luxury with all the wealth in the world, it would have worked, she thought drily. He'd moved out of their apartment days after they'd returned home and they hadn't spoken at all in several months. She massaged the matching body wash onto her skin, filled her senses with the zesty scent of the foam. And as the start time of the festivities drew closer, her brain filled with thoughts of champagne flutes and fireworks and Miles was forgotten, like the soap suds she swilled away down the drain.

* * *

'You look *magnifica*,' Gaia heard Federico exclaim from behind her as she fastened her sapphire earrings in place. The asymmetrical floor-length dress fitted her perfectly, the one-shouldered, cut-out-midriff design accentuating her toned physique, and the knot motif at the side of her waist making a playful nod to the fact this was the only one being tied tonight at the non-wedding.

'*E anche tu*,' she said, catching his eye in the mirror. His shirt was the shade of Derwentwater at midnight, and when he moved, the shape of his muscles was visible beneath.

He wrapped his arms around her middle and kissed her neck, just below her left earlobe, making the teardrop jewellery she was wearing tremble. She twisted her head so her mouth met his lips, the luckiest girl in the world. She had everything she could ever wish for. Couldn't help feeling as though it might have been a mistake to delay the marriage. Really, what were they waiting for? The sooner she was Mrs De Angelis the better—

Federico's phone began to vibrate on the bedside table.

He stepped back, went over to the nightstand, but didn't answer the call, just put the mobile in his trouser pocket.

'Everything okay?' asked Gaia, fixing a curl of hair that wasn't falling just so.

'Yes, it was only Si,' he said. 'Probably ringing to wish us a good time. He'll be sad to be missing tonight.'

'You can speak,' said Gaia. 'Call him back.' She knew how much he cared about his team's welfare. Didn't even employ a permanent security officer, preferred to treat the bodyguards that he hired to escort him to industry events more like friends, not members of staff. He refused to have a PA, because he believed in being as self-sufficient as possible. 'See how he's doing,' she encouraged, giving Federico a nod. She knew he'd been upset by the fact that Si had fallen sick a couple of days before they were due to fly, felt bereft he wouldn't be here to attend the thank-you party. 'There's plenty of time before everyone arrives. And I've got a couple of questions to run past Rachel anyway so I can leave you to it,' she said, bending down to unlock the safe at the base of the double-doored antique wardrobe.

'It's fine. Don't want to make him jealous,' said Federico, spritzing cologne on his wrist. 'He should be resting anyway,' he added with a shake of his head. 'I've told him he works too much.'

Gaia smiled up at him.

'Oh, can you pass me my watch, *amore mio*,' he said as she twisted the combination lock to the date of the day they'd first met.

'Of course,' she said, as the numbers aligned and she opened the door to hand it to him. Then she reached inside for her engagement ring, the finishing touch to her showstopping look. She'd missed having it on her finger while she'd been performing in the play, felt naked without the weight of it.

She swept her hand from side to side against the cool metal interior. Leaned closer. She stared. The safe was empty.

'It's gone,' she said, a shiver travelling down her spine like an ice cube had been slipped down the back of her dress.

'What has?' said Federico, coming to stand beside her.

'My ring.' She pinched the part of the fourth finger on her left hand where it usually sat as though she could make it appear again, like a magician. 'It's not there.'

'What, it's vanished today, while we've been out? Could you have dropped it somewhere?'

She shook her head. 'No, I definitely put it in there.' She nodded at the safe. 'I know I did,' she added with a frown. She crouched down to have a second look. It was completely bare.

'Are you sure?' asked Federico, kneeling next to her. 'Hang on, we need to be able to see better.' He took out his phone to switch on the torch app. But the screen was already lit up. An unknown number was displayed at the top. Gaia watched as he cancelled the call. The twitch in his jaw told her this had happened before. If only he had someone like Rachel to shield him from such things, he'd save himself a lot of trouble, she thought with a surge of irritation. She'd told him so, so many times.

He turned on the flashlight function, but desperation was making her impatient. 'Can I have it, please?' she asked, snatching the phone from him and peering into the safety deposit box first, then into the bowels of the wardrobe. But she knew she hadn't dropped it. She had a photographic memory, unmatched powers of recall – could recite an entire play line by line. She wasn't mistaken. The ten-carat cushion-cut diamond had been stolen.

Chapter 52

'It's okay,' said Federico, wrapping her in a hug.

It's only a ring, Gaia forced herself to think. It wasn't a kidnapped person. Nothing had happened to either of them.

'I'll go to the reception desk downstairs, speak to Katrine about it,' said Federico, stepping back.

Gaia nodded. 'Thank you.' She touched the area of skin where the ring ought to be, again.

'We'll sort it out, all right?' said Federico as he walked towards the door.

He was a good influence, she thought as she watched him leave the room. Had a calm logic, which was a helpful foil to her more impulsive method of problem solving: immediately involving Rachel.

She sat down on the bed in his absence, tried to stop her mind from spooling through worst-case scenarios. Surely no one at the Lake Island Hotel could have taken it. But she hadn't exactly been the ideal guest the last time she'd visited, and there would more than likely be a way of resetting the safe if the number combination had been forgotten by a guest.

But there was a nagging in her gut that she couldn't ignore, an inkling that there could be more to the situation.

Most of all, she wanted to make sure her family were safe. She pictured her mum and dad arriving, delighted to be setting foot on the idyllic island in the middle of the lake. What if she was putting them at risk? She stood up. With no Si, there was only Chris in charge of security. She needed to talk to him. The ring was of little consequence in the whole scheme of things. It was an expensive item, of course, but she had insurance she could claim on. It would be all right. But her loved ones, they were irreplaceable.

Rachel was at the top of the stairs, one hand on the burnished curve of the banister, about to descend to the entrance hall below. 'Is everything all right?' she asked as her boss appeared on the landing, looking dazzling in her carpet-skimming, palest-blue ballgown, the one Rachel had thought she might choose from the bespoke selection of designer creations she'd collated ahead of the occasion. She congratulated herself fleetingly, but then noticed the expression topping off the look. 'What's wrong?' she said, retracing her steps and trying to pre-empt what could be the matter.

'Have you seen Federico?' asked Gaia, her gaze flitting down to the ground floor. The reception area was empty apart from Katrine, sitting at the front desk.

'No,' replied Rachel. 'He's probably checking everything's ready for the party,' she said with a smile. He was so proactive and personable; he really was like something straight out of a fantasy. 'Is there anything I can help with?' she added. As far as she knew, she had all bases covered, but it was a matter of personal pride to triple check.

Gaia shook her head. 'No.' She resolved to forget about the ring for the time being. Money and material possessions were resolutely not the focus of the night. Her beloved guests would start to filter in through the hotel's front doors any minute now, and there was no point blighting the evening over a missing ring.

Gaia cleared her throat and cast her eye around the buzzing terrace. The sky was a peach-haze blaze of pinks and yellows. The lake below was flecked with flickering gold.

Federico was grinning at her from in between her parents and Mrs Watson. '*Ti amo*,' he mouthed. Love didn't need proving with a ring, she realised that now.

She straightened her back and smoothed a breeze-loosened strand of hair from her cheek as she looked around at everyone standing on the flagstones in front of her. These faces before her were what made her fortunate. How she had failed to see it any earlier, she didn't know. She opened her mouth to make her speech, careful to meet the eye of every single invitee present as she spoke. She glanced at Rachel, and at Chris beside her, and thought of all the ways they went above and beyond in order to ensure her life was as easy as possible. It was long overdue that she showed some appreciation, and this evening was at least a start.

Rachel saw Federico making his way over to his fiancée and tried not to stare, but it was hard not to in the presence of such a pair. She glanced over at Chris, who was constantly checking the periphery, the only guest still one-hundred-per-cent on duty. She'd spoken to Gaia about a suitable bonus; it only seemed fair in the circumstances. She took a sip from her sparkling flute, felt the liquid gold hit her system like she was physically drinking in luxury. *This was the life.*

Chapter 53

Chris's forehead was so deeply creased, it reminded her of Crinkle Crags. 'You'd better come in,' he said, with a quick flick of his hand to motion Gaia through the door.

Hopegill was much smaller than the Blencathra suite, but its more modest dimensions soothed her, made her feel cosier, like she was in a silk-lined womb. She sat down on the splat back chair beside the desk and turned to face Chris, his features so familiar he was virtually a family member. But as she glanced around, at the toiletries neatly lined up on the dressing table, and the paperback police procedural by the bedside, she realised she knew next to nothing about him, despite placing her safety in his hands every day. She ought to make more of an effort. Take a leaf out of Federico's book and take an interest in her staff. The financial reward for all of his hard work that Rachel had suggested was an excellent idea.

'This isn't easy to say, and I imagine it's harder to hear,' Chris began, scratching his chin.

It took all of Gaia's newfound restraint not to tell him to hurry up and just blurt out whatever it was. It was nearly one in the morning, and her feet were aching.

'But I'm afraid I've just spoken to Si on the phone . . .'

Gaia frowned. His tone was so serious she wondered if his condition had taken a turn for the worse. If that was the case, Federico would be so concerned. It surely had to be why Chris was telling her, instead of him. She pressed her fingertips to her lips as she waited for her bodyguard to continue.

'Actually, I think we'd better get Rachel . . .' he said, already reaching for his phone.

Chapter 54

The storm was so wild Gaia wondered whether their flight would even be able to take off. She put a hand on her stomach in anticipation of the turbulence to come. Swallowed the wave of worry that rose up inside her.

'I can't wait to get back to LA,' she said lightly, looking out of the window of the Land Rover at the sideways slants of rain.

'Me too,' said Federico, reaching for her hand across the backseat. The bare skin where her ring had once been seemed to burn as she laced her fingers with his.

Gaia bid goodbye to the Lakes through the glass from her passenger-side seat. The tops of the mountains were shrouded in cloud, as though they couldn't bear to look. She couldn't quite believe what the last twelve hours had made clear.

The rest of the journey to the airport passed in a blur of damp grey.

The further they got from Cumbria, the more drained she started to feel, like she'd left some of herself behind in the county. It wasn't so much the ring she seemed to have lost, but the sense of being Grace that she'd gained.

She slipped on her shades as they approached Departures, and the sky outside the car turned to black.

'Don't be sad, *amore mio*,' said Federico as she pulled on her baseball cap too. 'You can come back soon.'

And as the Land Rover drew to a standstill, Gaia took solace from the fact that was true.

Rachel had only half watched the rom-com on the in-flight entertainment system, and hadn't even touched her meal, despite the first-class food being so good. She glanced over at Gaia, but she had her face covered with an eye mask, the rest of her body cocooned in a blanket. They'd be landing soon, and her brain fast-forwarded to what would happen once they arrived at LAX. She glimpsed Gaia's passport in her handbag alongside her own as she reached for her organiser; running through events in her mind helped settled her. She was always prepared, equipped for every situation. Except this one.

The plane seemed to bounce down on the tarmac more harshly than usual, as though demonstrating they were coming back to reality with a bump. Gaia felt the impact in her bones; being in this part of the aircraft couldn't entirely shelter you from the outside world. She understood that now. And she knew her life as she knew it was about to crash down with force.

They disembarked first, as priority passengers. Gaia followed Federico down the aisle, desperate to breathe fresh oxygen after the unnatural, over-conditioned environment of the flight. But it wasn't the same pure, foliage-fragranced air that had filled her lungs in the Lake District that she experienced when she passed through the plane door. She missed it already, the aroma of home. Craved its fortifying earth-scented essence. Could really have used a blast of it now. But even that wouldn't have helped quell the nausea in her stomach.

The atmosphere in the air bridge was equally as stuffy. Her feet moved automatically, but she felt faint. She looked across at Rachel, by her side now as they approached the terminal, but her proximity wasn't a comfort. Nothing could be. Her chest thudded the same way it had when she'd rescued the Cumbrian swimmers, but this time she was saving herself.

Gaia had seen the films, she knew more than most how it worked, but when it actually happened for real it made her whole body shake with shock. The second they stepped inside the airport building; the signal was given and the uniformed officers descended. And despite her affluence and her A-list status, all she really wanted in that moment was to be transported back to Borrowdale to be with her mum and dad.

Chapter 55

Even the chandelier in the entrance hall gave the impression it was shedding a tear, as it scattered confetti-like sparkles across the sweeping staircase. The bride took each step slowly as she made her way down to the reception area below, showcasing the flowing white gown to its full potential, much to the delight of the Lake Island Hotel staff who had gathered to catch a glimpse of her wearing it. With an elegant empire line and a square neck, the wedding dress was opulent yet simple, and the spectators craning their necks from the corridor that led to the dining room collectively stifled their gasps of admiration.

'Do you think you'll go for something like that?' whispered Harry in Katrine's ear, and she nudged him in the ribs to preserve the reverential silence.

'It'll be you next,' mouthed Anna from her other side, and Katrine couldn't help but smile.

Light was spilling in through the front doors and windows, filling the entrance hall with brightness, giving the illusion it was a sunny day outside. But the hotel staff knew better;

that the Lake District weather could be as unpredictable as people were.

As Gaia reached the foot of the stairs, the seamstress who'd handstitched her dress rushed forward to make a final adjustment to the sleeve, then leaped back again, towards the hotel's lounge.

A chain of signals from various assistants travelled round the foyer in sequence. They were ready to leave for the ceremony. The bride's father took her arm, and the hotel's front doors were flung open, just as the director shouted 'Action!'

Chapter 56

'That's a wrap!'

Gaia grinned as her team broke into a round of applause and the staff of the Lake Island Hotel joined in.

Jackson gave a strident whistle of relief from where he stood at the back of the dining room, before Anna could shoot him a reprimanding look. 'What? I'm only thinking the same as everyone else,' he said. 'I can't wait to get back to normal.'

'We're lucky we can do that,' said Katrine, glancing over at Gaia. 'I don't envy being her at all.'

Anna shook her head. 'Me neither. She's certainly been through a lot since the last time she was here.'

'She's coming over,' said Jackson. 'I'm outta here,' he said.

'This hotel's future is secure because of her,' said Anna, putting her hands on her hips, but he'd already disappeared off towards the kitchen.

'I have to say, this is a *perfect* film location,' said Katrine, gazing out at the stone balustraded terrace. 'I still can't believe it's going to be in a *blockbuster*, though.'

'Fingers crossed it will be in some more,' said Will, beside her, winking at Anna.

'Hi,' said Gaia, encompassing them all with her smile, before turning her gaze to Harry and Katrine. 'I wondered if I could speak to you both for a second?' she said.

'Of course,' said Katrine, taking Harry's hand and following Gaia out into the hallway and onwards through to the foyer.

Everyone was gathered in the restaurant to celebrate the end of filming, so the reception area was empty.

Gaia gestured for them to sit on the sofa, and she took a seat herself on the chair nearby. 'I just wanted to say that if you'd like to stay at my house in the Caribbean for your honeymoon, you'd be very welcome.'

Neither of them spoke, and jovial shrieks of laughter drifted along the corridor from the high-spirited crowd in the dining room.

'Obviously, I won't be offended if you'd prefer not too, but the offer is there, as a wedding gift.'

'Wow, really?' murmured Katrine.

'We couldn't . . .' said Harry.

'You can,' said Gaia with a nod. 'If you want, that is,' she added. 'I've got a beach house in the Bahamas that's yours for as long as you'd like it.'

Katrine clasped her hands together. 'Are you *sure*?'

'Absolutely.'

Harry cleared his throat. 'That's really kind. Thank you.'

'It's nothing,' Gaia swatted the air. 'Rachel will sort the arrangements if you send her the dates. I'll be pretty tied up promoting this –' she wafted a hand to indicate the movie they'd just finished shooting – 'so it's all yours. I haven't even been there since . . .' She trailed off, and Federico's name hung in the air like a cobweb caught in the chandelier.

Katrine leaned forward impulsively, as though Gaia was a friend not her fiancé's ex-girlfriend. But she felt compelled to comfort the woman in front of her: all the finery in the world couldn't protect anyone from heartbreak.

'How are you . . . after all that?' ventured Harry, voice almost a whisper in case she didn't want to answer.

Gaia sighed, and to Katrine's surprise, she reached for her hand.

Katrine squeezed her fingers, knew what it was like to need another's touch, recalled the way Anna had held her close when her dad couldn't hug her himself.

'It's been hard,' said Gaia, blinking rapidly.

Katrine's brow creased.

'You'll have seen it all in the papers . . .' said Gaia.

They had, and the tale was wilder than the plot of most films.

But Harry sensed that Gaia needed to get the whole story off her chest, that it was cathartic to tell it to someone who wasn't a journalist, or a stranger, but someone who actually knew her.

And so, he and Katrine listened as Gaia told them how Federico had been arrested at the airport for committing a whole string of offences, from falsifying taxes to relationship fraud. How he'd scammed Victoria Cole's parents out of millions of dollars after inventing a fictitious property development that he promised would be a fabulous investment. He'd dated their daughter for her money, well aware she came from a dynasty of very successful actors, desperate to pay off his mounting debts from several flopped films. He'd finally come undone when Rachel and Chris had sussed that something was up at the summer party, after a number of strange phone calls.

'Si wasn't even a real bodyguard,' explained Gaia, eyes wide. 'He just hired him to pose as one, but when he didn't pay the bill, the guy stopped working for him. He rang Chris to give him the heads up.'

Katrine gasped.

'I'm so sorry,' said Harry, shaking his head. 'You couldn't even make it up.'

'And he stole your ring . . .' murmured Katrine, still holding Gaia's hand, her fourth finger free of any band.

Gaia nodded. 'He was a better actor than I am! Even went off to speak to you about finding it.' Katrine looked over at the reception desk as she remembered it.

'Oh, I think someone's waiting to speak to you,' Harry said to Gaia suddenly, noticing another actress hovering behind her shoulder.

Gaia turned around and smiled. 'Oh, yes, meet my friend and on-screen sister, Victoria.'

Epilogue

'*Everything your heart desires,*' read the tagline at the top of the poster, above a picture of Gaia and her co-star in Regency costume, the inimitable backdrop of the Lake Island Hotel behind them. The advertising campaign was a triumph, thought Rachel, feeling a swell of pride at having come up with the quote herself, as she crawled past the billboard in her cab.

She could probably walk there quicker, she thought, checking the time on her phone. But she still had almost an hour till the meeting, so there was nothing to worry about. She always left a sizeable buffer in case of emergency. She'd been able to move closer to Gaia's apartment after the last pay rise, but still seemed to spend an inordinate amount of her life shuttling there and back in a taxi. Miles had always said she might as well move in, but instead of smiling at the memory of his joke, now more than two years had passed since their split, she was struck by an uncomfortable feeling that the scales might have tipped too far.

She'd blurred the lines between her and her boss so much in the pursuit of a privileged lifestyle that the balance had gone, and she'd lost her sense of self.

Her satin camisole top was sticking to her back and she sat forward on the black-leather seat. Perhaps she'd feel better if she got out, stretched her legs. She hadn't been for a run or even a walk in forever. The exercise would probably do her good. 'If you just drop me here, that's great,' she said to the driver, already leafing through her purse for a tip.

The cab pulled up in a side road and she climbed out, feeling the LA heat sear her bare skin. She double checked the directions on the maps app on her phone, so used to being chauffeured around the city she wasn't quite certain of the best route on foot – and Rachel hated being unsure of anything.

She put her mobile away, was about to start walking along the pavement, but paused for a beat as she saw a man stop still to look up at the billboard displaying the ad for Gaia's new film. He stayed there for several seconds, staring up at the poster, and as Rachel made her way along the street towards him she was already imagining reporting what she'd seen to her boss: someone physically halted in their tracks by the brilliant movie promo—

But then she realised it was Miles.

'Rachel,' he said, almost dropping his takeout coffee when she tapped him on the arm.

'How are you?' she asked, studying the well-groomed stubble and the shine to his hair. He looked good. Happy.

'Yeah. Fine. Great.' He hitched his satchel up higher on his shoulder. 'How about you?'

She slicked an escaped tendril of hair from the nape of her neck. 'Okay.' She nodded, wanting a sip of water from the bottle in her bag.

'Good to see you,' said Miles. He pointed up at the billboard. 'Well done. I guess you're still the one making it all happen behind the scenes.' He gave her a grin, but to Rachel's surprise she didn't feel her usual burst of satisfaction.

'Yeah, it's been a smash hit so far . . .' She pulled at the hem of her top.

'I'd say do you want to grab a coffee but I guess you'll be rushing off somewhere important,' he said, raising a hand.

She felt an unexpected tug in her stomach. Didn't want him to go. She was reminded of the oak tree she'd seen on the shore of the island in Derwentwater, the way its roots reached for the lake.

'I've got time,' she said, noting that he already had a coffee right there in his hand.

'Have you?' Miles said, raising his eyebrows.

'Yeah,' she replied, realising the Lake District had in fact shown her many things, including that time was the greatest luxury of all.

The Lake Island Hotel Triple Berry and Honey Ice Lollies

Deliciously fruity and refreshing, these ice lollies take five minutes to make, feature only five ingredients, and taste like holidays!

Preparation Time: 5 minutes
Makes 4 ice lollies

Ingredients
120 grams fresh strawberries
120 grams fresh raspberries
120 grams fresh blueberries
120 ml natural yoghurt (8 tablespoons)
60 ml honey (4 tablespoons)

Equipment
Ice-lolly mould (for 4 lollies)
Blender

Method
Measure out your strawberries, raspberries and blueberries and wash them well.
Blend with your natural yoghurt and honey in a blender.
Sieve the mixture into a measuring jug to ensure it is smooth.
Pour the mixture into your ice-lolly mould.
Freeze for at least two hours and then enjoy!

Acknowledgements

This book is for my family, who are also friends, and my friends who are like family. It's these relationships that have nurtured me through life's peaks and troughs, and I'm forever grateful to have such a good group of people around me. Writing a book is a marathon process that wouldn't have been possible without you by my side.

Thanks in particular to my mum for reading every chapter as it was produced, and for her unerring encouragement. Thank you to my dad for always supporting me in pursuit of my dream to write. Thank you to my brother for the laughter and late-night calls. To David for being proud of me and shouting about my books from the rooftops. To Richard for rare hugs and putting up with me writing around the house. Thank you to my wonderful circle of friends including the brilliant Niamh for always being there for me. Life is a wild ride but I'm so glad you're all on it with me.

Thank you to Genevieve Pegg and the whole HarperNorth team for believing in my writing and being so enthusiastic about this book. I'm thrilled to have now published three novels with you.

Thank you to my agent Anne Williams at KHLA for championing me from the beginning.

Thank you to my amazing readers: I'm truly touched by your love for the characters and their stories, and your kind words about my books – they only truly come alive in your hands. Every message and review means the absolute world to me.